T0304917

BABY TEETH

Celia Silvani is a communications director and freelance writer, who has written for *Stylist*, the *Telegraph* and *BBC Future* on topics ranging from weddings to hurricanes. *Baby Teeth* is her first novel.

This book contains discussions and references to pregnancy and infertility. There is also a scene of pregnancy loss.

BABY TEETH

CELIA SILVANI

ORION

This hardback first published in Great Britain in 2025 by Orion Books,
an imprint of The Orion Publishing Group Ltd
Carmelite House, 50 Victoria Embankment
London EC4Y 0DZ

An Hachette UK Company

The authorised representative in the EEA is Hachette Ireland,
8 Castlecourt Centre, Dublin 15, D15 XTP3, Ireland (email: info@hbgi.ie)

1 3 5 7 9 10 8 6 4 2

A CIP catalogue record for this book is
available from the British Library.

ISBN (Hardback) 978 1 3987 1441 0
ISBN (eBook) 978 1 3987 1443 4

Typeset by Input Data Services Ltd, Bridgwater, Somerset

Printed in Great Britain by Clays Ltd, Elcograf S.p.A.

www.orionbooks.co.uk

For my mum, Anne Jones, and her constant love

PROLOGUE

TheSecretGoddesses
[ADMIN HAS REMOVED THIS POST]

Comments:

Lucy_Loves_Life: *Moderators, I don't think this post should stay live. We've all worked so hard to ensure our little corner of the Internet is full of positivity. Pregnancy is such a delicate, special time and us Goddesses must help nurture each other's minds and bodies, without exception. This is a place to feel held and supported.*

MindFullOfLove: *While what's happened is terribly sad, I've got to agree with @Lucy_Loves_Life. This page celebrates the beauty of births. Mentions of funerals unfortunately belong elsewhere. I think many of us have felt very triggered.*

SanneHoward: *Does anyone know her address? I'd like to send some Rhodonite. I'm an angel mother too (with two children earthside) and this stone really helped me recover from grief.*

Growing_Nicholls_Fam: *Ladies, has she been online recently?*

I can't stop thinking about how terrible this all is and how she might feel if she logged on and saw these comments.

CrunchyMumma: *Hi all, I've got moderator rights and have ac-tioned the request to remove the post. A reminder of the rules for everyone:*
1) We do not encourage, endorse or support women engaging with healthcare systems. Please do not, under any circumstances, suggest a medical intervention. Users who do this will be asked to leave.
2) This is a private forum and everything discussed is not to be shared beyond the group.
3) Posts and comments must be productive and informed by our lived experiences. We do not tolerate anything that disrupts the calm of this space. For many women, it is their only outlet to discuss their wild pregnancy.
Sending love and light to you all.

Part 1

Chapter 1

Claire locked the toilet cubicle and turned her phone into a mirror. She fussed at her top, willing the neckline upwards, and frowned at her reflection. She'd noticed someone from IT – she still didn't know everyone's names – staring at her while she used the fancy barista equipment to make a coffee. For the hundredth time that day, Claire wished she could just be alone at home instead of in the office. She held the phone closer. Her breasts definitely looked bigger. They felt heavy and uncomfortable. This change in her body was no longer exciting. She'd allowed hope to overwhelm rational thinking again. It was like her body and mind conspired against her each month, testing her further and further to see what she could endure.

Claire heard a door slam and the clicking sound of heels.

Whispers came from the next cubicle. 'Did you get it?' Her manager Holly's clipped tones were unmistakable even at this volume.

Claire's arm hair stood on end. *What was happening?*

'Yeah, I got the super-quick one. No one saw.' Ali was rushing her words more than usual.

Claire tried to make her breathing as quiet as possible. She was desperate to hear everything. Holly and Ali must both be in the toilet together. Ali was Holly's little crony; they regularly coordinated their work wardrobes. That morning, they both turned up in matching Breton-striped t-shirts.

'I feel so gross right now. Like, what if it's, you know? Like what do I do then?' Holly sounded upset. It made Claire focus even harder.

'I'm here whatever, babe.' Ali's voice was gentler than Claire had ever heard it. Ali rarely deigned to speak to Claire.

The trickly sound of nervous urination was just about audible.

Claire's heart started to race – *could this be what she thought it was?* She tried to stop her thoughts as they spiralled, but it was impossible. James, her husband, recently suggested she was starting to get obsessed. *But was it?*

'Can I just check, are you late?' Ali asked the question Claire was dying to find out herself.

'Kind of,' Holly replied. 'This app said so, but I keep forgetting to update it, and you know it's been a weird month. So much has happened, it's hard to keep track.'

'Oh God, Holly. You should have said. My heart's going! Why am I more stressed out than you?'

The reek of fear slithered across the tiles. Claire swallowed down the tickle of a cough and willed her body to remain quiet. She held her hand against her mouth just to be sure. She hoped none of the team had noticed she'd been away from her desk for too long, that the two girls didn't realise how easily their voices carried. Claire didn't need to look at the device in her hand to tell the time. She had experienced the agony of this wait so many times she could pace it in her sleep.

Just yesterday Claire had sat in the same spot with a test of her own. She put her phone on her lap, started a three-minute timer and wedged her headphones into her ears – she didn't want to risk the alarm going off and attracting attention. Even though it was early in her cycle, something had compelled her to check – and she believed in gut instincts. At lunch, she'd walked for twenty minutes to ensure she wasn't seen by any colleagues before buying the special test that provided early results. The excitement consumed any hunger, so she raced back to Uno Energy headquarters and straight to the toilets.

Every shred of Claire's attention focused on her screen, the countdown. She didn't want to look at the result before it had a chance to develop. When the timer went off, she took a deep breath before silencing the irritating, repetitive trill.

Her heart thumping, Claire turned the test over and used the light from her phone to scrutinise its window. There was a thin grey line to the left of a pink one, Claire was sure of it. She took photos from all angles and sent them to the ladies on her favourite trying-to-conceive forum – the TTC Tribe. 'Can you see this too? The second line?' she asked. She wanted confirmation that this was really happening.

'OMG! I think I see it! Exciting! Congratulations!' one woman replied.

'Ahh, I'm pretty sure that's an evaporation line, that brand is famous for it. Could you try again tomorrow? Please let us know how you get on!' commented another.

Most women seemed to be in the negative camp, but the few affirmations made Claire's heart swell. She kept running back to the toilet to see if the test had got any darker, bringing her bag with her each time. For once, she didn't really care what her colleagues thought. She loaded up her phone, refreshed for messages on the group, and looked again at that shadow of a line. Her line.

Claire decided she would show James in person instead of

messaging. She pictured his face when he saw that hint of their long-awaited future. Jude, they'd decided for a boy – years ago, right at the start of their relationship, back when true adulthood felt so far away. Jude the dude. *Hey Jude, don't be so sad*, they'd sing if he ever felt unhappy. Claire had already played these family scenes out in her head. And for a girl, Emily. A classic name; a beautiful person's name.

She arrived at their apartment first and wiped down the kitchen counters in need of something to do. The test lay on top of her bag, ready to be celebrated. She jumped when she heard the tell-tale signs of the door being unlocked, beaming at him once he entered the kitchen.

'Someone's pleased to see me!'

'James! Look.'

She handed the test to her husband.

James brought it closer to his face.

'Another negative?' he said, his eyebrows in a frown.

'No, look!' This wasn't the response she'd expected. Where was James's huge smile? The happy tears? Instead, his eyes showed no signs of joy.

'Claire . . . I can't see anything there.'

'Here, use my phone torch, look!'

'I don't think that's how it works. Shouldn't there be two lines? I can only see one pink one?'

'No, James, look here! When you turn it to the light, see?'

James only glanced for a second. 'I'm sorry, I just don't see it. Should I . . .?' James moved towards the bin.

'No, no, don't do that. I want it back.'

'Oh. Are you OK?'

Claire felt winded with disappointment. 'Just wait,' she eventually said, and watched as her husband nodded. He didn't look convinced.

Claire knew what she'd seen. After they ate dinner in near-silence, she opened the group, re-read the handful of supportive messages and felt crushed anew that her husband had dismissed the test so quickly. She could barely sleep with the thought of what she believed would greet her when she woke up, and what James might be able to finally see. This was it: the turning point so many women on the TTC group mentioned. So many signs were there: the wonderful tenderness of her boobs when she turned in bed, the dry throat that no amount of water would relieve, the little twinges in her pelvis.

But just five hours ago, when Claire finally tried again with her best, most concentrated morning urine, she was confronted by empty space where the second line should be. Her body had misled her, betrayed her again.

James pulled her into his arms when she handed him the new test, sobbing, and kissed the top of her head. He didn't say anything – he didn't have to. He rocked with Claire in his arms, as they'd done so many times before, until they both had to leave for work.

Claire hadn't worn much make-up to the Uno office. Normally, she spent the commute trying to make her face more presentable, but she kept her head down on the journey from Dulwich to Soho, swiping away tears. No one commented on Claire's raw skin when she sat down at her desk. In fact, the girls didn't seem to register her presence, and continued babbling about last night's TV. Claire didn't say hello. She didn't trust her voice not to wobble. Instead, she focused on the screen and willed her tear ducts to behave. Somehow, she made it through the first half of the day without incident. The first few hours were always the hardest after another big fat negative.

Holly and Ali, barely a metre away, remained silent.

Three, two, one, Claire counted.

'Yes!' Holly squealed, right on time. 'Yes, yes, yes!'

'Let's have a look,' Ali said.

Claire wished she could see too.

'Oh, that's great, Hol. Hey, you had me worried there.'

'Thank God.' Holly's relief was palpable. 'Wow, is that the time? I've got so much to do this afternoon.'

The girls slammed their way out of Holly's lucky escape with the carefree aggression that only the young and the beautiful can get away with. Claire stayed sitting on the closed toilet lid until her breath became even. It took a long time. She felt a uterine squeeze of longing alongside hatred for her colleagues.

All her life, she had wanted to be a mother. The urge had been there for as long as she could remember. She'd loved caring for her younger sister, Lily, and wasn't put off by the various squalling children she babysat as a teenager. Claire had asked James early on, just to be sure that he wanted kids. Still, she wanted to be sensible about things. Wait until they could definitely provide, until they had the right jobs and the right home. She didn't want to push the conversation too much, back then. She knew there would be a time James would be ready. Where he'd also coo at the unbelievably small perfection of a newborn. So, like clockwork, every day she took her pill at the exact same time just to make sure it worked. Her body had been cleansed of those artificial hormones for a long time now, but it still wasn't functioning as it should. Her dreams had been crushed like clockwork for the past fifteen months.

And there was Holly, gleeful to not be carrying a child.

The gulf of the age difference between Claire and the two girls had never felt so pronounced. According to LinkedIn sleuthing, Holly was four years Claire's junior, and Ali had only graduated from university three years ago. Claire wasn't sure how Holly had managed to land the senior communications manager position – she had yet to see evidence that Holly had more knowledge or practical experience – but she'd needed a new job to support their move to London so accepted the first role offered and never asked about the team structure. With their affected tones and disregard for anything that truly mattered, the all-female communications department at Uno Energy seemed like a bunch of children masquerading as adults. For a split second, Claire was glad they didn't seem to accept her as one of their own.

The pod of desks was lively with chatter when she returned. Claire made herself smile at her boss when she sat back down at her desk.

'What's up with you? Are you ill or something?' Holly asked, as she played with a blonde curl.

'Oh, nothing!' Claire replied. 'It's just so bright outside, isn't it?' Claire was glad Holly hadn't commented on her watery eyes.

Holly's perfume filled the air. She must have applied it liberally after coming back to the desk. It smelled of leather and wood smoke, like the excitement of an evening after the sun sets. Claire took in a mouthful as she sighed. Some girls are just better at making themselves attractive and presentable. As she batted a clump of dark hair away from her eyes, she was reminded that she would never be the polished, perfect girl of her aspirations. She opened her emails and tried her best to ignore the sense of injustice that threatened to make her scream in the middle of the cavernous Soho office space.

Holly's reaction to a negative pregnancy test was all Claire could think about as she made her way home. Summer had started to creep in, daylight yawning later and later, stretching out the possibilities of each day. Claire felt alone as she walked past the park full of groups sprawled on picnic blankets. The air carried wafts of barbecues and booze and satisfaction. This communal giddiness felt so out of reach.

Claire could see James was in their apartment from the street level: they lived in the second and third floors of a Dulwich town house. He was standing by the beautiful bay windows. She didn't wave. She missed the excitement that used to fizzle inside at the prospect of their new city adventure, all sparked by that first visit together years ago. The looks they gave each other when they briefed the estate agent on a child-friendly place to rent. The belly-flutter when the agent launched into descriptions of local primary schools and the squeeze James reciprocated that this was really happening, they were going to move from Gateshead to London, and this place would have a spare room. Over four months had passed since they'd been handed the keys and there were no signs the room might be occupied soon.

'Do you want to talk about it? What happened this morning?' James asked, as soon as she unlocked the door and sat down on the sofa. James looked so sincere, so handsome, it made Claire's heart ache. He must have left work early to comfort her. She hated how he had to do things like this. She thought of the bathroom bin, the graveyard of their failures, and crumpled onto James's familiar chest. She would have to ask him to empty it again.

'Something must be wrong,' Claire whispered, as she turned a patch of James's t-shirt from royal blue to navy. 'It should have happened by now. It should be working. Everything should be working. Why isn't it working?'

'It's going to be OK, Bear. It's going to happen. It will happen soon,' James whispered. He'd used that nickname liberally for well over a decade, ever since they'd met in the second year of university – he was the only one she let get away with it.

'I just don't understand,' Claire said. 'We did everything right this time.' Claire had followed every piece of advice she could glean from the ladies online this cycle. She'd filled his-and-hers containers with new vitamin combinations and encouraged James to eat two Brazil nuts a day. Once they'd passed the narrow window of ovulation, she'd gorged on so much pineapple that her lips went numb. She'd even stopped placing the laptop on her lap, using a cushion to intercept any dangerous rays. And for what?

James opened his mouth. Closed it again and cleared his throat. 'You know, it could be the stress of the move, uprooting everything, all the change. I've been thinking that we don't have to stay here, Bear. We can always move back home if it'll make you feel better – or go for a visit? I hate seeing you like this. Do you want to talk about it? Home?'

Claire shook her head. She thought of the life they'd left, its comfort and familiarity. The goodbye party brimming with colleagues and friends. Claire's sister and mam helping them drive the six hours down and unpack everything over one frenzied weekend that was so full of potential that Claire could hardly sleep.

Claire was so sure she would enjoy it here in Dulwich, where her local high street featured pastel shop fronts and the park minutes from her doorstep was always busy with buggies. But each day made her feel less deserving. The long line of people shaking their heads at the local café after she'd launched into conversation with the barista. The invisibility of the overground as it chuntered into Central London, packed with blank expressions and grim-set mouths. The gut-dropping sensation when she realised none of her new colleagues would ever follow her back on Instagram. Claire tried to stay hopeful things would change and the city and its people would welcome her. Her doubt was increasing with every day.

Claire took her time to reply to her husband, her throat choked by the failure the question implied. They couldn't – no, wouldn't – turn back now. Claire had so many more things she wanted to achieve in this phase of their life. They had been married for five years and every month was a reminder that Claire was running out of options, of time. She knew her husband meant well, but his suggestion was painful.

'No, we can't do that! We've got our flat, our jobs, all your new friends! I just need this evening, then I'll be better. I just really thought this was it. I just . . . Well, I thought it was our time.' Her voice came out more brittle than she'd hoped.

James placed his hands under Claire's eyes and stroked away the tears dangling from her lower lashes before kissing her. 'I love you, and it's going to happen. It's us, Bear. It's us, and together we can do anything. Now, are you hungry? Should I order pizza?'

Claire nodded. It didn't matter that the flat was sticky with dusky, polluted heat, this was now their ritual: a rich indulgence every month.

When the two boxes arrived, Claire resisted the urge to take a photo of her husband mid-bite, his face hidden by dough. She did this sometimes: try to obscure the bad memories with carefully chosen images that showed the small, fleeting happiness. Claire didn't want to spark another lecture from her husband about her obsession with social media. His comments had ramped up since she'd joined the latest group.

The ladies online kept suggesting professional assistance. They were well over the NHS threshold for investigations. She opened the TTC forum and was pleased by all the new notifications that would keep her occupied that evening. Claire first discovered this online world through a chance google a year ago, almost six months into their journey, and she'd never looked back. As anyone who has ever befriended someone in the club toilets knows, strangers are the best audiences for your darkest fears.

Claire sank deep into the sofa and away into the online chatter while James tuned in to a programme about second homes abroad. A young couple said they wanted a two-bed in Fuerteventura because they were expecting. Claire put down her phone, careful to close the page full of other women's secrets, and looked up as the camera panned to a rounded belly held by four bronzed hands. Their place was a two-bed, with both bedrooms upstairs, perfect for tending to a child. James changed the channel without a word.

In bed, in the darkness, James told her again that it *was* going to happen. That they should try and enjoy all the time they had while it was just the two of them. Claire lay still, her head full of the day's tumult and the latest advice she'd received online. The reassurance, but the realism. She nearly voiced these strangers' suggestions of looking into assistance, even though the thought of being prodded and poked filled her with almost unbearable anxiety. She almost told him about Holly, and what she'd give to be flippant about testing again, to be able to turn back time and try sooner, with more ovarian reserves. Instead, as James drifted off beside her, she opened her phone and lay awake, her face illuminated by blue light as she scrolled and scrolled, searching for something that might quieten her aching sadness. She would do, try, anything to have a child.

Chapter 2

Claire didn't test again the following morning. She couldn't bear the disappointment. As James lay beside her, sound asleep, she wanted to shake him awake, join her in mourning the cramps she could feel brewing. It had been a bad night: Claire spent hours tossing and turning in the heat. She dragged herself out of bed and into the too-bright bathroom. Her skin felt bloated with tiredness and no amount of make-up could hide the fresh batch of sleep-deprived spots. She ran a finger over one as she patted down concealer and winced. James always swore he couldn't see them but they looked like barnacles, thick and with a life of their own. It was easier to complain about her skin than admit the other, less tangible causes of sadness, like the loneliness of her working day.

'Cheer up, Claire Bear. We're nearly halfway through the week!' James said, when he finally woke.

Claire eyed her husband suspiciously before she kissed him and left for work. He always had far too much energy in the mornings.

The heat deadened the usual hum of the office, making the morning stretch longer than Claire thought possible. It was as if time sensed her impatience. She had an appointment at lunchtime with the secretary of Emma Gray, the acupuncturist with over 100 five-star reviews on Google and a growing band of loyal followers on Claire's favourite fertility forum. It felt like things were aligning – this was the perfect time to get some guidance. She couldn't face another month of failure.

When midday finally arrived, Claire slumped down in the little park next to the office with her food, a box of vegetable maki rolls and tempura avocado laced with sweet, dried onions, and revisited some of Emma's recent reviews. The rice stuck to the roof of her mouth and her tongue felt too inflated and lazy to remove it. She let the rice dissolve and release its sickly, sugary taste while she read praise like 'Emma is a superwoman' and 'Thank you for kickstarting my fertile abundance!'

Apparently, Emma Gray could even help with Claire's anxiety that she might never be a mother. She hadn't dipped her toes in alternative therapies before – the closest she'd come was picking up a colourful leaflet about reiki healing left out by an instructor after a yoga class. Claire forgot about it until her mam spotted it in her bag and laughed so much that she still, years on, accused Claire of being into 'new-age nonsense'. She wished she'd investigated further back then and not cared so much about her mam's comments. Another lady on the group was convinced reiki helped regulate her inconsistent cycles, and Emma seemed like she really could be the answer to all of Claire's problems. It was just a matter of taking this first step.

In preparation for the getting-to-know-you chat, Claire brought her planner to the park. She flicked through it. The diary once burst with plans and the glorious quandary of being double-booked with work drinks and a meal with Sally, her best friend back in Gateshead. Now it was full of coded updates on her cycle. She could have won *Mastermind* with her knowledge about things like the luteinising hormone. She noted down everything: her mood, her periods, the days when she should be releasing her dwindling supply of eggs. The back page featured a list of specialist clinics recommended on the forums. Claire hadn't made any enquiries to these medical centres just yet. The idea of cold offices and their sinister, invasive equipment always stopped her from reaching out directly. Still, the names and the information on their FAQ pages gave her a sense of control.

Her phone buzzed. 'Hello, is that Emma Gray's office?'

'Yes, this is Sophia speaking. And Claire, what a pleasure to speak to you. Before I talk about what Emma can do for you, I need to let you know she has a significant waiting list and does ask me to ensure every future client is aware of the nuances of her work before signing up. Let's get into that now, shall we? Emma, as I'm sure you know, works with women's bodies to support their natural rhythms and flows, boosting blood circulation to certain parts of the body to assist each woman's unique journey. She's had brilliant success nurturing clients' palace of the child – that's what we call the womb in Chinese traditional medicine.'

Claire heard herself swallow. 'Palace of the child?'

'That's right. Now, I read all the information you shared about your situation. Thanks for going into such detail, most women don't give us anywhere near as much to work with! I think there's a lot we can do to assist you on your path to motherhood. I do need to tell you that acupuncture takes three months to have an effect on your eggs, and we recommend that patients seeking fertility support see Emma at least once a week.'

Claire looked around. The office entrance loomed in her periphery, and she turned her body so it was no longer in her line of vision. The nursery on the corner hadn't gone unnoticed either. Claire tried her hardest not to stare when she walked past the nursery in the mornings. All those happy parents; all those beautiful children.

'And how much would that cost?' she said.

'Well, the investment would depend on how regularly you see Emma, but her fertility clients tend to find that those weekly sessions are very worthwhile, and that would come in at around four hundred pounds a month. This isn't medicine as you know it, you see. Emma doesn't just consider your fertility through the lens of science, she also works with your emotions, lifestyle, and any energy she can feel from your early life. She's a firm believer that these elements have a huge impact on a woman's happiness and her ability to conceive.'

Sophia's voice was gentle and kind, exactly how Claire imagined someone tied to the profession would speak. Claire loved the sound of the treatment, so personalised and holistic, but she tried to imagine explaining this to James. He was someone who liked to know outcomes and odds, facts and figures. That would be the key to convincing him. She had her pen ready. 'OK, right, thank you, and what sort of results can we expect?'

Sophia's laugh fluttered through the phone; the type of laugh used to calm women reaching their breaking point. 'Ah, I'm afraid there are no guarantees with the body. But I recommend you read Emma's testimonials page if you haven't already. She's had some truly wonderful feedback. Women travel from all over for her help. And some men too – increasingly, we're realising the role men play in supporting their partner's fertile potential. Now, I'm afraid I've got to head to a meeting so would you be able to let me know if you'd like to join the waiting list before the end of tomorrow? It's currently sitting at around six weeks. We'd love to help, so how does that sound, Clara? Must dash, I have another call now!'

Sophia ended the call before Claire could respond.

Claire felt dizzy from all the information and the news of the waiting list. She used the unexpected extra time in her lunch break to calculate how much a minimum of three months of acupuncture would cost, and then totted up the rough quotes she could gather from the slick websites of Harley Street centres which boasted 30–40 per cent success rates. While Claire loved the idea her body might contain a hidden palace, she could already picture James's dismissal. A good gut feeling wouldn't sway her husband about acupuncture, not when they were supposed to be topping up their joint savings account which was depleted from the move. She knew she wouldn't continue the conversation with Emma's well-meaning secretary; there was no point pushing the point unless she had some hard numbers. She would have to work on building up her courage about investigations. As soon as her period started, she would try and initiate the conversation with James. They'd see what they were entitled to on the NHS first, of course, but have the private options as backup. She would need his support every step of the way to be able to even walk into a hospital again.

Claire sighed, tucked her planner back into her bag, and made sure she smiled when she breezed back into the office so no one realised how useless she felt.

She tried to keep up the pretence when she got home and kissed the tipsy, sun-warmed lips of her husband. James had hundreds of different smiles, and Claire could tell just how much he'd drunk over the course of the afternoon with his colleagues by looking at the lazy curl of his mouth.

'Oh no, you look stressed,' he said, when she wriggled under his arm on the sofa. 'What's up?'

'I'm fine,' Claire said. She no longer articulated all her daily experiences to the partner she once shared everything with.

She didn't want to bother him with tales of work woe or cut through his hazy happiness by mentioning the let-down of the acupuncture call. It was better for him to think she was OK.

'No come on, what's the matter?'

'James, I said I'm fine. It's just been a rubbish week, you know. Remember yesterday? The test?'

James hesitated, like he was weighing up how to respond to her. She hated that he had to coddle her. 'Claire, you're driving yourself crazy with this. Come on, let's just chill. Shall we open that vinho verde that's been in the fridge for far too long? Perfect night for it. The weekend is in sight!'

Claire shook her head emphatically. 'I'm not going to have a single sip this month. But you go ahead. Knock yourself out.' Claire couldn't help the barb. It was impossible to contain.

'I think it might help you relax, Bear. This stress isn't good for you.'

James had no idea how much work it took to give them both the best possible chance at success, and he had the nerve to complain about stress? All the things she'd given up, including the recent end of her weekly allowance of two glasses of wine. While she wanted a drink more than anything, to relish the delicate fizz of the Portuguese wine they first tried on their honeymoon, she knew she couldn't. She knew how dangerous alcohol might be to any embryonic hope, no matter what time in her cycle. She had to commit, give this her all, leave nothing to chance. She followed the advice that she should act like she was pregnant, and here was James, already drunk. The load was not evenly spread.

'I just want water. Maybe you should try that too.' She could feel small flickers of resentment gaining momentum. But she didn't want to start an argument, not tonight, not when she was so tired. 'Sorry, I'm just knackered, I didn't mean it,' she said, and James's face immediately softened.

That night, while James stayed downstairs and watched a film that carried the sounds of battle into the bedroom, Claire lay on top of the sheets and decided to do it again: read birthing stories. They could transport her to the visceral beauty of motherhood. Her favourite ones included the element of hardship – people who beat the odds to bring a child into the world. Who, like her, struggled to enter this inner circle. She often included the word miracle in her searches to unearth such gems. She'd always loved finding out as much information as possible about certain topics. Now, it presented as her insatiable appetite for all things motherhood.

Not for the first time, Claire was taken aback by the bravery of anyone who shared their innermost thoughts for the world to read on the Internet. She pored over an account written by a transgender man who feared scrutiny and bigoted comments from people complaining about male presence in the 'female space' of the maternity ward and so opted to deliver at home. He wrote about his experience giving birth to a beautiful baby boy while his partner looked on in awe and pride.

She couldn't stop there. She kept catching snippets of gunshot from the film downstairs. James was safely preoccupied, and her brain needed more. She read about an older lady who conceived just as people started to refer to her as a woman of a certain age. She was traumatised by malpractice during the birth of her now twenty-year-old son – the obstetrician made a mistake during her episiotomy and it became infected. This was a woman who simply wanted to reconnect with the unique and unparalleled moment where one life opens into two. For this baby, she wanted the nurturing care of midwives rather than doctors' prying fingers and scalpels.

Claire understood these concerns. When she was younger, she was kept in hospital overnight several times after terrifying asthma attacks, a mask clamped on her face while doctors screamed at her to stop crying, stop panicking, or her wheezing would get even worse. It felt like someone was sucking away all her air. She'd lie there, petrified, desperate for her parents, until doctors were satisfied by what they saw and she was allowed to go home. It was just a precaution, her parents would say, just in case. But Claire always felt like it was needless torture. Throughout her childhood – and still, occasionally into her adult years, though she grew out of her asthma – she had nightmares where she'd wake up thinking that mask was pressed back on. That she couldn't breathe. That no one was coming for her.

Thirteen years ago, Claire's dad had entered that same hospital and never left. In his last months, she forced herself into the building so she could see him, hold his hand, and do her best to keep him entertained. They would play rummy until one day he didn't have the strength to sit upright and hold the cards anymore, so Claire used all her energy and control to just sit there and tell him about university and the world and not show her horror that her dad, her strong dad, was fading in front of her. She would only ever make it a few steps out of the ward door before she started howling. She hoped her dad never heard. After every visit she washed her hair and clothes at least twice to remove the insidious smell that seeped into every pore and fibre – death, vegetable soup and cleaning products, all mixed together. Even now, well over a decade since her dad passed, just the thought of that smell filled her with dread.

Claire raced through one mummy blogger's account of how her husband assisted the midwife in the tranquil surroundings of a birth centre and imagined James doing the same, with no hospital strip lights in sight. She felt her sadness start to dissipate. The algorithm took her to an account of a woman who gave birth at home, with just a pool, her partner and a special playlist. It sounded divine. Claire lost the page when the door opened and James got into bed. She must have pressed it away when she put her phone down. She tried to find it again while James snored – he always did this after a few drinks – but technology refused to cooperate, and she gave up. She went onto Pinterest instead and browsed beautiful baby clothes.

One day, Claire thought, one day all this will be worth it. All the planning and preparation and hope and heartbreak. The last year had corroded something she knew she'd never get back. Claire stared at the ceiling and focused on her breath. She didn't want to get upset again, thinking about the innocence that coloured the first few months of this journey, the naive optimism. No, she thought. It will all be worthwhile. We will create a little world together. We will have our own birth story.

Chapter 3

Claire winced as she typed the words: *how to make friends*. Before she pressed enter, she checked behind her, forgetting that James was out with the so-called 'football lot' and unable to see her phone screen. Just as Claire remembered to ask if he'd won, James sent a picture of a sweating amber glass. *The sweet taste of success*, the message read, followed by the happiest emoji face. She smiled; James had a competitive streak that only surfaced during sports. She could imagine his pride at winning and the second-hand joy cheered her.

Claire didn't understand how James had managed to acclimatise so well. She had gone from being the more sociable one in the couple to a woman sitting alone most nights, FaceTiming Sally, her mam or her sister Lily, waiting for her husband to come home. She hadn't experienced this great expanse of alone time before. It made evenings feel so much longer. She'd had no problems bonding with former colleagues. After-work drinks were a given at her old place, especially towards the end of the week. Even in her first job after graduation – a recruitment agency – there had been a sense of camaraderie, a communal desire to decompress, a few nights out where Claire was the youngest by far.

Claire wished she knew what she was doing wrong at Uno. She always tried to join in conversations with the girls, but they seemed to end as soon as she swivelled her chair round. She'd brought up a diluted version of her concerns to Sally to get another perspective. Sally, who had been removed from workplace dramas for almost three years now – her maternity leave turned into permanent parenting of her son Rory – suggested Claire just wait for everyone to realise how wonderful she was. Claire appreciated the boost but knew the idea that Holly and Co. might one day sit down and suddenly want to be her friend was ludicrous.

Earlier that day, Claire had been waiting to refill her water bottle when someone she recognised as being from the design team – he was heavily tattooed with bleached hair – turned round.

'So, see you at The Crown and Anchor tomorrow, then?' the man said.

'Pardon?'

'Ali's birthday? You're on her team, right? She said everyone from comms was invited. We're all going to be there.' He gestured towards the design desks.

'Oh, right.' She tried to laugh in a way that suggested this wasn't the first time she'd heard of this event. 'No, sorry, I'm busy tomorrow. But I'm sure I'll be there next time!'

'Sure, cool,' the man said.

When Claire got back to her desk, she looked him up on the HR database. His name was David. After careful consideration, she didn't request to be David's friend on Instagram, or mention anything to Ali or the team. She knew she needed to earn these kinds of invites. It felt very important that she make an alternative plan. She had to be proactive.

Claire dared herself to reopen the Internet tab on her phone.

She clicked on the first article and exhaled as she scrolled down. She thought, not for the first time, how amazing it was that Google could answer any question within milliseconds. She owed a lot to the balm of the Internet and its ability to soothe. The article told her that there were easy ways to make friends in a new area. It was a simple matter of joining community groups, getting involved in team sports, and looking friendly and approachable. Claire wasn't sure about the last point. She tried to make her face neutral before looking in the mirror, but the results were inconclusive. She would have to ask James about the vibes her face gave off when he got back.

Further clicks revealed the most serendipitous gathering the following night. The Dulwich Darters, which claimed to be South-east London's most inclusive running club, was celebrating its third birthday with a run and pub jaunt. All ages and abilities were welcome. Claire considered the joy of a recent run with James around the local park, the happy burn of her lungs. She RSVP'd online and spent the evening glowing with excitement. She laid out all her potential gym clothes by the full-length bedroom mirror and tried on combination after combination of neon kit until she felt satisfied with her reflection. So what if all her team were going out without her? She looked forward to leaving the office with purpose, now she had plans.

Claire didn't notice James slink into the room until he announced his presence with a cough.

'You look nice,' he said, and looked her up and down appreciatively. 'But it's late, what are you doing? Come to bed, you loon.'

She gave herself one last glance before she wiggled out of the Lycra and joined her husband. She loved how he accepted her without question and didn't probe her decisions. It wasn't the right moment to tell him about the running. That was a tomorrow job.

When Claire got off the train at East Dulwich after work the next day, she sat on one of the cold benches in the station, hunched over her compact mirror, and applied just the right amount of powder to conceal the anger of her recent acne flare. She'd been so focused on leaving the office in good time, she hadn't found the time to conduct her usual make-up top-ups. She wanted to make the best possible impression on the Dulwich Darters – she really needed to make some friends here. James always told her that no one was staring closely at her face, and no one truly cared, but that wasn't the point. She didn't want anyone to feel sorry for her.

As Claire walked up to the café where the running group met, she realised that someone from the group might have caught her applying make-up. She was seized by the need to turn round, go home, retreat before she might embarrass herself further. She was more of a plodder than a dasher. But she so wanted to have people she could have proper conversations with on the weekends. Claire had a niggling fear that her family and Sally wanted that for her too – wanted her to stop trying to FaceTime home so much. She needed to put one foot in front of the other.

A dozen heads turned towards the door when Claire entered. A woman wearing full Dulwich Darters merchandise strode over and said how delighted she was to see a new face. She introduced Claire to everyone, including an athletic couple with matching outfits and abs, before launching into the instructions about this evening's route. Claire resisted the temptation to gawp at the duo's crop tops. Their muscles rippled with each breath. Claire tried to stand a little straighter.

'Welcome,' a woman who looked slightly older than Claire half whispered, while the rest of the group nodded along to that night's plan.

Claire grinned back and gave the stranger a thumbs-up. She regretted it immediately. *Who does that*, she chastised herself, before stowing both thumbs in her fists.

There was no chance to rescue the conversation before the group were out of the door and pounding the streets with swift, practised strides. The leader set a fast pace. Claire struggled to keep up, her breath rasping and rattling in her throat. She stared at the lean legs of the woman in front and wondered what hers might look like if she was ever brave enough to wear exercise shorts. She was a high-waisted leggings type of person, through and through. This woman bounded with such grace, it was hypnotising.

Thirty minutes of winding around the gorgeous tree-lined streets of Dulwich felt like a lifetime of torture. The pub gardens they passed were bursting with chatter, and Claire was relieved almost all the people she knew in this city – her Uno colleagues – were safely occupied in the Crown and Anchor with no chance of seeing her in this state. She hadn't kept up her normal running routine since they moved to London. She used to run home from her old office – one of the girls on her team who lived nearby was training for the Great North Run and it turned into their weekly routine, a chance to chat and gossip as well as get some exercise. With the exception of the recent run with James, her trainers had lain largely unused in their new flat. She regretted it. Her mouth burned with desire for water and her head thumped with each step. She could feel sweat crystallising on her forehead. Stop, she wanted to cry out, break time, please. But she kept going. The group was going to go out afterwards. She couldn't tap out before then. Inside, she recited things she'd read: *being active can boost fertility. Women who do moderate exercise on average conceive faster than women who don't.* It helped her keep going.

Claire was mortified by the number of people who asked if she was OK when they finished. *Just how bad did she look*, she panicked. All she wanted to do was lie down and gulp in mouthfuls of still air, not make polite chit-chat about the best running watches. She hoped no one noticed how she was propping herself up with an arm against the wall. Claire swiped a finger over her upper lip to remove the slug of moisture and sought out the kind face of the woman who'd made an effort earlier. She had sensed kinship in her sparkling eyes.

'God, I'm unfit,' Claire said, and pointed to her face. 'I bet I'm as pink as anything.'

The woman laughed. 'No, everyone was unusually fast today, I think it's because we've had to really pare it back the last few weeks with the heatwave. I struggled too.' She offered a well-kept hand and Claire shook it. 'I'm Taya, by the way. I haven't seen you around here before, have I? Oh, please don't tell me we've already met.'

'You're being kind,' Claire said. 'And no, we moved here a few months ago. I'm just trying out some new things. I didn't realise how out of practice I was!' Claire hoped the other woman didn't pick up on the reedy tone to her voice. It always happened when she was nervous.

'Well, it's a pleasure. God, my calves are seizing up, are yours? Those hills were brutal!'

'Everything's seizing up,' Claire said. It was the truth. She was too stiff to even try and stretch.

Taya chuckled generously.

'Are you staying for the drinks?' Claire asked. She looked forward to hearing more about everyone over a pint of soda and lime. She wanted to know how the hyper-fit couple looked like they hadn't expended a single shred of energy. She wanted to know what Taya did, and where she lived, and why she'd joined this running group. Taya had the look of someone who found joy and humour everywhere in the world. It showed in the soft lines by her eyes and mouth.

'No – no drinks for me,' Taya said with a little shake of her head.

Claire noticed Taya had her slim arms crossed around her stomach. *Was she?*

'Ah, that's a shame. I was hoping to meet new . . .' Claire stopped herself. What she'd said already sounded so desperate. Taya was smiling at her, most likely out of pity. Her loneliness must be so obvious, so transparent. She needed to leave before she embarrassed herself further. She scanned the room for her bag and spotted it in the corner. 'You know what? I don't know what's got into me. I promised I'd make dinner for my husband tonight! How could I forget?'

Taya's face remained so kind. 'Well, I'll be heading off soon too if you don't mind waiting a few minutes?'

'No, I really should go,' Claire said. This running club idea had been a stretch. She grabbed her belongings and waved to everyone as quickly as possible. She still hadn't fully caught her breath.

Claire felt like she was walking on stilts as she jerked her way home. She wished she could call her sister or Sally to laugh, but knew they'd just ask questions. Or worse, feel sorry her. She'd failed in her friendship mission entirely. James was eating dinner when Claire bashed the door open. She dragged her feet along the floor for dramatic effect.

'I don't want to talk about it,' Claire said to her husband, whose fork was poised mid-air, waiting for her to share everything. She'd told him about the running club earlier that day, of course, and he'd been excited for her. He knew how much she'd enjoyed the routine back home.

'Suit yourself,' he replied, and resumed his habit of using the fork as a shovel.

Claire waited for another probe from her husband but all she could hear was his overly loud chewing.

Claire let out a yawn as she spooned some of James's left-overs into a bowl. The run had taken everything out of her. She stabbed each piece of pasta. The jarred sauce was as bitter and metallic as blood. This was typical James: how could someone mess up a recipe like pesto pasta, and couldn't he have made a little more effort? Claire checked herself. She arranged her mouth into a smile and asked James to share the details of his day. He'd finalised a deal and enjoyed an all-expenses-paid lunch. Claire liked seeing the glint in her husband's eye as he shared every part of his experience. I'm glad one of us is happy, Claire thought. It would have been horrendous if both Hansens felt the same way.

'Who's Taya?' James asked, while Claire scrubbed stubborn flecks of sauce from the pan. James, as usual, had left that job for her.

Claire enjoyed an electrifying jolt of recognition. 'What?' she shouted over to her husband.

'Your phone.' He gestured to her glowing device. 'Who's Taya? And where's that name from?'

Claire abandoned the pile of plates and seized her phone from James's hands. 'Oh my God,' she said. 'Oh my actual God.' The lock screen notified her that Taya had both followed and messaged. *Hello! I didn't catch your name but Dani (our lovely group leader) passed it on. Do you fancy a coffee sometime? I'm busy this weekend but what about next?*

'You're mad, you,' James said, as Claire punched the air and started dancing around. Technicolour suds flew from her still-wet hands.

'Love you,' she replied, and then she spun around with her phone raised above her head, temporarily forgetting the ache in her legs.

Claire angled the phone so James could easily see the screen as they navigated Taya's online presence together. Two super-sleuths nestled on the couch. James was impressed by Claire's quick ability to deduce everything about someone's life from just a few select images. Taya was a lawyer, lots of nice holidays, childless, probably single. Claire didn't tell James she'd noticed something unusual in Taya's instinctive arm around her stomach when she declined alcohol; it would be another reminder of what they still hadn't achieved, and she didn't want to spoil the fun of the moment. Perhaps it was bloating, and Claire knew the discomfort of bloating all too well. Her own belly felt puffed after the pasta.

Disaster struck when Claire asked James to zoom into an image from five years ago. Taya in a polka-dot swimming costume, shin-deep in a slick of azure sea. His thick fingers touched the screen twice. Claire had *liked* the old photo.

Claire screamed and James flinched.

'Jesus!' he said, with one hand on his ear.

'James!' she could hear her volume, but it was out of her control. 'What have you done?' She knew that even if she pressed *unlike*, Taya would get a notification. It was a hopeless situation. And the worst part was it was totally avoidable. Claire felt her palms dampen against the cool metal of her device. 'Argh!'

'Oh, come on, Claire,' he said, and raised his hands in the air. 'She won't mind. No one cares about these things. Just undo it. Do your usual Internet magic.'

'Taya's going to think I'm a freak!' Claire knew she sounded hysterical, childish even, but she was unable to stop.

'No,' he said. 'Oh, Claire, are those tears? Hey, this isn't a problem. Come here, this is fine, I promise. You've only just met this woman!'

Claire shrugged off his attempt to put an arm around her. 'She's going to think I'm such a loser, James. I can't believe you did that. You don't understand.'

James's eyes widened. Claire scrolled until she could try and undo her husband's heavy-handed mistake. James continued to talk but she tuned him out so she could concentrate on the pressing matter at hand.

She heard him sigh. 'You know, Claire, for someone so keen on being a mother, I really hope you don't teach our kids to care so much about such unimportant things.'

Claire willed her face to not expose how much this hurt. The gentleness in his voice had gone. 'I don't know what you mean,' she said.

'It's you and that phone. It's not good to spend so much time on it. It feels like you're hardly with me anymore.'

The pain of allowing someone into the centre of your life was that they could make such incisive judgements. James had a habit of bandying around comments like that in arguments. As if he didn't clock up tremendous screen time gaming or watching sports. She stewed in silence, thinking about the hypocrisy. As usual, her TTC forum ladies were online, posting updates on their cycles and sharing top tips from the lucky ones who graduated away to the pregnancy page. After reading through a restorative amount of chat, and noting she needed to stock up on both grapefruit and pomegranate juice, she made a show of leaving her phone on the table. She gave her husband a look that she knew he would intuit: would a phone addict do something like that?

'Would you like a peppermint tea?' he said, instead of rising to the bait. 'I got some of those posh teabags you like. A little weekend treat for my non-drinking Bear.'

'No, I'm good, thanks,' she said stiffly.

'What are you going to say back to that new friend? It's exciting, isn't it?'

'Well, first, I've got to apologise for your actions, haven't I?'

'No one really minds about little things like that. And if they do, they're not worth a moment of your time anyway. Trust me, it's not the big deal you're making it out to be.'

While James turned his back to boil the kettle, Claire retrieved her device and typed and re-typed an explanation for her husband's gross misstep. James kept peering over as she attempted various drafts. She appreciated his silence while she concentrated. She couldn't handle any more comments. Eventually, she decided it would be best to pretend it never happened. She sent Taya the name of a local café she'd not yet visited that made fresh *pastéis de nata* each day.

Claire felt her shoulders relax when Taya replied minutes later to confirm a time and a date for their coffee and cake. She hadn't realised they had been so tense.

'See,' James said, with an infuriating grin, when Claire showed him the message. 'And I bet she'll end up loving you too.'

Chapter 4

HomeBirthHeroes

Flora_Is_Free

Ah, I can't believe I've made it to the third trimester already. The weeks have genuinely flown by. Pregnancy is just so much more relaxing when you're not interrupted by scans and tests and invasive questions.

I can't stop thinking about how different things are this time around.

With Freddie, I was so excited about our twelve-week appointment, our first chance to see him, that I practically skipped into the ultrasound room. But we were only allowed a few magical minutes watching our baby before the consultant told me she had some concerns and I had to come back in four weeks for diabetes testing. And no, she hastened to remind me, that was *not standard procedure*. Of course, when I came back, the blood results showed nothing was wrong.

At every appointment, I endured raised eyebrows when they checked Freddie's growth, told me I was in the top percentile for fundal measurements, snide comments about scans not being so clear. I had to just grin and bear it. I did it because I wanted the best for my baby, and back then, I honestly thought that these people knew best.

The final straw was when I was banned from the birth centre and told I could only deliver on a ward. This doctor didn't listen to me when I told him I walk every day, I swim. Instead, he just raised his eyebrows and said sorry, those were the rules, and my BMI meant the midwifery team would not accept someone so high risk.

That's when I realised that these people didn't care for me and my son.

Tom and I sat down that night and made our plan to arrange a birth at home – and I found this amazing group. Checking out of the system was one of the best decisions we've ever made.

I will never forget the serenity I felt during Freddie's birth. How empowered I felt when I turned to Tom and said we could do it alone, just like we'd practised. The sounds of the playlist we made of our special songs, the elation as I danced around and felt so held by the water in the birth pool, and didn't question any urge or surge over the 19 hours. Or the light as we lay together that morning when I gave Freddie his first feed. I was nourishing him, but he had already given me the greatest, most enriching experience of my life.

I feel beyond lucky I have the chance to repeat the experience in a few short months. I look at my body and am in love with its ability to bring life into this world.

For those following my journey, I'm still feeling great. All the little twinges, niggles and kicks (Bump loves to boot me any time I have any sugar) that are amping up now? There's nothing a bit of breath-work won't fix. There's a whole world of resources out there, and thank you so much to the wonderful women on this forum who've sent podcast and YouTube recommendations my way.

At the end of the day, as my lovely mum (who was far more lucid back when I had Freddie and not at all well now) used to tell me – this is how women gave birth for thousands and thousands of years.

It's how we came into existence. So why all these restrictive measures nowadays? We're taught that birth is this horrible, scary thing, but it doesn't have to be. It can be calm and safe and glorious.

All this is to say – I don't want to dwell too much on the past, but now I've hit this milestone and Bump's arrival is in sight, I wanted to reflect on how different things are. We are ready, relaxed, and beyond excited to meet this amazing kicking being. We love Bump so much already. And the best thing is we have no doubts about our birth plan. Freddie is our amazing proof that *we've got this*. We've done it once before and in just twelve weeks we get to do it all over again.

Here's to a wonderful final trimester.

Comments:

HappyHeather: Moderators, I don't understand why no one is responding to me.

I don't think this is appropriate content for our home birth page – it belongs elsewhere and is quite frankly dangerous. Does Flora have a medical or midwifery qualification? Of course HCWs know best. Home birthing doesn't mean checking out of the system! I've reported this account several times now, and her original birth story is still up. Please can someone get back to me.

JessPinto: *Oh, Flora, you sound much, much calmer this time around and this post is a real pleasure to read. I can feel your positive energy through the screen. I remember all your updates from years ago. Keep going, sweet mama!*

Rose_Oram: *Hello! I was just wondering how bub is doing? The way doctors spoke to you sounds so nasty but have you seen a midwife at all in this pregnancy to check everything's OK? Have you had a scan? Sorry, just a bit confused here!*

Rose_Oram: *Me again! I was just talking to a friend and she's seeing a wonderful, size-inclusive midwife if you're looking for any recommendations? She'd be happy to chat to you about the fatphobia she's experienced too – sounds like you've both been through the wringer. DM me.*

Flora_Is_Free: *Hi @Rose_Oram, thanks so much for reaching out, I really do appreciate it. We're all good here, thank you though.*

Chapter 5

Claire felt her heart skip when Holly came over to her desk and asked if she'd like to join her for lunch at midday. It was a wonderful sensation, feeling worthy of someone's attention. Perhaps Sally was right after all, and it was only a matter of time before people started to warm to her. She may not have been invited to Ali's birthday night out but she'd managed to fill her weekend with things that almost distracted her from going to the toilet every half an hour to check if her period had arrived. On her way into the office, she had prepared responses to any potential questions from colleagues just in case anyone asked. Yes, she'd mouthed into her compact mirror while reapplying lip balm, I had such a lovely weekend. We walked to the Horniman museum, have you been? It has a gorgeous food market on Sundays, we tried the biggest burritos for just six pounds. She was relieved to have manicured and perfected these stories; she was ready for Holly.

Claire tried to initiate a conversation when they left the office, but Holly kept striding out of earshot. Claire was grateful she was wearing plimsolls: she almost had to break into a trot in order to keep pace. She tried to not let the effort show and made a mental note to message Taya about the running session later that week. She needed to work on her fitness.

Holly smiled at Claire once they were tucked inside a booth in the new burger joint round the corner, where Soho met Oxford Street. She made an affected ahem noise. 'So, Claire, I'm sure you're wondering why I asked you here today. I thought it would be better if we caught up outside of the office. Everyone can hear everything that goes on in those meeting rooms. Did you want to order first, then we can chat through my issues?'

A waiter appeared, as if he'd overheard the exchange. Claire tried to concentrate on the menu but it was impossible. Her mind was swimming. *Issues?* The back of her legs started to stick to the pleather cover of the seat. 'What can I get you today? Can I interest you in any of our specials?' he asked.

'I'll have a medium-rare burger with no bun, some sweet potato chips and extra ketchup, please. Oh, and tap water,' Holly said.

'Er, same,' Claire said. She couldn't think about food. She felt so foolish for assuming this would be a positive meeting. She truly thought Holly wanted to get to know her at last. She tried to focus on Holly's face. Up close, her boss looked far less intimidating. Claire could see the real colour of Holly's skin in her hairline, the place fake tan was unable to reach. This made her feel better for a reason she couldn't quite pinpoint.

'So, I need to talk to you about the *choice* searches you conduct at work.' Holly unlocked her phone and tapped on the screen with a manicured nail as she turned it around. There was a photo of Claire's monitor. *Eight days post ovulation can I test.* 'See? This was last Monday. I wouldn't mind if you were excelling, but – and I hope you'll forgive my bluntness – you've hardly made your mark on the team. Last week's big announcement? Every time I walked past you were googling, not calling journalists to interest them in the news. You're a manager. You're meant to be leading by example. Imagine if everyone spent their work day searching every little thing that popped into their head? That's not right, is it? No one would get anything done.'

Claire found herself nodding. She didn't know what else to do.

Holly laid her phone down on the table between them. Another picture. *Is hunger a sign my period is coming?* Claire remembered typing this after her stomach rumbled throughout Friday's all-staff meeting. She thought she'd minimised Google before anyone could see. (It wasn't a fruitful search. The Internet was divided.)

Claire couldn't meet Holly's eyes. She looked at her lap and pulled the fabric of her top away from where it had gathered around her stomach.

'Part of me wanted to speak to IT about this and find out how much work time you're wasting. We've been paying for this, Claire. Uno has been paying. For this.' She pointed again at her screen.

'I'm really sorry, Holly.'

'Well, I'm glad to hear that. But I don't just want you to be sorry, Claire, I want you to focus during valuable work time.'

'I will.' The skin on Claire's face prickled. Don't cry, she willed herself. You're thirty-two, please don't cry. While she knew she wasn't Uno's best and brightest employee, she always wanted people to think she was at least good at her job. She felt so ashamed to have been caught in this way, for Holly, for anyone, to think she might be slacking. Why had she been so careless?

It was then that the food arrived, two mounds of beef that looked exposed without the usual coverage of buns. The waiter gave no sign that he sensed the air bristling with tension as he put both plates down. Something instinctively revolted her about the meat, which she assumed was either her curdling anxiety or a hangover from her vegan phase last year. She'd read that plant-based foods were optimal for boosting fertility. Instead, the diet made her hair fall out in clumps in the shower.

'Let's just eat. I'll trust you to not repeat this again, Claire. It goes without saying that there will be consequences if I see something like this happen. I'll have to escalate it.' Holly speared her burger and Claire stared at the pool of cow's blood and ketchup congealing on her manager's plate.

'Thanks, Holly,' Claire said. She had no appetite. She cut up a chip just to do something with her hands. When she finally brought it to her mouth, the taste was not pleasant.

The two women ate on in silence. Claire thought of Holly's invasion of privacy and the threat of greater monitoring. And what must Holly have searched in private before her own testing incident? It felt doubly unfair she had to endure this conversation.

'Oh, come on, don't do that,' Holly said, when Claire finally crumbled.

Claire looked around for a napkin and settled for the sleeve of her top when she couldn't find one. The polyester hurt her eyes as she wiped.

'Look—'

'No, I'm just sorry. I'm so sorry.'

'Here, use this.' Holly fished around in her bag and pulled out a pack of tissues. They had yellow chicks on them. 'My mum always gets me novelty things and, as you can probably tell, I never use them. These must have been in my bag since Easter.' She eyed Claire with what looked like pity. 'Oh, we can't go back to the office with you looking like that. I need you to be on your A-game. Do you want to take a minute? Bathrooms are that way, I think. I'll settle this.' She clicked to signal for a waiter.

'No, I'm OK. I'm all good now, thank you.' Claire stopped herself from making the kind of comment she would with former female colleagues: how she was due on any moment now – in fact, one of her many apps predicted her period should have started yesterday – and her hormones were probably to blame for her emotional state. She didn't want to draw any more attention to the mystery of the inner workings of her body. She hated how she still wanted to please the person who made her feel so small.

Claire was relieved when Holly turned to her outside the restaurant and said she just needed to pick up something, she'd see her in the office shortly. Claire used the walk back to try and gather her thoughts. She knew now that not only would she never be let in on the team's social confidences, but it was likely that most people knew she was trying for a baby. They must laugh at her unremarkable dreams, so ordinary and yet still so out of reach.

Claire put her headphones in for the rest of the afternoon and powered through her to-do list. Every task brought her closer to an evening away from Holly and the horror of the day. James had left the house that morning in his smartest suit: a grey wool that made his green eyes shine especially bright. He'd been invited to a client's party – the client, who James said must be facing difficult times if their summer bash was on a Monday – was taking over a rooftop mini-golf club. James had already sent Claire pictures of the sensational view, skyscrapers poking into clouds. Claire was thankful she'd have some time to digest what happened at lunch alone.

After Claire had sent her final email of the day, she nudged her way through crowds of tourists and selfie-takers in Piccadilly

Circus to enter the Boots by the station. Even though she had barely eaten, she wasn't hungry. Her body felt light as she tried to sweep past the hordes. She was on a mission to buy the most expensive face mask possible. She deserved it. The shop was an oasis of calm compared to outside. Claire always loved wandering the aisles stacked with products that would make her healthy and beautiful. She could never resist trying on the make-up samples despite James's protestations about their dubious hygiene status. A slash of highlighter here, a pop of lipstick there.

It was impossible to avoid the family planning aisle on the way to the cashier. *Why not?* she thought, as she picked up a pack of double tests. She hadn't bought any since the previous week's heartbreak. The disappearance of her grey line hurt more than she cared to dwell on. James once commented on the small fortune spent on her testing habit, so she usually bulk-purchased cheap ones from Amazon. But she had earned the right to scratch the expensive itch again today. One final check before her period announced its inevitable presence.

She held the packet close to her chest in case anyone from work was around. The man behind the till gave her a generous smile as he scanned the item. Claire allowed herself to smile back. She liked how this man didn't know how many of these tests she'd done over the last year. In his eyes, she could be an expectant mother. Not the kind of woman who suffered from acute monthly loss.

Claire took the bus back to Dulwich. The prospect of being crushed against someone's armpit hair on both the Tube and the Overground was too much for her stomach to handle. She was happy to extend her journey time if it meant she could breathe in some fresh air. She didn't quite understand some people's disdain towards buses. They were so much nicer than being trapped, crammed, among others.

45

As the number 12 wound its way past the architecture of Westminster and towards South London, Claire remembered the first time she'd really looked at the grey water of the Thames and realised just how many people filter their images of the capital. She wondered when London might start to feel like home. Was it normal to still feel like a stranger when you opened the front door of an apartment you've lived in for over a third of a year?

The vehicle hurtled down the chaotic Walworth Road, where greengrocers spilled onto the street, and a group of teenagers traipsed onto the top deck in school uniform. They were youths on the cusp of adulthood, with heavy make-up and borrowed voices. Claire's interest was piqued. She found the act of eavesdropping relaxing. When you tune in to the beat of other people's lives it calms the anxieties that otherwise jostle for attention.

Claire turned off her music and listened through her mute headphones as the group discussed plans to obtain booze for the weekend. Claire's own teenage years had been mis-spent on caring too much about her schoolwork. She'd exited college with an envelope containing a gleaming white row of As and celebrated on the floor of Sally's bedroom, a bottle of dark rum glugged between bites of pizza. They saw pictures of the party plastered all over Facebook the next day. Everyone in their year cheering a final blowout. She would do her teens differently if she had another shot at life. She would have tried more things sooner: kissing, drinking, letting loose. She would be like these girls on the other side of the bus deck, discussing how they'd syphon some spirits from someone's mum's kitchen, replace gin with water. Maybe if she'd done that, she'd be in a different position now. Perhaps en route to a social with Holly, Ali and the other Uno girls.

Claire resented the lack of distractions when she got home.

The slam of the door continued to ricochet in her ears as she padded upstairs to the toilet. Something encouraged her to do this. She'd done it so many times now. Claire tore the test out of its packaging and let the foil drop to the ground. She held the reed too close and it hurt her. She stayed on the loo while she turned it round and watched the window in the cheap plastic cloud over as it processed her future.

Claire had to blink many times when it developed. A straight line blossomed before her eyes before another immediately slashed through its middle. A plus sign, a cross, a stamp of success. This time, there were no ambiguities about its colour. Claire made herself breathe. She checked the packaging, just to be sure, even though that clear second line was all she'd ever hoped to see, all those times. It confirmed her state. It felt unreal. She picked up her phone and struggled to get her PIN right as she pressed through the fog of tears.

James's name popped up alongside pictures of the sunset views from his roof terrace. The sky looked bruised and there were too many women stalking around in the background for Claire's liking. Everyone carried brightly coloured cocktails. She had never felt so sober. She wished her husband was beside her right now and able to help her stand up and process what was going on.

She waited for a moment, then dismissed his notification.

Before Claire could really think, she loaded up the TTC Tribe and posted a photo. She was too stunned to include a comment or text. Her phone immediately sprung into life, and she stared at it. All these people who hoped for the same thing, grieved what could have been every month, yearned for this test, this picture, this object in Claire's hands, were writing to her. But their congratulations felt as intangible as the news. She needed someone with her. It was all too much.

She opted for the next best thing and pressed dial.

'Claire?' she was so glad to hear another voice.

'Sally. Sally, something's happened.' Claire's words caught in her throat and came out with a croak.

'Are you OK?'

'Sally. I'm—' Claire took a deep breath that pounded in her mouth.

'What, Claire, what?' her friend asked.

'Pregnant.'

'Claire! This is just the best news. Hey, you worried me there for a moment. Oh, this is immense.'

Claire was silent. A fearsome amount of adrenaline zipped around her body.

'You there? Oh my God. I'm just – wow! What did James say?'

Claire's throat was dry. 'I – I haven't told him? I'm here with the test in my hand and I don't know, Sally, I don't know what I'm doing. Should I hang up?'

Claire's oldest friend laughed. 'Oh Claire! Yes. Yes, you should. Hang up and call your husband!'

'Sally?'

'Mm?'

'Is it normal to feel this . . . strange?' Claire could hear Rory mewling in the background.

'When we found out about Rors, my hand was shaking so much I had to put the test by the sink in order to read it. So, yes. Whatever you're feeling is very, very, normal. And exciting!'

'Sally . . .'

'Claire,' Sally's voice changed. It was her parenting voice. Stern. 'I love you. But I think you need to call James.'

'I know,' Claire said. She wanted to cry. She always wanted to cry. 'How do I tell him?'

But Sally had already gone.

That was the problem with Sally. She had moved forward first; she had bigger, more important commitments now. Claire would never admit it, but she missed the total access she used to have to her friend. Claire used to be able to offer Sally support, too. But when Rory arrived, Sally naturally turned to other mothers for little things, like where to buy the best nursing bras, and that turned into big things. There was the time Sally forgot to tell her that she'd had to rush Rory into A & E. 'He's fine now!' Sally had said, but to Claire it signalled a shift. Maybe now the gaps would shrink. The full friendship would return.

The flat was plunged into total quiet. The late afternoon sunlight highlighted the fragments of dust and skin hanging in the air. Tiny parts of Claire floating around, unacknowledged. Claire angled the front camera of her phone so it captured the vivid blue of the plus sign and her face. She needed to send something to James but the eyes that stared back at her looked haunted. The configuration of her features was all wrong.

James messaged again, *I'm way too drunk for a Monday*. Claire deleted the picture she'd just taken. Willed her husband to know that he needed to be home right now. She stared at the test until the cross burned into her retinas. She wanted her husband to hold her, to help her up, celebrate. The news was too big to convey to him over text. Pregnant, she was pregnant. It had happened! She allowed herself to sob from the depths of her gut. It wasn't the reaction she'd expected. For well over a year, pregnancy had felt like the end goal. Thinking beyond that positive sign had seemed almost impossible. All that scrolling, all that googling, it had felt so out of reach. It had been a form of escapism. But the test was positive, she'd arrived at last, and she didn't know what to do.

Sally sent a stream of pregnant emojis and happy faces and a: *Remember to take folic acid.* Claire smiled at that. She had been taking it for so long.

A sudden wave of exhaustion overwhelmed Claire's desire to do anything but lie down. She couldn't bring herself to even check the group. She left the foil on the bathroom floor and the bag containing her pampering ingredients in the corner and dragged her body into the bedroom, each step taking longer than the last. Despite the persistent heat, Claire pulled the sheets above her head. She only meant to rest a little before James got back. She curled up with the test in one hand and her phone in the other and fell deep into the ocean floor of sleep.

Claire didn't wake when James slumped onto the bed fully dressed and passed out on top of the duvet, his hand resting carefully on the outline of his wife's tender stomach. They were a naturally tactile couple, always instinctively touching each other, and after so many years together they knew the corners of each other's body perhaps more than they knew their own.

If Claire had checked her phone, she would have tracked her husband's increased concern about her uncharacteristic unresponsiveness. He had called seven times, messaged again and again, let her know he was worried because something clearly wasn't right. The phone glowed beneath Claire's pillow. The positive pregnancy test remained in her fist all night. According to the last website she'd looked at, the baby was only the size of a poppy seed. James had no idea he was going to be a dad.

Chapter 6

Soft light trickled into the bedroom and the clock on Claire's phone confirmed her suspicions: it was 5 a.m.

Claire allowed one hand to trace her flat-ish belly as she performed her morning phone ritual, checking all social platforms and forums. Her post had over a hundred messages of well-wishes from around the world. She positioned herself away from James in the unlikely circumstance he woke up before his alarm, before deciding it was too risky. She focused on Instagram instead. Sometimes Claire wondered if anyone studied her profile as dutifully as she did others'. She'd once known a former colleague was pregnant months before it was announced: the woman had started following baby pages on Instagram. Claire uncovered the secret while seeing if the woman was digital friends with one of the latest joiners to their company. It had taken all her willpower to not give the secret away with a knowing look over their desks. A shiver of excitement ran through her as she sought out and pressed the 'follow' button on those pages now. Accounts with names like Mumma Method, Baby Beans, or Acorn. It was her time at last.

Claire's body reminded her again that she'd gone to bed

without dinner. She looked over at James to check the rumble hadn't disturbed him. She was struck by how strange this moment was. Their whole world had changed but her husband had no idea. To him, this was just another Tuesday morning. She tried to think about all the delicious ways James might respond to the news, but a panic started to creep into her fantasies. Shouldn't she have just *known* she was pregnant? Why had she needed a test to confirm things? The prospect of any question being answered within seconds was too tempting. A global network of women had searched for the same thing.

Still, Claire wasn't fully satisfied. She shuffled into the bathroom where the second pregnancy test lay in its box. James must not have batted an eyelid if he'd noticed it the night before. It had been a long time since they represented anything but disappointment. Anxiety strengthened its grip. Perhaps last night was a fluke, or she'd jinxed things with the new Instagram follows. Claire needed to double check before she spoke to her husband. She tore at the wrapper and examined the stick for any existing lines. Maybe she'd misinterpreted yesterday's result? She tried to remember advice she'd read about catastrophising. Imagine your concerns written down on the sand, and water lapping all the fear away. She kept her eyes closed while she waited for the test to develop but instead of gentle waves, all she could picture was being confronted by the punch of a negative, and having to tell Sally and all those women online it was all in vain, and the huge future she'd already pictured for her family would disappear before it even had a chance to start.

When Claire finally found the courage to open her eyes, she saw the second line was even darker. She felt giddy with relief. This was actually happening. No more tests, she promised herself, while she waited for her breathing and heart rate to regulate. No more. She couldn't take the emotional turmoil.

Downstairs, Claire arranged the latest result on the table so James would see it, but it all seemed a little in your face. She hid it by the kettle instead – much better for a big reveal – and took a photo to send to Sally.

James was out last night so didn't get a chance to chat (yes, I know, on a school night). He's going to get such a surprise with his tea this morning.

Eeeeeek. Sally replied almost instantly, despite the still-early hour. *You've got to tell me EVERYTHING later!*

James often woke late after he'd been drinking, so Claire tried to coax her husband out of bed through a soft assault on his senses. She wondered if he'd even set an alarm. She started preparing his favourite cooked breakfast and allowed herself to be loose-handed with the pots and pans. She turned on the radio and increased the volume.

Claire had just flipped the bacon and was reading through the TTC Tribe messages when she heard James groan along with the stairs. She put her phone on the counter to give this moment – their moment – her full attention.

'Christ alive, I am not well, last night was heavy,' James said as he fell onto the sofa. When he turned to face Claire, she could see his hair was flattened on one side. 'Oh, is that what I think it is? How did you know?'

Claire nodded and held up the pan of eggs so he could see the deep red streaks of sundried tomatoes, his favourite. She wanted to prepare a feast. This was going to be a core memory, no matter how bad her husband's hangover.

'A cooked breakfast this early? You spoil me.' James sat up with outstretched arms and recoiled in pain. 'No fast movements,' he added in a small voice.

Claire's mouth was suddenly too dry to respond.

The plates wobbled as Claire walked over. She cleared her

throat after she set them down but before she could say anything, James pounced on the pile. She picked the slashes of
tomato out of the mound of eggs. They were the only thing she
could bear, hunger or no hunger.

'May I?' James asked, after he'd finished. He grabbed the rest
of her food.

'James?' Claire said, as she watched her husband overload his
fork. The way he was eating was revolting. 'Stay there.'

'Bear, I'm not going anywhere any time soon.' He yawned.
'How am I going to work today? I'm done in.'

Her arm trembled as she gathered the test from behind the
toaster. 'Look,' she said, and thrust the plastic towards her
husband.

'Is that . . .?' he said, staring at the plus sign.

'Baby,' was the only word Claire could get out. 'Our baby.'

Claire allowed James to nestle his head on her shoulder. She'd
only ever seen him cry once, when Newcastle United escaped
relegation from the Premier League and he'd wept with relief.
She hadn't dared to expect this reaction.

'We did it?' James's eyes were glistening. 'What . . . what
do we do now? Am I like, should I wash this up?' He gestured
to his plate. 'Oh wow. I can't think. This is the worst and best
hangover ever.'

Claire pulled him closer and inhaled his musty boozy scent.
'I think we're meant to just enjoy this.'

'OK, but I'm going to do all the housework now, Bear. Mark
my words, you won't lift a finger. This plate, every plate, it's on
me now.'

'Oh really?'

'Leave this to me. You focus on yourself. On our little secret.
Oh, this is just . . . It's just amazing. Oh, Bear, I'm all over the
place! I can't believe it.'

Relationships are full of surprises. Often the years reveal things forgotten or discarded in the initial throes of attraction: James's tendency to never wash the bedsheets, or his comments about Claire's phone-checking habit. But sometimes, time uncovers new things to love, like the sea buffering away a shell's blemished layers. James's face showed pure joy as he digested the start of their new life. At no point did he ask when she took the test, and Claire appreciated his simple trust. She hadn't meant to tell him third; that had never been the plan. If he had asked, Claire would have denied the post, denied contact with Sally, just so she could preserve the look on his face and the way he bent down and kissed her stomach after he finished the washing-up – that perfect moment – forever.

The whirlwind of happiness gave Claire new buoyancy. She left the TTC group and shared her sincere hopes to see other long-haulers in the graduate forums soon. Claire had wanted to write this message for so long. She let every congratulation sink in and almost showed James some of her favourites, but managed to rein herself in. He barely used social media. He wouldn't understand the extent to which these people had helped her through the darkest moments of their fertility journey, or the way she shared some of the most intimate parts of their life online. But here they were, on the other side.

At home, James kept referring to the pregnancy as their amazing secret. It made Claire's heart both sing and sink. It had always been a given that the mams would be told right away, but James wanted a little more time. When Claire said she was worried her mam would somehow just intuit the change, just like how she'd known Claire's period had started just by the look on her face one morning when she was thirteen, James said he completely got it, but could they have just one week where the news was theirs and theirs alone? Claire made all the right sounds but inside she thought: Oh no. She started leaving her phone face-down, just in case another one of Sally's messages like *Are you not replying because pregnancy exhaustion has hit?* came through when he was nearby. She knew she'd missed the opportunity to tell James about Sally. It wasn't the lie – James would have understood her need to speak to a loved one – it was the continuation of the lie that was the problem. And he never needed to know that people online had found out their news first.

Thankfully, most times Claire checked her phone, her worries were superseded by the sheer pleasure of their new reality. The unlock button opened a world she'd only dreamed about. On the recommendation of one of her new and exciting groups, she downloaded every pregnancy app she could find. One told her the baby was the size of a grain of rice, another said it was so tiny it was like day-old stubble on a man's chin. A symptoms tracker warned her about nausea, changes in appetite, and profound tiredness. Claire felt a sort of superiority that she wasn't one of those women who vomited day in, day out from the very beginning. She felt fine, wonderful, even. It was coming naturally, as she'd always hoped it would. As she left the house each day, she said to herself, *I'm pregnant, I'm pregnant, I'm pregnant.* When she ordered her now-decaf coffee, she hoped the barista noticed the change, noticed her new purpose. *I'm pregnant!* And at work, Claire made sure any research was conducted strictly off Wi-Fi, or off premises. She didn't want to risk another Holly encounter while she checked whether smoked salmon was safe to eat.

At first, her googling was wide-ranging, like confirming her make-up wasn't toxic, wondering how long you can fly on a plane for, or discovering the best ways to announce to your family, but it steadily became focused on one thing: Claire's old favourite, birth stories. It was different now. She no longer read indiscriminately. Perhaps the new influx of hormones guided her, but she much preferred learning about the home birth experiences.

There was something so wonderful that wove through these stories and made her bookmark them. It wasn't just the distance from the horror of hospitals – although she truly couldn't imagine feeling calm while in a building housing so much pain – it was more that they enabled the mother to have so much more power over their destiny. That thought alone was so comforting. She discovered a recent account of a woman who delivered with just her husband and her children by her side, her eldest son handling cups of cooled boiled water to top up the free-standing bathtub every fifteen minutes. The mother's pride jumped off the page. Here was a woman who endured one of life's most difficult tasks without any pain relief. Claire had to pop a couple of ibuprofens on the first two days of her period, without fail. She would have to work on her pain threshold if she wanted to experience this ultimate show of feminine strength.

Claire bookmarked the article. She planned on sharing her dossier of carefully curated research with James later. He was still so awestruck, so these kinds of practical conversations could happen when they were further along. She hoped the idea would enchant him too and he'd also see it as a chance for them to have their version of a tale as old as time itself, body begetting body. In the meantime, she would learn to be more resilient. Forgo the painkillers if she had an ache, build up a tolerance, perhaps undergo the mystery of hypnobirthing to unlock a hidden reservoir of power. She would do it. Something about those stories felt so right.

Chapter 7

James was out again on Thursday evening. Claire couldn't quite remember where. Her memory was all over the place and he hadn't updated the shared wall calendar that was typically full of scrawls like *five-a-side in Vauxhall* or *drinks with floor three*. Claire scrolled through her phone, wondering what to do to fill the expansive quiet. She didn't trust herself to call her mam or her sister. How could she hear those voices asking how she was doing and not mention the momentous change happening inside? It would be torture.

Claire received regular text updates from her sister Lily: old classmates spotted in the local pub, the countdown to Lily's departure for her big trip backpacking around the world, pictures of the special cubes her sister had purchased so she could stuff her possessions into one rucksack. Claire had always been careful to protect Lily from additional worry. When they were growing up, she made sure Lily wasn't exposed to the most difficult truths. It was a role she'd gladly occupied after their dad's illness, his death. Lily had always been fragile. It was why her adventure abroad was so important: it was her time to finally flee the nest and enjoy herself. Claire's thumb hovered over the green phone symbol by her mam's name. She so wanted to video call home, see the comforting sight of their living room, but no, it would be too difficult. She clicked away.

A notification on Claire's phone reminded her that, twelve years ago, she was with Sally, toasting the last few weeks they could officially get away with bad behaviour as students. Claire went to York, Sally to Newcastle, and they spent countless weekends taking the hour-long train between the cities. The pictures were a memento from the era where people brought digital cameras with them on nights out and took umpteen versions of the same pose before uploading them to Facebook under album titles like *Gulping down the last dregs of freedom.* Sally and Claire both sported bad fringes and ill-fitting body-con dresses. She texted Sally a screenshot of their faces crushed together, the flash highlighting the beads of sweat in their hairline and the slick of spirits on their teeth. *Remember being young?* she asked. Her friend started a video call within a few minutes.

'Claire Hansen, you've been ignoring me.'

'Sal. I am so sorry. James is off somewhere and he – well, I've accidentally promised we'll keep it between ourselves for a while.'

'Right.'

'As in, I forgot to tell him that you know already and now it's too confusing.' She didn't mention the online groups. Sally always regarded the Internet with slight suspicion. To her, it was a good tool for storing photos, finding lesson plans, reading about the many uses of bicarbonate of soda for cleaning. It wasn't its own universe of interests and passions.

'OK. So, in conclusion, you're as mad as ever.'

'You're meant to make me feel better!' Claire heard her voice go shrill.

'Say hello to Aunty Claire!' Rory popped up on screen and immediately ducked away in a blur of yellow dungarees and watery eyes. Sally's face returned to the screen. 'Claire, my love, all relationships are built on white lies. James doesn't need to know. And I've been worried about you. I thought you might be having one of your . . . down times.' Rory reappeared and tilted his head to one side. Sally bounced him on her lap. 'Come on Rors, it's Claire! Say Claire. Cl-aire.'

'Hello, bubba! Is that the most dashing man in Durham?' Claire cooed. She adored Rory. He was the only child she really knew, the first baby she'd held, cradling his neck with stiff, fearful arms, admiring toes so plump and tiny that it almost hurt to see something so perfectly formed. And she'd watched those toes grow, always kicking off any socks or footwear, while Sally went from strength to strength as a mother.

She tried not to be too offended by Sally's down times comment. That was the problem with friendships that last a lifetime: the friends know all the parts of yourself you keep locked away. Claire had a history of trying to hide when things turned difficult. She'd refused to answer the phone for weeks after her dad's diagnosis. She presented herself as a functioning member of society, but spent her evenings howling instead of answering the phone. Sally's flippancy was born from the privilege of having both parents still alive. Claire didn't want to mention or discuss it further.

'Listen to me, Claire, it's all totally fine! Just don't say anything to James. I know what you're like. And thanks for that picture, by the way. Weren't we gorgeous?'

Claire sighed. 'I can't even recognise that version of myself anymore.'

'No, I mean, we're still smoking hot, but isn't it sad we didn't realise it back then?'

Claire started to angle the phone to show Sally her latest burst of angry spots.

'Claire, I swear to God, if you show me your skin one more time, I will hang up. Focusing on it makes it worse. You need to chill! Zen for you and your baby. Hey, Rors, you're going to have a friend! Ooh, imagine if it's another boy!'

'Shush! Sally!'

'Oh, come on, Conor knows. And Rory doesn't really understand what we're saying, do you, Rory?'

Claire heard Rory giggle off-camera.

'Sally!'

'Partner rules. A secret's a secret but he's in on everything.' Claire heard a clatter in the background. 'Oh, someone's hungry! Got to go, love you. And call me soon. Or even better, can you come and visit? Maybe you can get some practice in. God knows, I could have done with some. So, no more ignoring me, OK?'

Claire spent the evening flicking through those ancient albums, the relics of her past self. Sometimes an old boyfriend would pop up, or worse, a former love interest who never felt the same way. Eric Taylor in the corner of a group shot, celebrating the end of their first-year exams. Eric, who once asked her if she wanted a drink and she felt her heart soar and then he said cool, can you give me the money? She googled Eric, just to see if time had also slapped him with a face-full of adult acne. Age had been kind: the black-and-white headshot on a law firm's website showed a man who looked like he owned a penthouse flat. Somehow, she ended up on his company's recent results in the London Lawyers' Royal Parks 5K. He didn't achieve an impressive time; at least she had that up on him. Back home, she'd been quite speedy. She just about stopped herself from searching him on her running app. Sometimes the

Internet satisfied curiosity cravings a little too easily.

Instead, she opened the notes on her phone. She was collating a bundle of information on home birthing ready to discuss with James on whichever evening he managed to spend with his wife, not sweaty men. She'd encountered some terrible stories about hospitals that showed what she was suggesting was right. Horror stories. Forceps blinding babies, C-section wounds festering, cases of negligence at the hands of doctors leaving children and families traumatised. These were all included in the master document. But the most important message she wanted to share was the one repeated time and time again wherever she looked: home births are natural, safe, and are how millennia of women led to where we are today. James had finally finished his copy of *Sapiens* – it had only taken him a year – so she knew that would really strike a chord.

The perfect opportunity arose when James got home the following night. He was drenched – a storm had punctured the heat at last – and dripped his way through the kitchen.

'I've got ingredients!' he shouted.

'James! Shoes!'

'Sorry, sorry. Will some toad in the hole wipe that look off your face? I'll clean up in a bit.'

'I want to tell the mams, James,' Claire said.

'Does that mean, yes, toad in the hole sounds wonderful, and thank you so much for going to the shops in this monsoon, what would I do without you, lovely husband?'

Claire took a step back. 'James, I'm being serious.'

'Oh, what did I have for lunch, you wonder? I had a champion sandwich, a Friday treat. Ham, cheese, pickle, the lot.'

'James, can you stop it? I really think it'll make their days. Their months, years, maybe!'

He reached for her hand. His voice took on a serious tone.

'Sorry, Claire, I just don't think it's a good idea right now. Can we wait one more week? A compromise?'

Claire sighed.

James wrapped his still-damp arms around her middle. He kissed her ear, which made her shiver. It always had.

'I think we should wait a little longer, until we've seen a doctor. I don't want to get anyone's hopes up until we've spoken to a doctor.'

Claire frowned. 'You can't say things like that, James. And a doctor's not going to tell us anything new. I was tracking everything; I know exactly when we conceived.'

'Ah, come on, Bear. Come here. Look, we'll tell them soon. Really soon. And it is going to make them so happy. Almost as happy as me.' He smiled for effect, but Claire could tell from his eyes it was forced.

'James, it's like you think something bad will happen.' She paused for a second. 'It's like you're expecting it.'

'Sh, sh, sh,' he said into her hair. 'I promise you, that couldn't be further from the truth, my Bear. This is the best thing that's ever happened to us. But you know how I get superstitious. I just think it'll be even more special if we wait just a tiny bit longer. Now, should I get cracking with dinner?' He gestured to the kitchen counter.

Claire felt herself soften. Toad in the hole was one of her favourites. 'OK,' she said.

She tried to bring up the idea of a plan as they tucked into two heaped plates of food, but the TV was too distracting, and it felt like too much of a statement to turn it off. James kept flicking through channels and sighing. The news was too depressing, he said, the weather forecast (predicting more rain ahead) was also deemed too miserable, and even *One Born Every Minute*, which Claire suggested they stayed on due to its educational purposes, was dismissed after it showed a woman being rushed from a houseboat to a hospital. 'Hippies, the lot of them,' James said, and Claire knew tonight was not the time to bring up her dossier. It was all right, she rationalised, there was more she had to learn, and it was best to prepare as much information as possible. They switched to Netflix instead.

Later that night, despite the failed mission, Claire registered her profile on a site called HomeBirthHeroes. *Because pregnancy is a natural process not an illness*, the strapline read. The phrasing struck her as slightly odd, but she continued with the process. Who thought it was an illness? A banner saying *All parents welcome!* flashed at the top of every page. She was DulwichGirl. The anonymity of these forums was always so exciting.

While James brushed his teeth, she rushed out a message in the *Introduce yourself, mama* thread. Her husband loved to spend luxurious amounts of time in the bathroom. Never-ending showers, serious attention to the correct flossing technique, an occasional habit of squatting fifty times while going over his teeth. She'd been known to query the timescales, but she'd loved him for it then. Her thumbs moved instinctively.

The phone lit up all night, flashing with messages of encouragement. It continued to chime over the weekend. Among these women, for Claire was sure they were all women, Claire felt at ease. No one judged her when she asked how she could try and convince DH (darling husband) this was the right thing. No one made her feel inadequate. Instead, they shared their experiences and offered words of comfort. It was so nice to speak freely and openly, without fear.

Claire took her phone with her when they went to Dulwich Picture Gallery on Sunday and snuck glances at the forum while James read out the descriptions of paintings by Old Masters. It was only human to want to learn more about the tiny life inside her. The reception within the gallery's thick, oak-panelled walls was so poor she had to pay £6 to connect to the Wi-Fi. Rembrandt could wait until next time. He'd waited four patient centuries before Claire even saw his work, these were cultural baby steps.

'How often do you reckon you're on that thing?' James asked, while they walked back. She had her phone out, ready to take a photo. The hydrangeas in the park were at the perfect stage of blooming, rich with colour.

'A normal amount?' Claire said.

'Want to bet? Can I look?'

Claire reluctantly handed her phone over. As it left her grip, she realised what she'd done. What he might see. She stood very still.

James turned the screen to her.

She exhaled. He'd only dug up her screen time report. For a moment, she was scared he might have seen the forums. The things she'd typed there weren't to be shared.

'Bear, it says eight hours a day! You spend eight hours on this little piece of plastic!'

'I think it's metal actually.'

'Eight hours! You've had more screen time than the man who invented screen time. Shall we do some phone-free evenings this week? I don't know how you fit it all in, you know. I'm actually impressed.'

Claire agreed to the idea of this digital detox because she hoped that James would forget. He seemed content with her response. He kept babbling on about how she managed to find the time to do so much. Claire resisted the temptation to explain why: how she had great empty caverns of time now, and was desperate to fill them with the closest thing she could find to friendship. It was too complicated to describe, and it was such a nice afternoon, and James was holding her hand in the way she loved, stroking it with his coarse thumb. He continued this hold as they walked past pastel doors and street art and all the special things that made Dulwich so impossibly pretty.

James turned to her as soon as they arrived back home. Past his head, Claire noticed a spray of breadcrumbs on the kitchen counter that would attract mice unless she cleaned them up immediately. Remnants of lunch. James could be so *careless* sometimes – he'd promised he would tidy that up. But before Claire could comment, he surprised her by suggesting they give the mams a call there and then. He'd received a slightly concerning message, he said, and thought his mam would appreciate some nice news. As an only child, James always felt very responsible for his mam's moods.

Husbands, Claire thought, always come around in the end. It didn't sit totally right with Claire that James thought this news, their news, was a mere pick-me-up, but still, it was something. They could finally share the surprise they'd been incubating, a joy that seemed too big for just the two of them over the last week. She let herself feel the excitement start to build and when she wrapped her arms around James's neck, he scooped her up and ducked down so her back nearly grazed the floor. She shrieked with the kind of laughter that comes from deep inside and allowed her brain to plan the scripts.

But when James's mam answered the phone, she said, 'Oh, that's lovely, that, so lovely, oh I'm thrilled for the both of yous, but . . . my loves, don't people tend to wait until their first scan before announcing this kind of special update?' and James shot Claire a look that made her want to scream. All those months of her mother-in-law asking when they'd give her grandchildren, for her to respond in this way?

She couldn't concentrate for the rest of the conversation or remember what else was said. When it was over, she immediately called her mam so she wouldn't have to speak to James about the comment. Her mam squealed with delight and asked if she should be a grandma or a nanna but Claire felt like she was not fully there. It felt like she was pretending.

When her mam cried and said, 'Oh, if only your dad could be here, he couldn't wait to be a grandad,' James had to nudge her so she would react.

'Yes, Mam,' she said, and James looked at her in a strange way.

Afterwards, James asked Claire if she was feeling all right, and she didn't tell him that the anticipation had been far better than the actuality. To Claire's relief, James didn't bring up what his mam said. Perhaps he felt stung too. It took a long time for her to find the energy to get up off the sofa, tidy up the crumbs, and join her husband upstairs. For the first time since the nerve-wracking second test, she'd been reminded that this could all come to an end.

Chapter 8

HomeBirthHeroes

Flora_Is_Free

Hello all you lovely Heroes! Warning: an angry post ahead. Please scroll past if you're not in the mood to hear a rant today. You know what it's like, a hormonal woman in a heatwave needs to get on her soapbox and vent sometimes!

Something's been playing on my mind over the last few days. Now, I don't want to get all burn-your-bra on everyone, but I've been thinking about all the ways I've been controlled throughout my life and let me tell you it's a sobering experience . . . And I've been as sober as a judge for a good 30 weeks now. Poor Tom's had his ear half chewed off so, for the sake of our partnership, I thought it would be better to get the rest of my thoughts down here.

It all started with little things when I was younger. Like how I was forced to take certain subjects at school, including maths, my GCSE nemesis. Or how we were banned from wearing strappy clothes in sixth form, presumably because the sight of a girl's shoulders is too much for some young minds to handle. I used to spend summer term in a constant state of panic that I had sweat patches. My general access to clothes has always been limited by higher powers.

I remember when I first met Tom, he asked me why I always wore black, and it dawned on me that I *just had*, ever since my mum, God love her, told me it was the most slimming shade. Whether it's well-meaning comments from mums still shaping our images or the insane cost of childcare restricting the return to work, we're directed from all angles – it's just so common we can't see it.

Right, now to the actual point of this point (sorry everyone, I warned you I was on one!) . . . I think that's why I've gravitated towards this path. There are few other times we get to do things on our own terms, where we have any kind of say.

As you all know, Tom and I are doing things slightly differently this time, although we're obviously planning another birth at home.

We were repeatedly stung by HC workers when expecting Freddie. Every time it felt like they were just desperate to have control over my body, our baby. Many of you know about their insistence I went down a consultant-led path and what we eventually chose, but I don't think I mentioned how the sonographer told us Freddie's sex even though we explicitly said we didn't want to know. We contacted the patient advice and liaison service to complain but nothing could retrieve the sense of wonder that had been stolen from us. When else in life is something a total surprise?

We've opted out of scans with Bump. I've got a Doppler at home (I know, I know, but I'm well versed on the risks and I know what I'm doing) and I hear little one's heartbeat galloping away when I use it every other day, so I'm keeping an eye on everything that way. And for anyone who asks about screening, we will love and care for any child. Even if we knew something was wrong, we would continue with the pregnancy. But this way, it's our decision and whatever happens will be on our terms. Although the constant wriggling suggests we've got a very active baby, so I'm not worried in the slightest.

I understand this isn't for everyone, but for me, it all goes back to regaining my voice. Younger me, the timid girl who allowed school bullies (including the boys in that heinous GCSE maths class) to make me feel so embarrassed just for existing, would be so proud.

If I have a daughter, I want to teach her how to advocate for herself. How to exert control in the small ways that amount to a real difference.

Anyway, if you've read this far, thank you for listening. I'm so proud to be part of this community. Us mothers show our babies we'll do everything in our power to ensure they arrive in a place of true, incomparable love – home – even if it means going beyond certain rules or norms. Is there anything quite as wonderful as that?

Comments:

AmyIreland: *Oh God, you've got me on one now and I'm fuming! I remember my mum used to tell me not to sit in a certain way as it wasn't 'ladylike'. What even is ladylike? Who decided we have to make ourselves little while men can be as large as they'd like? One of the few benefits of galumphing around at 36 weeks is that when I plonk myself down, I can spread my legs and rest my bump on there and no one bats an eyelid. So here, here, Flora girl!*

McBuckley_E: *Argh, Flora, I was so on board here until your part about no scans. What has your midwife said?*

Taylor-Rew: *Hello! God, so much of this resonated and I totally agree that home birthing is just so good at making you feel a little bit in charge of the craziness going on inside, it's exactly why I can't wait for mine (I'm a first-timer!!!). I was so tempted to get a Doppler too but NHS and NCT advice (just double checked to be sure) is that only trained practitioners should use them. Are they really hard to use? Do you definitely recommend? I'm just nervous because at my 16-week appointment it took the midwife so long to find baby's*

heartbeat (I was in FLOODS with worry) and I don't know if I can
handle that again. Thank you in advance!!!

Flora_Is_Free: @Taylor-Rew I've DM'd you, one of the best decisions I've made this pregnancy! No feeling quite like it, it's mine and
Tom's favourite part of the day.

Chapter 9

Claire's sister Lily and their mam Rosemary were arriving the following Saturday. They were not invited. They simply knew, in the way that only family members can truly predict each other's behaviours, that Claire would want to see them. They told her via a hurried mid-week call with a chorus of 'surprise!'. Claire had been halfway through a podcast where two doulas spoke to women and their partners about home births. She was so charged by the news that she forgot to return to the episode she was enjoying. Instead, she shouted, 'James! Can you come here?', found the nearest piece of paper and made a list of everything they had to prepare. She needed to order prints of family photographs and buy some frames, ensure the spare room was no longer a dumping ground for all the *bits* they'd somehow accumulated, and so much more. The list occupied the whole of the back of an envelope. James just nodded when she talked him through it all. 'Ah, it'll be nice to see them, won't it,' he said when she finished.

In the days leading up to the visit, Claire fizzed with a combination of excitement and nervousness. When she woke up in the middle of the night to go to the toilet, she struggled to get back to sleep because she found herself thinking of new tasks that had to be done, like making sure they had Earl Grey tea for her mam (who always called it Earl Gary) or searching for a restaurant name she knew she'd noted down somewhere. Throughout their relationship, James never quite understood why she cared so much about visitors' opinions – especially her family's, considering the permanently cluttered state of the house she grew up in. If it was up to James, their home would only be lightly tickled by a duster before anyone arrived.

The night-time bursts of worry meant Claire no longer glowed her way through the working day. The productivity decline from the previous week must have been noticed: Ali emailed and offered to get Claire a coffee. She only realised she'd missed this olive branch when Ali placed a latte on Claire's desk and said, 'Here, I think this is your usual.' She thanked Ali profusely but had to dispose of the drink when she next went to the loo. As one app kept reminding her, it was better to just avoid all caffeine. Claire felt a profound sadness as she tipped it away.

Claire missed the clarity coffee gave her. As she muddled through an inbox full of red urgent icons, her mind kept turning to conversations she might have with her mam about motherhood. It was difficult to know how they might go. Claire had often alluded to wanting to start a family and her mam was always encouraging, but these conversations were shallow, light-touch. Several women on the podcast mentioned friction from mothers convinced there was only one right way to give birth – their own method – and Claire realised she had no idea about her own story. She'd seen a photo of her parents in hospital, eyes moony with happy tears as they held her, but had her mam wanted a home birth too? She wished the podcasters would share the cues they followed to broach these conversations. And more than anything, she hoped her mam would support her in whatever she chose to do. These were the types of thoughts that took precedence over Uno's press office demands. Concentrating on her computer was tricky when so much *life* was happening. To help her focus, she didn't listen to the podcast series on her commute in on Friday. It had little to no effect.

When Saturday finally arrived, the two Brooks women bundled out of the car with a joint squeal of 'Claaaire'. James helped them with their luggage, and everyone made a show of not allowing her to carry anything. It felt wonderful to have three loved ones acknowledging this, but Claire didn't quite know what to do with herself. No one wanted a cup of tea, so she lingered in the corner while bags were plonked on clean surfaces, until everyone started hugging again.

Up close, Lily looked thinner than Claire remembered. The last time they'd all been together was just before Easter, before Claire and James left their beloved flat in Gateshead. Claire had got too used to the image of her sister, the mirage in FaceTime, rather than flesh and blood. She'd forgotten how elegant Lily's movements were, or how her sister's prominent hipbone was practically the same height as her chest. Claire hated being short. She got that from her dad, who was as compact as her mam was willowy. When Claire reviewed the photos she'd asked James to take of her wedged between her mother and sister on the sofa, she hated how she looked. She held her phone in her lap and scrutinised the series of stills, zooming in and out, in and out, while the rest of the family babbled away.

'That one's lovely, isn't it?' James whispered. Claire looked at the picture one last time before placing her phone screen-down on the table. She had no idea what James could think was nice about it. But conversation had moved on; there was no point in requesting a reshoot.

Claire and James sat on the chairs that were normally tucked underneath the kitchen table. In the preparation process, Claire realised they'd welcomed no guests since moving, well over five months ago. She was surprised by how quickly she'd adapted to only socialising with her husband, to being alone. Looking around, at the room that was finally full of company, she felt sadness brew within. This, this soundtrack of familiar babble, was what she'd been missing.

'So, Claire, James, would you like to hear some pregnancy stories?' Rosemary said.

Lily groaned. 'Mam . . .' She looked at Claire. 'She's been like this the whole drive down. I think I reached peak anecdote around Nottingham.'

'I'm all ears,' James said.

'You'll regret that,' Lily said.

'Charming, Lil. So, you don't want to know about the time I joined a mad group of women for NCT classes?' Rosemary winked at Claire and James.

I'm so glad she's brought this up first, Claire thought.

'Sis, trust me, you don't. The course leader made them knit patterns to show how a Caesarean works and mam thought it was grim and crazy. And now I can't get the image of Caesarean surgeries out of my head, so I'm saving you from it too.'

'Lily, madam, you've spoiled my best story! Oh, I hope you don't have to have that operation, Claire, pet, it's a terribly long recovery. Janice, you remember Janice from up the road, she couldn't get up or down stairs unassisted for weeks. So, have you thought about what you might like?'

'No, we've not actually,' James jumped in, just as Claire was about to speak.

'Good, good, no point in planning.'

James laughed, but he sounded unsure. 'What do you mean?'

'I've always said, anyone who thinks it's possible to control anything is kidding themselves. I wanted to tell all those NCT ladies, your baby doesn't care one jot about your birth plan, what will happen will happen.'

'Deep, Mam,' Lily said.

'Did you hear that, Claire?' James said, and put an arm around her. 'No point in planning, so we can just kick back for the next eight months, eh?'

Claire shot him a glance. His arm felt heavy on her shoulder. He had no idea how much time she spent learning, reading, absorbing. She hadn't shared the home birthing research with him – with anyone – yet. It was still a work in progress, and she was waiting for the perfect time. But she didn't like how he assumed that her mam knew best when her knowledge was decades out of date. Everyone on this new podcast had a plan. She needed a plan.

Rosemary continued, 'You'll never guess what I read about in one of my magazines. Apparently, women are eating their placentas these days. Turning them into pills or something. You won't be doing that, will you? Can you imagine it? Oh, the smell, Claire, wait until the smell. Your poor dad nearly fainted like a Victorian lady when it flopped out of me. And they just leave it there, the great mass of it.'

'Eugh!' Lily said.

Claire couldn't stop herself from grimacing.

'Right, well, thanks for that Mrs B.,' James said. 'Time for a walk?'

While everyone busied themselves finding their jackets and bags, Claire opened up the notes app on her phone. *Placenta? Ask Sally, ask HBHs.* She didn't notice her mam appear.

'Have you looked into that, pet? NCT? It was good, you know, despite those loons. And when's your first scan? What did the doctor say? And how are you feeling, any nausea? I was sick to the high heavens with you, you know. The only thing I could keep down was cheese on plain crackers. It was the same with Lily too, although olives were my thing with her. And you know, of course, the other time . . .'

'Oh, Mam,' Claire said. She remembered. She looked around, but there was no sign of James or Lily. She had only ever alluded to this part of her family history with him, never discussed it with her sister. Some things are so sad they must be permanently tucked away.

There was the announcement of another sibling over a picky tea one afternoon after school, and Claire had to explain to Lily what it was like seeing a baby grow inside their mam's tummy. But their mam went away, and their dad was so sad he forgot to turn the oven off when making dinner and the house smelled of burnt fish fingers for days. Claire and Lily were sent to their grandparents' house for what felt like an eternity. Lily wet the bed almost every night and their grandma would issue barbs about Lily needing to act her age as the two girls stared at a rack of toast and marmalade, and their grandad just turned his newspaper pages. When they got home and asked when they'd meet the baby there was a terrible silence. Sometimes, when Claire was sleeping in the top bunk of her shared bed, and Lily was fast asleep, she'd hear sobs coming from her parents' room. Claire both did and didn't want to know more about this memory, one she'd stowed away so deep. It was too awful back then, even more appalling now.

She looked at her strong mother, whose face was so open and kind despite the horror just recalled. 'I'm fine, don't you worry about me,' Claire said with a hug. The NCT conversation was no longer important.

'It's a mam's job to worry. Just you wait, it never ends,' Rosemary murmured.

Later that day, they all wandered around Dulwich and Claire pointed out her new running route. Lily looped her arm into Claire's, just like always. The younger sister's enthusiasm propelled Claire forward as they walked by shops and cafés. When they passed one of the many estate agents on Lordship Lane, Claire's mam lingered by the window, her mouth wide as she registered the cost of one-bed flats in the area. Each caption mentioned the *vibrant heart of Dulwich*, as if a suburb had an organ. One tiny two-bed with a west-facing patio was on the market for three quarters of a million pounds.

'I know,' James said. 'Everything costs so much money here. And yet everyone I work with is tighter than a knicker leg.'

Rosemary and Lily enjoyed that. James was so good at making them feel at ease. He'd always fitted in well with the Brooks women. Claire knew her dad would have adored him too.

Over lunch, at an excellently reviewed Italian, Lily shared the latest version of her travel itinerary. Claire had heard so many iterations of this trip over FaceTime, but in person, she could see just how much the anticipation made her sister glow. Instead of fiddling with her hair, something Lily had done for as long as Claire could remember, she used her hands to present screenshots of every country on her list. The rest of the table watched as she tapped through pictures of animals, beaches and paradisiac views. James asked all the right questions about whether Lily had booked any flights yet or if she'd already started packing. He already knew the answers, but it was clear that Lily was so proud of her organisation, her upcoming independence.

Vietnam, Cambodia, Thailand, Malaysia, Singapore, Australia, New Zealand: the route was all mapped out. Claire wondered how their mam felt about being alone for the first time.

Lily had never gone to university, and she'd always been there in that cosy house. Soon, Rosemary would have one daughter three hundred miles away, another three thousand. Claire didn't mention that Lily would miss the arrival of the baby. It was the type of thing that would always remain unspoken among their family.

'Enough about me,' Lily said, when the waiter brought out the dessert menu. She'd never liked being the centre of attention. 'How's work, Claire? Is that boss of yours still as nasty as anything?'

'What?' James and Rosemary said, almost in unison. Two of the closest people in Claire's life.

Claire had trusted Lily to keep this a secret, implored her not to tell their mam after a throwaway comment about Holly and her surveillance methods slipped out during a call. Lily had no idea what office life was like. She'd done shift work in bars and restaurants and had spent the best part of the last year working in the local supermarket to save up for her adventure. Claire knew her sister would be horrified if she heard the full extent of Holly's behaviour.

Claire forced a smile. 'Oh, that was nothing.' She focused on cutting the arancini on her plate, so as not to catch her mam's eye. 'You just caught me on a bad day. I've actually got a work friend now, one of my juniors. We get each other hot drinks in the morning.' Claire didn't mention how this was a one-off, and how insignificant she'd felt when she realised she was the only person on the team not invited to Ali's party.

'A friend's cool, sis! Hey, are you OK?' Lily asked. 'Your face has gone . . . well, you look like a piece of salami?'

Claire chuckled but she could feel her sister's eyes on her for a long while afterwards. Sisters, through the shared combination of DNA, can always tell when something is wrong.

That night, the flat felt crowded instead of complete. Lily knocked over a bottle of Coke when she reached for a jumper and the drink erupted everywhere. James just watched as Claire mopped, seemingly forgetting that she was meant to be taking it easy. 'Don't mind me,' she said to everyone on the sofa, as she detached the mop head and accidentally stained her cream jumper. She didn't bother changing.

When everyone finally said they felt hungry, Claire jumped at the chance to be able to acceptably get her phone back out. *James is being SO annoying,* she texted Sally, and it felt good to externalise a feeling that had festered all day. The reactions to the pizza place Claire chose, her and James's favourite, weren't what she'd anticipated. Rosemary scrunched her face when she tried the sriracha aioli Claire paid £2.50 for and asked for ketchup for her crusts, then complained the pizzas weren't like the new takeaway that had opened down the road back home. 'Great, thanks Mam,' Claire sighed. They couldn't agree on a film, even after James tried to make the case for various award-winners, so the room flickered with the lights of Saturday night TV. Her mam and sister excused themselves to get ready for bed before the celebrity talk show was over.

'Bear, you've got to be nicer to them,' James said as they tidied the plates and pizza boxes away, 'They've come a long way for you.'

'For us.'

'No, for you, Bear.'

Claire considered this for a second. 'I've been on my feet since the crack of dawn, cleaning up, offering drinks, making sure we followed the itinerary that I came up with. What's not *nice* about that?'

'No, no, I know, but you've just been a little . . . tense. Look, forget I said anything,'

'But you've made me feel bad now. And why didn't you let me speak when my mam asked about plans? I wanted her advice, but you just cut me off.'

'Did I? Well, you've got all tomorrow to chat to her about it, haven't you.'

Claire raised both eyebrows. 'Great.'

'Oh, come on, let's not do this now. It's been a full-on day for everyone.'

Claire made sure her voice was low. She didn't want her family overhearing. 'These are the kind of things we need to talk about first, James. It's not just my responsibility to look into how our child might be born. You embarrassed me.'

'Sorry, Claire. I was probably just trying to make conversation. I can't even remember what I said. Shall we go to bed?' He reached out to touch her face. 'You look tired, my beautiful Bear.'

'You go, I'll finish up here,' she said, and James seemed more than happy to oblige.

Claire didn't sleep well again. She lay beached on her side for hours, picturing the burst of life inside her and what kind of future it might have. Rosemary tried to broach the topic of NCT once more over their Sunday roast. Even though the podcast suggested NCT was prescriptive, outdated and a waste of time, the tiredness meant Claire said 'Of course,' about NCT, and the GP, and the scan, and any updates on sickness or aversions or anything, when her mam asked her never-ending stream of questions over the gastropub table. It was somewhere Taya recommended. According to Taya's recent texts, the beef short rib was to die for.

Claire noticed that her mam left most of her lunch untouched. The family had a joke about picky eaters: they asked if they'd been poisoned in a former life. Claire didn't say it, though.

James made her feel like she'd done something wrong the day before. She was taking extra care.

They all had ice creams from the gelateria afterwards. The man behind the till looked horrified when Lily asked for 'monkey's blood' on her cone of vanilla. The group huddled in a fit of giggles on the pavement, re-enacting his face, his raised eyebrows, and Claire's explanation that it was just strawberry sauce. It was the hardest Claire had laughed in a long time. And it felt special, to be among her family, doing what she used to do. She almost forgot her pique towards her husband. They hadn't held hands all day.

The visitors left later that evening in a flurry of luggage and Lily's promises she'd visit again before her trip. Claire had been in the bathroom washing her hands and slicking down her unruly eyebrows when she heard James say, 'It's all good, Mrs B. I think she's just a bit stressed at the moment because of all the changes and she's not sleeping that well. Yeah, I'm sure it's all good.'

Claire walked as lightly as her frame would allow down the stairs, holding on to the banister to absorb the sound of her weight.

She caught her mam saying, 'She seems very on edge,' and heard James murmur something that sounded treacherously like agreement. *Breathe*, she reminded herself.

When the conversation turned to silence, Claire clattered down the remaining steps. Neither reacted.

Her mam held her tight, with a too-firm grip digging into her shoulders, and said over the top of Claire's head, 'It's been hard going for the both of yous, but you must be so excited.'

'It's all I've ever wanted, Rosemary,' James said.

Through the corner of her mam's arm, Claire saw her husband's sincerity. He truly meant this.

Claire realised she couldn't remember the last time she'd asked how James felt. The guilt unsettled her, and she felt annoyed that someone else had exposed the right way to behave. She would talk to him later.

Lily was already in the car, and she shouted out, 'Come on, Mam, the traffic's only going to get worse! This app's saying it's going to take over seven hours.' She blew Claire a huge kiss from behind the window.

Claire waved from the pavement for a long time after they'd driven away. The familiar smell of home stayed around for a few seconds before it evaporated and all that was left was the scent of late-summer decline. Inside, on the wall planner, Claire ticked off the hurried *MAM AND LIL HERE* capitals scrawled over the weekend section, as if they were another completed job on her to-do list. She tidied away the teabags Lily had left in the sink and closed her eyes. She soaked in the silence. There was no one asking for a drink or following her around. Claire wondered if anyone had truly enjoyed all the time they'd spent in each other's company and sent a long message saying how much fun she'd had, how much she'd appreciated them coming down, and how she couldn't wait to see them again very soon. Lily immediately responded with so many hearts that it filled the screen with the image of love.

Chapter 10

'What's your work like?' Claire asked Taya on their next park run. It was a gorgeous, mellow Sunday afternoon, the last weekend of August. The sky was on the precipice of pink, the clouds lit from within. Flying ants had swarmed the previous day and Claire saw the specks of their once-hopeful bodies on the pavement and amid the grass. She tried not to step on their remains. Claire hadn't been back to the running club in weeks and instead ran with Taya alone. The two women didn't ever discuss their breakaway from the main group.

'It's not too bad at the moment,' Taya said between pants.

They had incorporated sprinting into their schedule, and Claire felt a satisfying trickle of hard work fall down her back. She looked forward to these sessions so much. Taya's brightness had a way of spreading its shine. Claire always felt like she had her friend's total attention and that made Claire feel like maybe she could be interesting too. It was so exciting to use that word, even in her own head: friend.

'We've got a big disclosure deadline coming up, but my boss is great. He always sends me home on time, which sounds silly but it's actually extraordinary in lawyer land.'

'Really? You know what, I've never met another lawyer before.'

Claire knew more about Taya's employment than she would ever admit. The Internet contained Taya's entire backstory: she went to international school, which explained the slight American twang to her words, before she studied Law at UCL, then took the LPC, and had been qualified in commercial litigation for nearly a decade. Claire even knew the sort of salaries to be expected; staggering, life-changing sums of money. She longed to be invited over and see how that type of salary manifests in the way someone turns a house into a home. Did Taya's wine glasses trill if you ran a finger around their rim? Did she have a bathroom with an actual bath?

'So you've never heard the horror stories? I call these my battle wounds.' Taya pointed to the skin under her eyes.

'You'll have to tell me.'

'That's best shared over a bottle of something. And I'll need space: some of these re-enactments are physical.' Taya took in a big mouthful of the afternoon air. 'But I'm lucky to have my boss. He's been very kind in the past. Very understanding. Men like that are rare, I think.'

Claire waited for Taya to turn the question round and ask about her work, and when she didn't, and the only sounds were the padding of their feet and the low roar of cars driving past the park, she said, 'Like when?'

Taya took another deep intake of breath and wiped her nose on her top, exposing a ripple of taut stomach, a body that contained quiet, elegant strength. 'Oh, just health things. Women's troubles, the usual.'

Claire saw a flash of something move over her friend's face and knew to stop asking questions. It wasn't the right time to bring up any of her problems either. Their relationship was too fledgling for Claire to admit she was less worried about work than being around women who still didn't accept her. Instead, she pictured what it would be like if Taya worked at Uno. Would they grab lunch every day? Would Taya be friends with Ali, who Claire recently bought a coffee for in return (a matcha latte, to be precise), but there had been no sign of a counter-move. The olive branch seemed to have reached its growth limits. This daydreaming helped distract from the fact this was the furthest the two of them had ever run together, the furthest Claire had run in nearly half a year, and her shins were crying out for attention.

When they finished and stood next to each other stretching, Claire told Taya about her family's visit and how they had loved her restaurant recommendation, even though that wasn't strictly true. The two women arranged to meet again, and Claire updated the wall calendar when she got home. She added a little heart next to Taya's name and immediately crossed it out. The next step was to invite her over and she couldn't bear the idea of Taya seeing such a strange flourish.

Taya messaged in the middle of a video call with Claire, James and Lily. It made James scoff. *I'm ravenous! I've just been out to buy my second round of snacks!* it read.

'I can see why you like her,' James said.

'I want to meet this Taya!' Lily said, when Claire read the message out.

'Who's Taya?' Claire's mam grumbled out of shot. 'Why does no one ever tell me anything?'

Claire's mam kept calling, always choosing the least opportune time to reach out. She had been retired for several years and already she'd forgotten the rules that restrict an office worker's day. Claire's phone nearly vibrated off the table in a meeting to discuss the launch of Uno's new energy bill app. Holly shot her a glance before Claire grabbed the device, nearly knocking over a jug of water in the process. *Talk at lunch!* she messaged underneath the boardroom table, expertly touch-typing while looking at Holly. Not that Holly maintained eye contact. Claire's boss spent the meeting volleying with their broad-shouldered, squat CEO who usually spent his days swaggering around the office and preening himself in the reflections of meeting rooms. Holly held her own deftly, as the CEO, Neil, tried to shoot down all her ideas.

Holly's ace move was when she presented the last suggestion to the group and said, 'Now, I know Neil's playing devil's advocate today, but he was *very* excited by this idea over email last week, so I'm sure this is the one.' Neil grunted when she finished. Before the meeting ended, Holly raised her voice slightly to ask Neil's PA to make sure the minutes reflected they'd be going down the final launch route, 'As per Neil's verbal agreement.'

When they left the room, Claire tapped Holly on the shoulder and said, 'I thought you handled that so well.' Claire's nerves were fried and she'd not said a word. Maybe this was why Holly was her senior, despite her age. She couldn't help but be impressed.

'I need a cigarette,' Holly said. 'Or I'm going to explode.'

Claire hadn't realised that Holly smoked. It felt like something she should have noticed. When she stepped outside to get lunch thirty minutes later, she spotted Holly slumped against the building, holding her phone with one hand and a cigarette with the other. It was the first time she'd seen Holly look fazed by anything.

Claire waved when she walked past but Holly didn't look up from whatever was absorbing her attention and grooving deep lines into her normally flawless forehead. When safely out of earshot, Claire called up to schedule the doctor's appointment for Friday. Her mam's mid-meeting call had prompted her into action. Just in case anyone from Uno was around, she stood in an alleyway. She realised when she checked to see how long she'd been waiting in the queue that she'd pressed the device so close to her face that she left smears of foundation on the screen. When she finally connected, she found herself unable to speak properly. It all suddenly felt so real. The receptionist repeated herself and Claire whispered, 'Oh, just a check-up please.'

GP booked, she texted James, once it was done.

Yesss, he replied.

Later, over a bowl of chicken salad, plopped down on the table with, 'An extra big portion to feed an extra special guest,' James told Claire that his boss had given him a knowing look when he'd asked to work from home on Friday morning so he could accompany his wife to a medical appointment. 'He patted my shoulder so hard I think I'm going to develop a bruise.'

'That's nice,' Claire said. The chicken was dry and so plentiful she wasn't quite sure how she'd manage to finish without asking for a refill of water.

'What did your manager say? Was she OK? What was Lily talking about the other day? Sorry, too many questions. I'm just excited!' His eyes were huge.

'Oh, yeah, she was OK,' Claire said, and jammed her fork into yet another piece of meat. *I do need to see a proper handover,* Holly emailed when Claire put the doctor's appointment in Holly's diary alongside a request to work from home. *I can't let anything slip, OK? Neil expects big things here.*

'Just OK?'

'Yeah, that's what I said,' Claire said as she cut off pieces of leftover skin, flabby and clear like jellyfish remains. James, as much as she loved him, was not a natural in the kitchen. She thought about Holly's fraught expression and chain-smoking, and the extra-strong perfume scent that lingered by their desks that afternoon, probably to cover up the smell. She would renew her focus at work, make life easier for Holly. That could be the key to winning her over. Maybe then she'd receive the same kind of support and tenderness from Holly as James did from his boss. Being honest with herself, she had allowed things to slip. After a lifetime of desperation to get top marks, she'd accepted hovering below average at Uno. She needed to impress.

James and Claire held hands on their walk to the doctor's surgery. Claire's stomach had been too full of panic and hope to eat the cereal James laid out in the bowls his aunt gave them as a wedding present. He'd eaten from the *Mrs* dish and if Claire hadn't felt such a churning sensation in her belly she would have taken a photo. Now, she was starving, but she didn't have time to pop into one of the bakeries that pumped out heavenly scents on their route. Neither of them wanted to be late.

'You know, Bear,' James said, with his eyes on the pavement, 'I was worried something was wrong with me. When you showed me that test, I wanted to say: Yes, it works!'

'James!' Claire said. He never usually spoke in this way. He made insurmountable problems pocket-sized. He was Claire's personal Atlas, their world on his shoulders.

'You know, all the comments my mam would make, how sad you'd always get when your period started, it scared the living daylights out of me. I don't know if you remember, but I started taking those tablets. The zinc. That nasty one, fenugreek. Like a mouthful of bitter liquorice.'

Claire didn't remember this. She only remembered the agonies of the negative tests, the deflation of her hope, the sense that her body was revolting against her will. She held his hand

and thought of how strange it is to exist alongside someone, sleep by their body, eat their meals, and yet sometimes feel like total strangers. Marriage was like that. You know everything and nothing.

She'd once read an article about how social media spies on everyone's conversations and monetises the words we say to each other and the secrets we type. It was why she started saying certain phrases whenever James left his phone in the room: *My husband is ready to be a dad,* she'd whisper in the device's direction, careful not to speak too loudly and rouse James's suspicion, *He will be a great, loving dad.* She got into a routine of saying these little mantras in her head whenever her fertile window approached: *We are ready, this month is our month, we will be fantastic parents.* Through the power of technology or telepathy, she'd hoped these messages would somehow spur her husband on to try a bit harder, make more time for the intimacy she meticulously scheduled, turn off the endless rounds of football on TV. She had added to his own sense of personal failure. All the conversations, the leading questions prompting him to say he also wanted this took on a different dimension in her memory now. She'd never thought how he might feel. The guilt twisted in her stomach.

In the waiting room at the doctor's surgery, Claire leafed through magazines, but the words kept swimming off the page. Every story, every double-paged splash of celebrities caught off guard seemed too bright, too insignificant. James played his beloved football game on his phone, acting god to assemble fantasy teams. Claire tried to focus on the glossy images of perfect bodies. She hadn't consulted the ladies on the forum to ask what to expect; she wanted to experience the excitement without any spoilers. All she knew was she would probably have a pregnancy hormone test, and she hoped it required a urine sample rather than blood. She chewed on the edge of her index fingernail and checked her phone. No new notifications from people she cared about, but her podcast app said a new episode of her home birthing series was available. She still needed to have that conversation.

The sound of something hitting the floor interrupted Claire's thoughts.

'Ahhh,' a woman said, as a water bottle rolled towards Claire's feet. 'Leo, what are you doing, you silly sausage?'

Claire grabbed the bottle before it could spin behind a seat. 'Here,' she said.

'Thank you,' the lady mouthed. She passed the bottle back to the gurgling child in the pram. 'You're just loving keeping me on my toes today, aren't you?'

Leo looked at Claire, his brown eyes crinkled at the corners in delight, and giggled. But before Claire could say anything, a middle-aged man shouted her name from behind the front desk.

'James.' She nudged her husband, who was transfixed by his game. 'Come on, we're up.' He shoved his phone in his pocket and jumped to his feet.

'How cute was that baby?' she said, when they were out of the mother's earshot.

'What baby?' James said.

Claire had never met Dr Faulkner before, and she was shocked when he not only forgot to congratulate her but also asked if she was here to discuss potential *options*. When James cut through Claire's silence with reassurance that this was very much wanted, the doctor asked why they were there. His jowls wobbled while he told the couple they were taking up a valuable slot in his very busy day, when he was looking down the barrel of a no-lunch, 7 p.m. finish. Why, he asked, through a furrowed brow that sent a ripple of wrinkles across his face, hadn't they been referred to the local midwife services by reception when they called up?

Claire's heart beat faster and faster as Dr Faulkner explained the chain of events to come: a twelve-week scan, blood tests to rule out or reveal genetic defects, a twenty-week scan, a long wait, a birth. He emphasised the importance of some screenings that really should be done before she reached the upcoming ten-week mark. James took out his phone and made notes and Claire just sat there, hearing the thud-thud-thud inside. She allowed James to hoist her out of her seat with his smooth, strong hand, and didn't respond when Dr Faulkner said 'Good day.' She fumbled her way out of the building in a blur of grey walls and automatic doors, thankful that James was able to guide the way.

'Come on, soldier. Let's get some scran,' James said, as they stood outside the surgery and Claire wrapped both arms around herself against a non-existent breeze.

'It just doesn't feel right,' Claire said, when they sat down on intentionally ramshackle wooden chairs underneath the awning of the nearest café. It was the kind of place that had a coffee menu split into countries of origin. She busied her feet crunching the leaves under the table. 'It's like I'm on a conveyor belt. He didn't even test. He didn't say congratulations. How did he even know?'

'He's a medic, Bear. He's not going to hug you and say well done, now, is he? Don't you remember my friend Dom at Uni? He's the straightest-talking man I've ever met, and he was a doctor, wasn't he?'

'No, but—'

'No buts. I'm starving.' James smiled at the waiter who lingered close enough to regard Claire with a suspecting smile when he came to take their order. She just pointed at the menu when it came to her turn, and scuffed James's ankle with her trainer toe when he said, 'Do you have any marshmallows for my wife's hot chocolate? She's had a tough morning.' This rankled. She didn't need him ordering for her.

James set his phone down on the table after they'd eaten. It was a meal that provided sustenance rather than pleasure, despite the marshmallows. James showed Claire the calendar app he'd updated already. It was all mapped out, all done so quickly. The sequence forced upon them, without consideration of what they wanted, and why. In cancer, Claire knew all too well from her dad's experience, each treatment was personalised to the person. Why were the months ahead so uniform? Where was her tailored plan? Where was the acknowledgement that she'd tried so hard, learned so much, come so far to achieve this baby?

'Ah come on, now. What's wrong? What's the matter?' James said.

'Nothing's wrong.'

The waiter reappeared and Claire couldn't meet his eye. She clenched her teeth against a sudden anger that was desperate to escape. Claire had expected to come away with *something*. Something that confirmed they had done so well.

When James left to go into work, leaving Claire feeling freshly abandoned, she loaded up HomeBirthHeroes and started typing. Her shoulders fell further down with every new paragraph. She shared every detail about her experience so no one else would have to go through it blind again. *Warning*, she wrote, *read this before you go to the GP!*

'Oh, DulwichGirl, I wish you'd told us,' the other women said, and it soothed Claire to see the three little dots dance at the bottom of the page as they all replied. She imagined what these people might look like. What would it be like if they were all in a room together, talking? Claire lay in bed with the laptop balanced on a pillow atop her stomach and immersed herself in the commiserations. These women knew how to make her feel better. They shared the disappointment and reassured her that the maternal health service wasn't fit for purpose. It lacked empathy and compassion. *Exactly!* Claire typed.

Holly's name kept popping up with new emails. Claire knew she needed to concentrate. It wasn't that she was trying to avoid work, not when she was on her new mission to impress Holly; it was just so easy to lose track of time. The group consoled her with all the things Claire wished her husband had said after they left the surgery. How could that compete with messages from Holly asking for updates on the energy bill app? There's a limit to what a pregnant woman can endure in one day.

'Sorry, Mam, but can you please just speak to James,' Claire said, when her mam rang for the fourth time, and hung up before her mother could finish her happy hello. Now she'd experienced the release of writing the emotions of the day down, she didn't want to tell the story from scratch again, not to her mother.

'Claire,' her mam said on a voicemail minutes later, her voice stern, 'I've always tried to encourage you girls to think beautiful things, learn to deal with whatever life throws at you, and let the past live in the past, and I'll never stop trying there. You'll be the same when you're a mam too. I didn't manage to get through to James but I know you, I know what you're like, and you've been funny about doctors ever since your poor dad got ill. I wish you'd grow out of it, my pet. You're not just making decisions for yourself anymore. Now, stop ignoring your mother and call me back. I want to know everything. I've been looking forward to an update all day.'

Claire knew she was being rude, but she texted James *Can*

you please speak to my mam? I'm too tired and feel too shit. She just wanted to wallow. Her mam was too stoic to understand her disappointment.

When James replied to say of course, he'd call right away, but he was so sorry, he'd forgotten about a colleague's leaving party and was Claire OK to have dinner alone? Claire didn't mind. In fact, she welcomed the opportunity to process everything with these people who understood that medical settings can be complex and triggering. James never really seemed to grasp the impact of her dad's death, laughed off her stories about her asthma-related visits when she was younger. She couldn't shake the memory of him staring in amazement when she refused to go to hospital after she cut her hand chopping onions, not listening when she explained her aversion, her dad, and eventually, after the application of plasters and Savlon, the argument was filed away with all their other spats into a place they tried to forget. So she continued her online discussions in peace and felt something like relief.

Chapter 11

HomeBirthHeroes
Direct messages for DulwichGirl (1)
From: Flora_Is_Free
Hi DulwichGirl,

I hope you don't mind me getting in touch. I had to reach out after reading about your godawful experience. I did a double take at my screen because the exact same thing happened to me a few years ago. Judging by your name, I don't think you're in Sussex like me, but doesn't that just show how women all over the country must be treated like this by doctors day in, day out. It's not fair, is it? Having our moment ruined by people who don't have any time in their miserable days for happiness. My heart hurts at how damaging the system is for us mothers with big dreams.

I'm sorry to say that the first GP appointment was just the start of my series of leaving offices and rooms and hospitals in distress. My partner learned to always bring some tissues along. I genuinely hope this doesn't happen to you but I do want to pass that on because I wish someone had warned me what to expect from the early stages. I would have done things differently from the get-go.

For me, the humiliation and suggestion that I had no say in what was best for my lovely Freddie eventually became too much. By the end of the second trimester, I walked out of my last hospital appointment and never went back.

I don't know why it took me so long. I guess it was the naivety of being a first-time mother. The session before that, my partner and I were ushered into a room where a midwife looked me up and down, handed me a leaflet about how I'm only meant to have an extra 200 calories a day from the third trimester onwards, and slithered out without another word. We waited for over two hours in that room, reading and re-reading about the BMI risks that I knew weren't true, slowly getting hotter and hotter without any windows or a fan, before a different midwife came in and said, 'Oh, you're still here? We need this room now I'm afraid.' When a letter came about another appointment, we thought we'd give them the benefit of the doubt (!) and returned, only to be ushered into that same room and told that there was no way I could be admitted to the birthing centre.

The whole conveyor-belt feeling you mentioned only stopped when I became my own advocate. I went to that final meeting full of knowledge and empowerment. Thanks to this community (and others, but that's a conversation for another day), I was reminded that us mothers always have a choice, the importance of truly informed consent, and how I should trust my instincts.

I'm afraid I've heard so many stories from other women who felt like decisions were forced upon them at all stages of their pregnancy. I'm so glad I managed to remove myself from the cycle as it was really damaging my mental health. But I don't want to overwhelm you, you must think I'm bonkers pouring my heart and life story out here!

I know things must be raw for you right now but I'm here to chat about any of this whenever you'd like.
Flora xxx

Chapter 12

Claire was excited to get out of bed. This Saturday felt so full of promise that even the birds who twittered by their windowsill cheered instead of irritated her. The last week represented a significant shift in her mood, with every day lighter than the one before. The HomeBirthHeroes group, the new friends at her fingertips, changed everything.

Flora's direct message had popped up as Claire searched for the perfect post-work reality TV episode on her laptop. After the Dr Faulkner encounter she was looking for a holiday for her brain. She recognised the name of the account instantly: Flora was the author of the beautiful birth story in a pool at home that so enchanted her when she found it months ago. It was strange to go through introductory pleasantries when she knew some of the most intimate details about this stranger's life. But she did it, and the conversation was seamless, perhaps even better than anything she'd experienced with a female friend face-to-face, because she didn't have to worry about the normal things, like whether she might have something in her teeth, or said too much, misjudged a tone.

When James came home from his work drinks hours later,

Claire found most of her anger had melted away in the catharsis of her new connection, and she hadn't even pressed play on *The Real Housewives*. 'You seem better,' James said, before he kissed her nose. And he was right: she was better.

Claire spent a week going back and forth with Flora, peeling off more and more virtual layers. Flora was now her confidante, the person she turned to when she wanted to share how strange she felt about James immediately registering her with a midwife at King's College Hospital post-GP disaster, without asking if that was OK. Flora offered a faceless, receptive ear when Claire said she found herself struggling to listen to the voicemail messages left by the antenatal team. *Just take things at your own pace,* Flora advised, *and make sure you're in a good mental place when introducing everything to your husband. He'll be more receptive if you're calm.* They talked about everything, from pregnancy pillows (Claire needed to buy one), to symptoms (Claire still felt fine, apart from increasingly vivid nightmares), and Flora's experience with nausea demons. It was so nice to be able to be her true self with someone. To externalise every thought and know someone not only understood but would guide her in making the right decision.

As Claire lay under the sheet – it was still too hot for a duvet, even a light tog – she was warmed by the prospect of a day where she'd get to see the lovely Taya again, while continuing the seamless chatter with Flora online. She hummed to herself in the shower, taking care to run the water at a lukewarm temperature. She continued the tune as she got ready. 'You're glowing,' James said from the bed, looking at her appreciatively as she rummaged through the chest of drawers for a top that would skim her changing figure. She left the house without a jacket, one of late summer's true joys, and thought about his comment. She loved this new stage, the way it lit her from within.

*

'So, how's work?' Taya asked as they waited for their food. 'And how's that handsome husband of yours?'

The two women were together for brunch. The location was Claire's choice and it was perfect. All the surfaces in the café seemed both soft and glossy: lamb's ear plants, as sleek as cashmere, were propped up in glazed ceramic pots; slab-like tables had ostrich-feather corners to protect the patrons' limbs; and everywhere, those endlessly inviting sofas. She had already posted pictures on Instagram and tagged Taya.

Claire stared at her friend across the table. Taya had the kind of face that people fall into. Her hair was the colour of autumn leaves and her eyes were like brushed bronze: brown and gold, melted together. Claire could always find beauty in anyone other than herself, especially in women. James often joked that she looked like a meerkat, staring on trains, at the beach, on social media. She did try to be subtle, but curiosity tended to get the better of her. She only zoomed into body parts on Instagram when she knew James wasn't around. She'd done this to Taya's online profile many times now. In the flesh, she noted her friend's toned arms, beautifully boned clavicle and the little hoops in her ears that looked so chic. She made a mental mark to order some immediately. White gold, not sterling silver.

Brunch was the loveliest of meeting options. Things tend to remain light-hearted at eleven-thirty in the morning. Even the word 'brunch' was nice and aspirational; it had always been a favourite. At university, Claire and James used to heat frozen waffles until they crisped golden and delicious and ate them as soon as they could bear food in the early afternoon, their stomachs reeling from cheap alcohol. They used to call those mounds of stodge brunch and it made them feel a little more grown up. Twenty-year-old Claire would not recognise the woman she was now – someone who wondered aloud about whether to have extra halloumi or heirloom tomatoes with her smashed avocado, before ordering both.

'Work's . . . OK,' Claire said, her mind temporarily stuck on the past. 'No, I mean, it's good.' Brunch is easy and non-committal. You don't talk about the worries that sneak into your dreams at brunch.

'Good, as in please let's not discuss further, or actually good?'

Claire considered this for a second. 'Actually good. I've had a productive week and I feel like my boss is finally starting to respect me. It's just – well – a girl I work with saw something personal on my phone, and, yeah, it's not great timing.' Claire felt her cheeks burn. Her skin could be so traitorous sometimes.

'Ahh. I could tell something was up. Like messages? I once sent a complaint about someone to someone. Utterly mortify-ing. We both still pretend it didn't happen.'

'Oh, no, not that, just personal things I didn't want to share yet.'

Ali had emailed earlier that week. *CONGRATULATIONS*, the subject read. *I hope you don't mind but when you put your phone down I saw the podcast on your Lock Screen. Don't worry, your secret's safe with me! I'm happy for you! What do you Geordies say again, why aye man! Does that mean good?*

Claire waited until the following day to reply. She had been listening to one of Flora's recommendations, *Reframing pain in labour.* The notes app of her phone was full of draft responses and attempts to try and not sound heartbroken by the fact that this news, the most precious news, had been ripped away before she wanted to share. Her right to tell the company on her terms, when it felt safe, had gone. But she was to blame. She had been so careless, leaving the podcast visible like that.

Instead, she'd responded with *Thank you – and please don't tell anyone yet, it's still early days*. She added a thumbs-up emoji, which she thought would make it impossible for Ali to detect any devastation.

'You poor thing.'

'Oh, I'll be fine.' She would tell Holly next week, although she was sure Ali would have said something already; the two girls were so close. And surely Holly must expect this from Claire after her search history intervention. She tried to stop this thought from avalanching through her mind while in such lovely company. It had already occupied so much of her time. There was something about Taya that made Claire open up. She asked questions she seemed to really want to hear the answers to.

Taya looked directly into Claire's eyes. 'OK. I hope you're OK?'

'Forget I ever said anything. I'm just annoyed with myself because this girl's pretty much the only person who gives me the time of day in the office.'

'Oh, Claire, bless you. Some women can be absolute vipers. It's not the same, but where I work can be vicious. I was given the cold shoulder for months because I once asked a partner if a "lunch and learn" talk was optional. Turns out it was her son giving the presentation, so she excluded me from any department socials. Hideous stuff. Now, shall we see what's happened to our orders and maybe get another round of those orange juices? We can toast to whatever's bothering you being resolved on Monday?'

Claire was so relieved for Taya's pivot. It was so nice to just let conversation flow. She thought: Wow, she's really letting me in here. Wait until James hears about this. 'Yes! And you asked about James before, sorry. You need to meet him. He's a good egg.'

'I do! I must meet the famous James. I was thinking that just yesterday: I need to invite you both round.'

'I'd – we'd love that. And you need to come to ours! I keep telling James we need to invite friends over. It's just been so funny, starting afresh.'

When it was over two hours later and the waitress asked if they'd like any drinks otherwise the venue would be closing before evening service, Taya said, 'Mimosas! Come on, let's do it!'

Claire said, 'Just one moment,' and smiled until the waitress got the hint and retreated. Still in the cosy caress of how lovely the day had been so far, Claire leaned over the table, her stomach grazing the tickly feathers, and told Taya that she couldn't drink because she was pregnant. It felt so wonderful to say it out loud. To have the opportunity to tell someone face-to-face, on exactly her own terms. But instead of joining Claire in her grin, Taya looked downwards and gulped loudly and visibly. For a moment, Claire panicked she'd said something wrong.

Finally, Taya looked back up. To Claire's relief, she was smiling. 'That is – wow, that's really something special. I wasn't expecting such happy news today,' Taya said. Her voice was as joyful as ever, that slight American twang turning everything into an uplifting statement.

'I can't believe it!' Claire said.

Taya kept nodding her head. 'It's really lovely, really lovely indeed, well done you,' she said.

When the waitress returned, she ordered an espresso martini for herself and 'the fanciest sparkling water you've got for my friend here'.

They both used their phones while they waited for their drinks to arrive. Claire messaged James and suggested he should pop down, meet the much-discussed Taya, sample the cocktail menu. Claire didn't tell Taya she was doing this. She wanted it to be a surprise. And it wouldn't spoil the mood, Claire knew, because Taya was the first to bring up James.

Taya's cocktail came before the water. She drank it all in one smooth sip, wiped the sides of her mouth with a napkin and ordered another when the waitress returned with a glass bottle of Perrier and two glasses full of ice. 'I needed the caffeine,' Taya said. 'Although I shouldn't complain about being tired to a pregnant woman, sorry! I bet you feel absolutely exhausted?'

Now the news was out there, Claire couldn't contain herself. She was buoyed by conversations with Flora and the other Heroes, all those hours typing bubbling over at last into real, physical conversations. 'I want it to be natural,' Claire said. 'I don't love the idea of a scan in hospital. It just feels so clinical. You know they only use it to date you? Like, I know I'm pregnant, you know? And due dates vary so much, it just seems a bit much?'

'Mm, I do know that.' Taya tapped on the table. Her fingers playing an invisible piano.

'And, well, I haven't even told James this, but I'm not sure I want them to tell me about the baby's development. What if something's wrong? I don't want to know. It's like if someone offered you a crystal ball and said: Do you want to find out if you've got a terrible disease? I'd definitely say no. I just – I don't think I could bear it if something was wrong. Could you?'

'Mm.' Taya was rummaging through her bag.

'Are you OK?'

'I'm so sorry, Claire, I've just remembered I've got a thing later. I'm going to have to cancel that extra drink. Bear with me one moment, sorry. I'm so hare-brained sometimes! It's with – you remember that trip I went on to Greece? With a woman I met there. Sorry, one moment.' Taya seemed a little unsteady as she walked over to the bar. She was so svelte, Claire imagined alcohol had a big effect.

Claire felt ashamed when she messaged James to say *Don't bother coming*. How had things gone from *Come, come, come!* to *Don't bother*? Claire wanted to rewind ten minutes, remove this strange veil of awkwardness, try again. James replied to say no worries, was she going to be home soon, and she hated him for not asking what was wrong, because something was clearly so wrong. Had she been droning on, boring her friend?

'I've just settled the bill,' Taya said when she sat back down, all fast movements and fragile smiles.

Claire wasn't sure what to say in response. She hadn't expected the meeting to end so suddenly. When she said, 'Next one's on me!' the sentence seemed too bright and generic.

Their hug was shallow and brief, and Claire had so many things she wanted to say but couldn't. They left the café and walked in separate directions.

When she opened the front door, Claire was dismayed to see James was wearing his best jumper, an ivy-green that made his eyes look even more spectacular. It made her frustrated, to see this effort, to know he'd tried but been too late. When he asked what happened, she said the truth: Taya forgot about another plan.

'Why have I never met your work friends?' she asked, and he said Claire could come on their next night out, but only if she was prepared to be the centre of attention as everyone knew about all their stories.

'No, not this one,' he whispered to her hardening tummy, his nose against her navel.

She always thought love was something furious and strong. But James had taught her that love could be gentle. It was the knowledge that he would always be there in the morning, with his musty breath and soft limbs, or say something that would quieten her mind. It wasn't the ball of lust that she'd once mistaken for something bigger and admit to terrible men at even more terrible times of day: over the thud of bass in a bar, when they were saying they wanted to go home for a good night's sleep, when they wanted to start seeing other people. Love was so integral to her life that she only remembered it in these extra gestures.

'You're going to be a wonderful dad,' she said to James.

'Oh, I hope so,' he said.

Taya messaged later that night and said what a fantastic time she'd had, and they must get a date in the diary for her to meet the man of the moment. When Claire played and replayed and fixated on every moment of the conversation, she couldn't work out why it hadn't gone to plan. Perhaps, she wondered, she'd imagined Taya's shift in mood. She typed as much as she could remember to Flora.

Direct messages for DulwichGirl (1)
From: Flora_Is_Free
Oh Christ! I'm sorry to be the bearer of bad news but this kind of judgement is classic. Some people really just don't get it. It's like they think there's only one way to do things and they're scared to even imagine all the other options out there! What happened to going with your gut and what feels right? It sounds like this friend is closed-minded, unfortunately, and the saddest thing is these types of people make up the majority. It can be so difficult to know who to open up to. I hope you're OK?

Claire wasn't completely sure what Flora meant – Taya seemed like she was a very open type of person, didn't she? – but she agreed with her online friend anyway. She set the date for a meal at Taya's and allowed herself another run through Taya's profile, and then all the images she'd been tagged in. There was nothing about Greece. But she did get to see some of Taya's old partners. She wished she'd asked if Taya was single or not. Navigating these kinds of questions was so much harder in real life. With Flora, she could just ask anything outright. Claire forced herself away from the app after a close shave perusing the profile of the wife of a man Taya was pictured with six years ago. She would have given anything for a clue about what she'd done to upset the beautiful flow of their brunch. Perhaps Flora was right, and Taya didn't quite understand her. Either way, it was too late to say anything now.

Chapter 13

Eva was the name of Claire's midwife. Claire found this out when, prompted by James's nudging, she finally listened to her voicemails and returned the call. There was something about missing calls. If you've done it once, it becomes increasingly harder to pick up. Eva wasn't one for small talk. In a monotonous voice, as if reading from a script, she told Claire she needed to choose where they'd meet. Claire heard a sigh when she said she'd call back with her answer. 'OK, but I'll need a response by tomorrow. You're already late for the booking appointment,' Eva said.

Claire wanted to ask Sally what to do. While almost all of her pregnancy questions tended to be directed to the cosy space online, it felt important to have this conversation over video, gauge responses in real time. It was nice, Claire thought, to have reasons to stay in touch. To have a real purpose to her interactions with her oldest friend.

'Advice please,' Claire said. Their relationship required no conversational preambles.

'Hit me. And how are you feeling? Still not being sick? I'm so jealous, mind. Remember how I used to have to keep a bin in the supply cupboard? The students definitely used to hear me throwing up. Grim times.'

'Oh, God, I remember that. All well here. No, I was just calling because I've got to decide where to meet the midwife. What would you do? GP, children's centre, home?' For obvious reasons, she didn't mention the hospital.

'What does James think? I'd just go to the GP if it's nearby, means you don't have to clean the flat beforehand. That's what I did,' said Sally.

Claire thought of Dr Faulkner's smug face and how she left the doctor's surgery struggling for air. 'No, not a fan,' she said.

'Suit yourself. Well, don't do home, too invasive. You don't want someone sneering at your work surfaces. What about the children's centre? I used to take Rory to one for his baby sensory classes. But Claire, listen, don't get too attached. Take it from me: the nicest midwives are never around when you need them.'

Rory's birth had been difficult. The two friends didn't discuss it, but Sally had ended up under general anaesthetic while Conor kept Claire updated through a series of uncharacteristically emotional phone calls. At one point, Conor sobbed down the line while Claire reassured him everything would be OK. The couple decided they were happy with just one child after that. Rory was their entire world.

Sally was yet to return to teaching post-Rory, such was her motherly dedication. Claire was proud to be part of an elite WhatsApp group of Sally and Conor's close contacts – the only friend involved, in fact – who received regular photo updates of Rory's milestones. Due to her phone-checking habits, she was often the first person (besides his parents) who got to see him smile, walk, watch the video where he chirped 'Mama'. When Claire pictured the future, as hazy as it was, she also saw herself remaining at home with the baby, being there for every key moment. She would love to follow in Sally's footsteps. She'd read about the cost of childcare and the importance of contact and conversation in a child's early years. She wasn't sure how James felt about this yet. Pregnancy, Claire knew, was all about stages, and the most immediate stage was getting through this midwife encounter.

Thankfully, telling Holly about the midwife appointment was a non-event. After much deliberation, she sent an email instead of setting up a meeting, out of cowardice more than anything. Claire didn't let herself turn round or even move until she received a reply. She did not want to have this professional conversation out loud, risk anyone else hearing. *I was wondering when you'd tell me,* Holly replied an excruciating near-hour later. *I'll let HR know. All systems go for this launch so please mark any time out of office in both of our calendars – and I'm going to need more notice about anything medical in the future.* Claire replied saying *Of course,* along with a smiley face emoji she instantly regretted. She filed the email under *Admin* and finally left to go to the toilet.

The waiting area of the children's centre smelled faintly of sick. Claire sat on a plastic chair in a corridor away from the main hub and tried to breathe through her mouth. There was only one other person there, inspecting her cuticles. Claire cleared her throat, just in case the woman wanted to chat, but the woman pulled a nail file out of her bag and started buffing.

Claire scrolled Instagram to pass the time. The algorithm was hellbent on promoting influencers' pregnancy announcements and babywear boutiques. She skimmed through page after page and tried not to think about the small parts of nail matter that must be floating in the air. Something about the woman's grooming made her feel uneasy. She wondered if it was really that many steps away from her doing her make-up on the Tube, an essential part of her morning routine. The thought was interrupted by a man who came blustering in. His face was flushed against bleach-blond hair.

'Ottie,' he said, and the woman zipped the file away.

He sat down next to Claire.

'I'm sorry, the queue for the showers after class was so long, I've not missed anything, have I?'

'Hm,' the woman said. 'Doesn't look like it, does it?'

Claire was struck by recognition. She knew this voice, this face, the tattoos. This was David, the designer at Uno who once asked if she was going to Ali's birthday drinks. It was a memorable experience for Claire because people rarely spoke to her outside of the firmly established office social structures. Ever since that moment, she'd waited for him to strike up conversation again. He was very good-looking, so Claire noticed him more than others. She knew that he also always responded to office-wide announcements of leftover meeting sandwiches, and that he had a particular fondness for prawn cocktail. But they'd not exchanged words since. And now he was here, next to her, in a children's centre in Dulwich, of all places.

She looked at him expectantly.

'David!' she said. 'What a small world.'

Claire felt David study her face. 'Hi,' he said, after too long.

'It's Claire. Hansen.'

His head bobbed up and down and he looked slightly terrified.

'Uno?' Claire continued.

'Oh, right, of course,' he said, 'of course, Uno, sure.'

Claire waited for him to ask something. Instead, he checked the time on his watch.

'So, are you expecting too?' Claire said.

'Our first,' the woman, Ottie, replied, without looking up. 'Can't go anywhere without bumping into anyone, can you, David?' she added.

Thankfully, a head peered out of a room down the corridor and said 'Claire Hansen?' Claire was relieved to be excused from Ottie's frostiness, David's lack of recognition. She wondered if their schedules would now be interwoven forever.

Eva the midwife gestured towards a chair as soon as Claire walked in. She ran through the whole routine: she weighed Claire, measured her height, probed James's family's health history, filled many vials with blood. Claire was handed a document reminding her of the series of appointments she should attend, classes she advised, and the timelines where Claire had to make huge, important decisions, 'With your partner, of course.'

The dossier conversation had finally been broached with James earlier that week. There was nothing special about the night she chose, but Claire felt like it was time to bring her husband into the fold of the idea that so thrilled her. She'd shuffled as close as possible to James on the sofa and talked him through her vision, all her research. At the end, there was a pause where James just closed his eyes and nodded. Claire found herself unable to intuit what that meant, even though there was a time she could guess his facial expression even when he had his back to her. 'I mean, sure, it's an option,' he'd said. 'It's just – well, would you not want to be around people in case something happened? We're a good 20 minutes from the hospital here. And wouldn't it be messy? Can you ask the midwife when you see her? Let's see what an expert thinks, stuff online could have been written by anyone.'

She had so wished for a more engaged response. She was ready to counter any questions about her resilience, her moaning about aches and pains, requests for hot water bottles over the years of menstruating, but not these strange, overly practical comments. 'Yeah, sure, I'll ask,' Claire said.

But Eva didn't bat an eyelid when Claire mentioned she'd been reading up on home births and felt like it was the best option for her. 'That's something that can be discussed closer to your third trimester. This is just to get you booked in,' Eva said.

At the end, Eva said she was glad Claire had come alone. She had some questions that always required partners to leave the room. Claire was horrified to hear Eva ask if she had any experience of domestic violence, and later, female genital mutilation. She refused to do anything but jerk her head to signal no when asked if James was a blood relative. She wouldn't dignify the question with words.

Claire dialled Sally as soon as she stepped out of the children's centre. There was no sign of David. Claire was glad. Her face always went blotchy, with livid red patches, when she was cross.

Sally's face moved around in the middle of the screen. 'Oh Claire, it's just a formality, please don't be so upset. Think how many other women that midwife is speaking to today! This may be your first child, but it'll probably be her ten-thousandth. They have to ask those kinds of questions, I'm sure they asked me loads of strange things about Conor too. Remember to breathe. It's all OK, you're OK!'

Claire had to force herself to keep walking and not allow her disappointment to totally take over. All she wanted to do was cry. Sally's comment didn't make her feel any better. It reminded Claire she was just another cog in the midwife machine.

'It's exciting! Don't forget to be excited!' Sally chirped, before she blew a kiss to the camera.

Flora was far more empathetic when she messaged:

Direct messages for DulwichGirl (1)
From: Flora_Is_Free
How terrible, I really hope you're doing OK, it seems like one thing after another with you at the moment, you poor thing. That vile doctor, this midwife, you've been through it all! Knowing your luck, you'll have a spiteful sonographer, just like me with Freddie.

You know, I've not seen a midwife at all this time. I didn't want to say that before, but this was exactly what I worried might happen. You're sensitive, like me. I think we're very similar, you know.

I wanted to tell you about something. I'm part of a group of women who advocate for their health throughout pregnancy. I've been meaning to ask if you'd like to join us. I think you'd really love it, it's all about empowerment around maternity decisions, and they were so lovely to me when I was expecting my first.

I'm not sure if you've heard of this term before but we all believe in the opportunity to freebirth. I'll send you the link and you can see if it might be your sort of thing. It's a bit out there so I totally get if it doesn't feel right for you. Let me know if you have any questions though. I have all the time in the world right now.

Claire checked the new group out as soon as she got home. This was Flora's second child, and Flora had helped her so much already. Claire recognised the antenatal approach instantly. She'd come across similar forums online a few times before during the desperate TTC months and remembered the throb of admiration she'd felt when she first read about the freebirthers' bravery. It was such a compliment that Flora, lovely Flora, thought she could fit in there.

This new group, The Secret Goddesses, helped turn Claire's day round. To join, Claire had to answer a few questions, like 'What do you think of the NHS?' and 'Is this your first child?'

Claire responded honestly, still smarting from the disappointment of her meeting with Eva.

The group wasn't some alternative religion thing: the Goddesses were just everyday women who cared about the way the next generation entered the world. They wanted their child to feel free and adored. They wanted the first image from wide, perfect, unfocused eyes to be of their parents, not the blue anonymity of scrubs or the cold glint of forceps. Who wouldn't want that for their baby?

Like Claire, these people also felt worried about the overwhelming amount of information available, making it too easy to fall down the doom-hole of irrelevant data and comparisons. Our bodies, they said, were purposefully built for the human fruit to grow, and we, as women, needed to have more faith in ourselves. This was a balm to Claire, who appreciated all reassurance. They offered proof of an alternative and effective system. Their very existence thrilled Claire. She had been chosen! *This* was the kind of language Claire expected around pregnancy, not the reductive, anonymised vocabulary of Eva.

'Yeah, it was OK,' Claire said when James got home, slung his filthy rucksack on the clean kitchen table and asked about the appointment. She wrenched her eyes away from her phone. There was just so much interesting conversation going on. A part of her was hurt that James didn't try to get in touch earlier. That he'd reduced an already rubbish experience to post-work, pre-dinner chit chat.

'I'm going to need more than that, Bear. Come on! What did she say? Did you talk about your home birth stuff?'

'Mm, but we didn't get into too much detail. They were too busy wondering if we were related and if you hit me. Oh, and I sat next to someone from work and he definitely didn't recognise me, so that was the icing on the cake.'

115

'Hey, what's got into you?' James said as he came closer. Claire was annoyed when he gently extracted the phone from her hands and put it on the table so he could hug her.

'Nothing,' Claire said, and she counted the length of James's embrace, waiting until she could be reunited and revitalised by the Goddesses' chatter.

'Come on, Claire. Don't leave me hanging here. Why are you in such a grump? Here, come here. Oh, don't be like this. I promise I'll come to the next one. Hey, this is supposed to be fun!'

Claire looked downwards as she left the room. She lay on top of her bed and allowed herself to be nourished by the novelty of this group, this new group. These women understood the great beauty of pregnancy, this experience. James, who Claire could hear cheering along to a pre-season friendly game downstairs, clearly didn't.

Chapter 14

The Secret Goddesses

Flora_Is_Free

Can we talk about trust? I love how everyone in this group trusts themselves, trusts the process. We know how to quieten these new anxieties around things like due dates and instead dig deep into the wells of strength inside us. We know that babies come when they're ready.

The energy in this space is so inspiring. I really wish I could say the same about other maternity forums. It's like they're afraid of catching self-belief. They shut me down without a second's thought that maybe there are other ways to give birth. Maybe this could work for them too. Maybe they'd end up loving it as much as us!

I've learned to change the way I talk about things outside of this circle. I never engage with negative comments on my home birthing group, HomeBirthHeroes. And I always type something like 'I understand this isn't for everyone' whenever I mention how my gorgeous Freddie came to be. What I want to say is: our great-grandmothers and great-great-grandmothers and all the women before them never gave birth in hospitals. And we all turned out OK, didn't we?

The pressure to conform to this new way of thinking is so big.

From all angles, we're told the only way a baby should enter the world is with the assistance of someone else. That's why I love you ladies. You're so resilient to all the judgement we receive. And when push comes to shove, you're ready, and you have a galaxy of strength inside.

When I delivered Freddie at home, I was so proud of myself for not calling the emergency midwife number. It meant I looked Freddie in the eye and I saw pure, true, authentic trust shining through. He knew he could rely on me for anything.

Can these other women truly look at their babies and say the same?

Comments:

DulwichGirl: *Ahh, Flora, this is so beautiful.*

Chapter 15

Almost overnight, it became too chilly to linger coat-less out-side for all but a few hardy souls. It meant Claire became well acquainted with an ever-increasing range of cafés around Uno during her lunch breaks. She let the steam from a peppermint tea coat her face while she logged on to The Secret Goddesses and cleared her mind of all the work stresses that built up each morning. She made sure she set alarms during these sessions. Otherwise, time would just melt away and she couldn't risk re-turning to her desk late. It's a special thing, to be accepted in a community.

The ladies were all invested in Claire's journey. They loved the rarity of first-time mothers joining the group and she loved telling them about the changes that were more and more notice-able by the day. Claire's stomach felt hard after every meal now. Sometimes, James would bend down and feel her belly and look at her with an admiration she hadn't seen since their wedding, when she met his eyes at the end of the aisle and watched as a gulp rippled down his throat. In those moments, she truly felt like a goddess. She was nurturing something perfect, deep within.

That feeling was always dampened during the working week. Around the half-strangers of her Uno colleagues, she felt a need to conceal, to pretend. She tried not to touch the curve of her midriff when she was in the office. She panic-bought a selection of scarves that were more middle-aged art teacher than chic early-autumnal pieces, but they helped hide the bloat that built throughout the day. It seemed to be working: so far, the only comment had been a hushed, 'You honestly can't even tell,' from Ali, as Claire adjusted her scarf by their shared desk. 'You look great!'

Claire wasn't sure if the rest of their team knew. She was confident that David wouldn't say anything. He caught her eye during the monthly all-team breakfast and winked, and Claire was thankful she had a large pastry in her hand so she could bite into it and obscure her blush. She wasn't sure what this gesture meant.

HR still hadn't got in touch despite Holly claiming she'd notify them the week before. This was a small relief. As Claire approached the twelve-week mark, she found it difficult to ignore thoughts about pregnancy-loss statistics. So many people, real people, now knew, and having to start employment proceedings while still in the first trimester would have been too much, too soon. Sally probably didn't remember it, but under the thick fog of a second bottle of wine, she'd once told Claire about her tragedies before Rory. The sudden, terrible bleeding that spelled the end. Claire had been so surprised to hear that her friend had suffered for all those years in silence, cocooned her grief within her relationship. They hadn't discussed it since, and she didn't dare bring it up now. Instead, Claire hung on to every tiny whisper of food aversions, cravings, and peakiness. Any sign that the baby was OK. *Not long now,* she kept channelling inside, a meditation, *Keep hanging in there. One more week and we should be safe.* Claire felt certain that her baby could hear.

James was by her side when the midwife services number rang again. Both her and James's work shoes were off and they were lying on the sofa, their phones within a lazy arm's reach, the cheers and whistles of a football match providing background noise.

'Go on, take it!' James said. He always loved the mystery and potential of an unsaved number. He muted the TV.

Claire recognised the number, knew it was the antenatal team, knew what it would be about. The number of missed calls had become too large once again. But there was nothing to do apart from answer now. As soon as she picked up, a robotic voice on the other end of the line said she was calling from the midwife team and asked Claire to confirm the upcoming scan. Under her breath, Claire apologised for being unavailable recently. She muttered something about work, the easiest scapegoat.

'Yep,' the new midwife said, 'well, we'll see you next week.'

Claire pictured the woman crossing off another name on a spreadsheet, counting down the minutes until her shift finished. Every one of these interactions made her more uneasy. Just the thought of having to enter hospital made her heart start racing. But when Claire opened her mouth and tried to articulate this to her husband, words failed her.

'Can you believe it?' James said. 'When is it again? Let me add it to the calendar.'

'Next Tuesday.'

'I can't wait. Ah, it suddenly feels so much more real. We get to see our baby!' He circled it twice and added arrows either side.

Claire dug an index fingernail into her thumb and counted to five. She stayed quiet.

Claire was thankful when James mentioned he was meeting up with someone, she didn't quite catch the name, to watch yet another football match (his second of the night) in Clapham. It afforded her the time and space to indulge in her new favourite pastime. He gave both her forehead and stomach a kiss goodbye, 'One for each of my loves,' before she settled into the familiar rhythm of scrolling.

That evening, many of the women were sharing stories about wonderfully supportive partners, boyfriends and husbands. One woman was on her sixth child, and her husband had been there, guiding each baby, totally there for the mother of his children. Flora didn't seem to be online yet, but she always talked about the impact her partner Tom had on her birth story. Claire decided to just observe.

Perhaps it was the subject matter and her tendency towards comparison, but Claire couldn't fully relax. Her mam kept messaging, clogging up the screen with questions.

Claire love, have you met any Caesarean knitters yet? James just told me about the scan! So soon! You must be so excited, pet. Will we get to find out if it's a boy or a girl? I always knew you two were girls, you know.

These texts grated. Claire wasn't sure when James set up this direct line to her mam. She should be allowed to share what she wanted in her own time. She edited her response for what felt like hours, her thumbs swift and adept. Surely her mam knew there was no way they'd know the gender just yet? Couldn't she have googled? Claire lay on the sofa with her phone raised above her head and squinted against the last honeyed bursts of evening light. She whittled away at the words to try and remove obvious traces of annoyance. Eventually, she settled on:

No, Mam. James is the one who's really keen to go. Can't say I'm particularly excited, hate hospitals.

Call me love, Rosemary replied.

Claire, answer your phone, pet.

Claire?

Claire flicked away the notifications. It's so important to make sure you only think of your pregnancy in positive terms, the Goddesses often said. Not allowing any space for negativity was all well and good in theory, Claire thought, but had they ever tried to evade the advances of a single Geordie mother expecting her first grandchild?

Claire??? This isn't helping my blood pressure!

An aura of irritation started to build. It wasn't like her mam had been able to shake off the utter horror of what happened to dad in hospital all those years ago. Their family home was full of reminders that a person was missing, that it was nigh on impossible to ever move on from so much grief. The coat rack was still full of her dad's cheerfully coloured raincoats that would never be worn again. As if he might come back and say, 'Hey, let's head out now, I bet it'll brighten up soon!' No, Claire did not want to discuss the matter further.

I've got a headache, sorry, love you, Claire sent back.

She didn't receive any further responses.

James found Claire napping, her phone beside her face, when he returned home later. He whispered, his breath sour with alcohol, 'Bear, Bear, wake up. It's ten o'clock, have you eaten? You're where I left you! Let me make you some toast.' He tried to scoop her up, all of her, but even with his biggest grunts as motivators he couldn't do it. It was a deeply unpleasant awakening.

James scrambled around in the kitchen, knocked over the carousel of utensils, and muttered to himself. Claire didn't feel hungry, she just wanted to be back asleep. Her body carried itself upstairs, leaning heavily on the creaky banister. The bed felt extra soft compared to her previous spot.

'Here, Bear.' Claire was startled out of a split-second half-sleep. James proffered a plate of charred toast on top of the duvet covers. The edges were black with thick stripes of still-solid butter. Toast ash fell off the edge of the plate. Claire was too tired to be disappointed; she had only washed the sheets a few days ago.

'You're back late,' she said between bites, while she thought of the effort required to go and brush her teeth.

'You're wearing yourself out. Willing horses take the heaviest load, you know.'

'What are you on about?' James regularly misused catchphrases.

He was on the end of the bed with her left foot in his hand, pummelling his knuckles into her sole. It wasn't very relaxing. 'You, snoozing on the sofa!' he said.

Claire looked at her husband. His hair was sticking up at the front and he seemed so young in that moment, it was like they were students again. James yawned, his mouth opening so wide she could see his old mercury filling. Her husband was in a soft, calm state of drunkenness, the type she knew immediately precedes a great night's sleep. The recent discussion on the group inspired her. She decided to try it out at last. It felt like the right time.

She put the plate on the bedside table and sat further up-right. 'James, you know that home birthing idea?'

'Hmm?' He dropped her foot and came and sat beside her.

'Well, I've been researching it, and what about—'

'Huh? Not now.' He held an arm out, and Claire nestled underneath.

'Well, I've been doing some more research, and I want to talk to you about something called freebirthing?'

He snorted, the sound exploding close to her ear. 'Is that a word? Free. Birthing? You say some funny things. Didn't you ask the midwife about a home birth?'

Claire shrugged off James's arm and reached for her phone. 'Let me show you. It's like home birthing, but better. It would be just us, here. Wouldn't that be amazing?'

He pawed the screen away. 'Bear, I think you should spend some time away from all those websites. We don't know the first thing about giving birth, do we? Oh Bear, you're silly.'

'What?'

'Always tapping away. Now, come on, can we go to sleep now?'

Claire sighed and walked into the bathroom, phone still in hand. She was fully awake now. Her reflection in the mirror highlighted bags like bruises under her eyes. James's instant dismissal stung. He had no idea how difficult it was for Claire to keep this amazing part of her life hidden away. She wanted him to know how accepted these Goddess women made her feel, to talk about the world they'd opened up for her, for them, for their baby.

She loaded up the familiar page. Someone had posted about a new research paper that examined women's motivations for freebirthing. Claire recognised the name of the journal, so she knew it must be legitimate.

MindFullOfLove
Girls, you're really going to love this. It's spot on about the belief we all have in ourselves and our bodies. Read the bit about how resolute all 85 women were . . . less than a quarter ended up going the medical way. I honestly can't believe this experience has been

documented, and in *Nature*, no less! That's a really big deal. It just shows how science is changing to recognise why we're doing this. I'd have loved to participate in this study.

Claire liked the post and opened the research paper. Amid the complex language and medical terminology there were beautiful, affirming quotes from the interviewees, with words like *peaceful* and *consent*. Claire sat on the closed toilet seat and continued to read. She thought of all the other Goddesses who were able to share this kind of reading with their partner and felt cross anew at James's immediate shut-down. How had the rest of the group managed it? What was she doing so wrong in her relationship?

When Claire finished, she commented:

DulwichGirl: Wow! So cool. I wish they'd say how the babies got on though? Anyone else? Do you think it's worth me popping the researchers an email?
Flora_Is_Free: @DulwichGirl you are actually too cute, you little worry wart. I'm sure all the bubbas are fine and doing better than ever.

Claire considered this plan as she brushed her teeth. She would message the journal's team and get the outcomes of these special case studies in writing. She was certain this would help James understand. Claire felt good as she tucked herself next to her snoring husband. While she'd hoped this particular hurdle would be overcome seamlessly, she knew she had to work to get James on board. It was important to just take things step by step. She put one hand on her stomach and said inwardly: *We'll make this happen, little one, won't we?*

Chapter 16

Bad news, call me, James messaged. Claire felt her pulse quicken. She rushed towards the toilets and shrieked when she collided with Ali. 'I'm so sorry,' she said, without turning round. She rang James four times before he answered. With each missed call, her brain exaggerated the potential crises that were about to unfold. Maybe his dad had finally decided to reach out after twenty-five years of silence. Maybe his mam was ill. Maybe he'd been in a lift where the cables had caught and crashed and this was the emergency services getting in touch with his most recent contact?

'Sorry about that, I was just in a meeting,' James said. The reception was patchy in the cubicle and he sounded far away. Claire was so relieved to hear his voice.

'What? What is it? You're scaring me, James. James?'

'Just one moment,' he said, and then whispered: 'Going somewhere I can talk.'

Claire heard James's footsteps against his office floor. *Come on, come on, come on,* she said under her breath. She hoped no one was listening. She knew from the Holly-testing-experience that the Uno toilets didn't provide the best sound barriers.

'OK, so, this is shit. I didn't want to worry you, but I've got to go to Singapore. I've tried and tried but I've got to go. It's on Friday.' He exhaled loudly.

'Singapore? This Friday?'

'Yep, in three days' time.'

'Wow.'

'Bear! I'll be back next Wednesday evening. Wait, no, Thursday morning. I've never understood time differences.'

'But James, you'll miss the scan.'

'Well, that's why I've been fighting so hard, but Helen . . . You know, my boss Helen? She says I've got to go. I don't think I have a choice.'

'Oh.'

'I'm so sorry. I'm so, so, sorry. Love you. I've really got to go. See you soon. I'm so sorry, Bear.'

Claire stewed over the news all day. She replied to Ali's email of *Everything OK???* with just a smiley face. She didn't know where to start. It was so unfair that James expected her to shoulder the hospital visit alone when he knew, he surely knew, her agitation about not just this appointment but even stepping foot inside the imposing building that loomed over the Camberwell skyline. Had he forgotten the nightmares she used to have, the memories she shared about the asthma machine sucking every last breath from her body? With each passing hour, her anger grew, and by the time 5.30 hit, it had reached boiling point.

She called Lily as soon as she left the office. She wanted to moan in the explosive way that's only really acceptable among family – and didn't want to reignite last night's difficult conversation with her mam.

But after listening to Claire rant, an experience which took Claire the entire walk to the Tube station, Lily just said, 'Ah, these things happen.'

'He's leaving me! That's not OK. You don't leave someone who's pregnant, do you?'

'It's just his work, isn't it? And I'll provide company soon, sis! Not long until I come down now.'

'Is everything all right with you both?' their mam chirped from what sounded like the other side of the room. Claire hadn't realised she was listening in.

She ignored her mother's question and redirected the conversation to what they were having for dinner that evening. Thankfully, she wasn't pressed further.

James arrived home later with two Waitrose bags groaning with goodies. 'Your favourites,' he said, as he filled their kitchen counter with his spoils. Claire folded her arms around her chest. Her affection could not be bought, although she did appreciate the way he knew precisely what she liked chocolate-percentage-wise and the specific brand of tonic water that kept the slight flickers of evening nausea at bay. Sally had always been jealous of what she called James's attentiveness. Just last week her friend said, 'If Conor had a gun to his head, he wouldn't know if I liked white or red wine. And I've not drunk anything lighter than a Pinot Noir since 2012.' Claire had to admit that this was a lovely gesture. She tried her hardest to look disinterested as James went about his preparation. She really wanted to take a picture.

More details about the trip were provided over plates of James's griddled vegetable tacos, each one oozing flavour. Helen, the boss (who Claire was sure had never been mentioned before), was forcing James's hand, or so he asserted. Helen had sat him in an empty boardroom first thing that morning, twelve seats away from her position at the head of the table, and explained how important it was for his *career* that he came along to Singapore. The long flight would show the potential partner based out there that the team at Holmesdown Capital meant business. James explained, with flushed cheeks, that Helen knew about their *circumstances*, but made it very clear that failure to attend would have consequences, before she got up and left James in that spacious meeting room with floor-to-ceiling windows overlooking St Paul's Cathedral, with James thinking, in his own words, 'Fuck'.

Claire just nodded as her husband spoke. She still didn't quite know what this meant, only that there had been a plan to go to the dreaded appointment together, and now she was expected to go alone.

Over the course of the evening, Claire was encouraged by the Goddesses to see things differently. She checked her phone whenever James looked preoccupied.

Flora privately messaged:

Er, Claire? This is amazing! Now you don't have to go anywhere you don't want to. Don't be down, this is seriously a best-case scenario.

This sentiment was shared by the other women. Claire flicked through the responses in the brief intervals when James turned his back. She needed time to fully absorb their suggestions. As persuasive as they were, her gut told her there was only one right way to proceed. Even though those scans made her uneasy, even though Flora and the Goddesses advised against it, she had to go. Yes, attending hospital alone would be horrific, but she had no other choice. The weight of not attending would be too significant to keep from James. Unable to find the words to say this to the group, she decided to say nothing at all.

The following night, Claire helped James pack. The Singaporean forecast showed a series of angry clouds and humidity levels of 96 per cent. She'd never known James to be so concerned by his appearance. He tried on shirt and suit-trouser combinations with a look of deep disappointment. 'Come on, you look great!' she said, from her vantage point on the bed, when James sighed for the seventh time and shoved a hanger into another suit jacket's shoulders. She swallowed down the desire to laugh. He looked so serious.

'It's no good,' James said. 'No matter what suit I wear I always look like I've borrowed something from my dad.'

Claire snuck a new boatneck t-shirt into James's suitcase. She'd sacrificed a lunchtime of online chatter in order to find the perfect piece of clothing. It was light green to bring out the colour of his eyes, and (if the shop assistant was to be believed) made from a bamboo fabric that was unparalleled in its breathable qualities. She sprayed it with her perfume before she folded it among the stiff greys and navies that were already packed in rows. She pictured James's face when he discovered the surprise. Perhaps someone would ask where it was from and he could say something like: 'Oh, my wife just knows what I like'. The thought made her feel good.

To stave off the creeping loneliness of a weekend without James, without someone who just helped time pass, Claire dedicated herself to baby preparation. She made a list of everything they needed to do to their second bedroom. She created a virtual scrapbook of inspiration and deliberated over the perfect problem of whether to go for the classic blue or pink or something more gender neutral, like taupe or lemon. She browsed Amazon's selection of linen toys and wanted to cry at how cute they were.

The weekend passed in bursts of online inspiration and companionship. There were so many guides to be read about the various baby must-haves and the Goddesses were more than happy to share their experiences and purchase-lists. Taya tried to tempt Claire out of the flat for a cinnamon bun at the new Danish bakery, but Claire blinked and three hours had somehow flown by and she was still in the same spot on the carpeted floor of the spare bedroom, the laptop whirring beneath her fingers, and had to tell her new friend that she was very sorry but she was busy. The strange way their last encounter ended still played on Claire's mind.

Meanwhile, James was busy exploring Singapore. Claire saw this mainly through his Instagram, which had lain dormant for well over a year. Suddenly, his account had sprung back into action. He hadn't mentioned three of the five jet-setting financiers were women. A group shot showed them all at a swanky bar. The women were in beautiful dresses, their polished fingers clasping cocktails. James was sandwiched between them, beaming at the camera. Who were these pictures for? Claire wondered.

'I hope you're not messaging James about all this baby crap,' Sally said, when Claire called. Sally had also been on the receiving end of many purchasing questions, like what type of mattress she had in Rory's cot, or how long Rory stayed in newborn babygrows. Sally was worried Rory was coming down with chicken pox, and Claire didn't know what to say apart from offer to send some calamine lotion to Sally's via Amazon. She remembered being doused in the stuff when younger. 'I know what you're like and he's working, so you've got to let him have his space. Oh, what I'd do to be sipping Singapore Slings on a rooftop right now. It's misery here, absolutely pissing it down, what's it like down with you?'

But Sally hadn't guessed Claire's behaviour correctly. Claire deliberately hadn't messaged James. Instead, she tracked every time he was online without getting in touch. Her resentment grew with every instance. James was a father, Claire thought, and he really needed to start behaving like one. But instead of checking in on his pregnant wife, he posted badly framed pictures on his Instagram. When he finally called, Claire was sure she could hear a female voice in the background. She wondered which of the beautiful women it belonged to. He only said, 'You too,' when Claire ended the call with the three most loving words. It broke her heart.

Chapter 17

Claire did not sleep on Monday evening. She'd found each beautiful colleague's Instagram account: Helen, Yasmin and Shahnaz. The discovery had been assisted by Sally, who was now on chicken-pox-scratch-watch and equally delirious through sleep deprivation. *There's nothing to see here, crazy lady* Sally messaged, after Claire demanded her friend conduct a full sweep for any new content. Claire couldn't check and potentially expose herself to these women; she was no amateur. *Stop worrying! What are you expecting to find?*

One in the morning slid into two, and then four, and suddenly the birds were chattering away and tentative autumnal light crept into the room. Claire hadn't told Sally today was scan day. She preferred not to dwell on it too much, keep things separate, and Sally hadn't asked anyway. When it was unavoidably morning, Claire pulled herself out of bed and made a decaffeinated instant coffee. It tasted terrible. The countdown was on.

She posted on The Secret Goddesses instead of speaking to her friend.

DulwichGirl

Help! Dating scan today!

    Hi everyone, I know you'll be cross with me for this, but I have to go to my scan this morning. I'm feeling so nervous. Is there anything I can say or do to be calmer? There's no way I can get out of this – even though my husband's abroad he'll want to know all about it and ask so many questions. Before you all ask (especially you, Flora!), I promise I'll talk to him soon about the freebirthing plans, he just needs a little more time. He always takes a minute to come round to things. Believe me when I say going alone is my idea of a nightmare.

Claire decided to walk to the hospital. She wasn't confident she'd be able to stay awake on public transport feeling so exhausted. Drizzle filled the air with a thick vapour. In Ruskin Park, she passed an outdoor gym that proudly declared it was made of recycled steel from knives taken off the street, so she took out her headphones and walked as quickly as possible through that joyless green space. It was school term-time but there were some families in the park. A football was kicked in Claire's direction but she had neither the inclination nor the skill to return it to the young body twenty metres away.

Her phone buzzed to say a woman called Lucy_Loves_Life had responded directly:

Darling, if you care about yourself and your baby, you need to stop what you're doing right now. Every second of your stress is producing adrenaline that is toxic. You need to pause and breathe and allow oxytocin to return. That's the love hormone. The calmer you are, the happier you are, and the healthier you will both be. Do you think stepping into a place that will make you even more panicked is a good idea? I really want you to think about this. Do you want your baby to feel love or stress? It's your choice.

The message made Claire feel even more shaky. All she wanted to do was turn round and stop her baby feeling anything but the purest, biggest love. But she knew she couldn't. James and her mam were counting on updates, and she'd already committed to the appointment over the phone, and even though she hated the idea of the scan she had no other choice. Her feet kept trudging along wet pavement and park, until she was sweating and crying on the slope of Denmark Hill while sirens and people blared up into the hospital.

Claire checked her phone. She still had time to make the appointment, plenty of time. In the group there were more messages advising against continuing. So many more messages.

Another member, MrsMellor, said: *Don't you know how many pregnant women pick up diseases from hospitals? Our immune systems are lowered. We're vulnerable. My friend is sure the radio waves from the scan gave her breast cancer. It's not a coincidence.*

Claire thought of her dad lying in the hospital bed all those years ago and the ground started to feel like it was moving beneath her feet. She thought of all the agony contained within the brickwork of the building up the road, and the lighting and equipment and the animal stench of fear. She couldn't take another step. Her phone was detonating itself inside her handbag, exploding with sounds and vibrations. 'Everything all right, angel?' a man leered through his remaining teeth. She couldn't look him in the eye, just tried to make her body inhale and exhale, inhale and exhale, and not keel over from the new surge of terror that was controlling every part of her. The breaths felt like they weren't reaching her head. Everything was spinning. She had to lean against a wall.

Claire saw ambulances race up the street, screeching their warnings, *Get out, get out!* She saw hungry patients wheel themselves into cafés in protest against the hospital food. She was unable to click the answer button while she received one, two, five missed calls from her mam. By the time she was sure she was able to pump the oxygen from her lungs around her body, it was too late. She'd long missed the appointment's start time.

Claire was thankful for the physical support of the wall when she finally called back.

'Hey, Mam. All fine,' she said. She hoped she sounded convincing.

'What's that, pet?' her mam asked. 'That was quick! Tell me everything! Oh, if I could just be there. You alone, it's not right, not right at all. I said that to Lily. Where are you, love? What's that noise?'

'Sorry. It's loud here. Just outside the hospital. Fine. It was fine. Look, I've got to go, James is trying to get through. Tell you everything later!'

James was not calling. James, according to the Instagram page Claire checked with rattling fingers, was now biting into a dim sum that spurted custard. She replayed the video again and again, the hollow sound of her husband's laughter on the other side of the world barely scratching the surface of the noise of Camberwell.

Claire had spoken a party line into existence: she attended the scan and it was fine. She had to commit to this now. The rain was incessant on the walk home. Her belly churned as she navigated her way past streets that suddenly seemed so full of happy people. When Claire finally unlocked the front door of the flat in a scrabble of wet fingers and exhaustion, she vomited onto the landing. This was her penance, she thought. This is what happens when you tell a serious lie. But there was no turning back, she had to keep going. She cleaned the area with multipurpose spray, opened her laptop, and logged on to Uno's work from home portal. There were several announcements that Holly said had to be issued post haste. Claire was grateful for the distraction.

It was easy to pretend from the safe distance of her empty home. A determination to prove herself at something, anything, took over, and Claire somehow managed to not cave in to the temptation to update the Goddesses until the end of the working day. Sally messaged to say that James was wearing a lovely new t-shirt in his pictures, where was it from, it would really suit Conor. Claire did not reply to that message, or the missed calls from her mam, Lily and James. She gave Uno her total attention.

When Claire finally reached inbox zero, she regurgitated every part of the day's horror to the Goddesses. They were more than understanding. The messages of support came flooding in. It almost felt like she had real company while she ate dinner alone.

Lucy_Loves_Life contacted her directly. *I'm so glad you took my advice on board, darling. You're really making the best decision for yourself and your beautiful baby. You're doing a wonderful thing.*

James messaged. *Bear, can you call me back? I don't think any of my calls are connecting. It's late here but I'll keep my phone on loud in case I fall asleep. Did you get any pictures? I can't wait to see. So sorry for not being there.*

Chapter 18

Claire sensed something was wrong as soon as she woke up. There was a warmth between her legs and an awareness that wasn't there before. She turned the light on and peeled off the duvet: there was nothing on the sheets, they were as crisp as ever. She stumbled towards the bathroom.

'No,' she whispered, when she sat down and saw. 'Please, please, no.' The toilet paper showed brown spots, the colour of rust. She held the paper closer to her face just to make sure her eyes weren't playing any tricks. The stains were definitely there. She was glad she wasn't standing. The possibilities of this were too big. She flushed the paper and reached out to the towel rack for additional support. The metal sweated under her fingers.

Claire continued to stare downwards at the certainty of the tiles beneath her feet until her face started to pulse with the extra blood flow. She had carried her phone with her in the dash to the bathroom and she could sense its presence. The idea of Google felt too difficult, too black-and-white in what it might confirm. She tried to focus on manually forcing air into her mouth. It didn't feel like the oxygen was doing the right thing and it panicked her even more. Claire had always hated blood: it was a family joke that she couldn't even watch *Casualty* and she used to loathe the mechanics of disposing of her period. She wondered what James would say if he was here. *Why wasn't he here?*

The phone was cold when she finally picked it up. Something deep inside compelled her to speak to her husband, even if it meant revealing the previous day's secrets. She needed him. She really, really needed him. Claire's screen told her it was nearly 11 a.m. in Singapore. James's WhatsApp status said he hadn't been online for almost an hour. The last message he sent, after asking again for more scan stories, was about a big meeting and his nerves. There was a pause before the dial tone, a reminder that he was on the other side of the world, before the phone rang out and she reached the voicemail prompt. Claire tried to record a voice note on WhatsApp but her mouth was so dry, the anxiety rasping at her throat, that when she listened back to the hollow sound of her own voice she had to delete it immediately.

Claire remained sitting on the toilet. She wiped again and it was still there. Less than before, but there nonetheless. A part of her always suspected this might happen, always wondered when her luck would run out. She thought of Sally's loss, her mam's loss. Had she tempted fate by avoiding the hospital appointment? By clicking purchase on the first babygrow over the weekend? The phone trembled as she typed.

DulwichGirl

Help!

Hi ladies, I think something terrible is happening, something truly awful. I'm bleeding. I don't know what to do? My husband's still away. I just really don't know what to do. Sorry for repeating myself, I'm so upset right now. Can anyone please help? I should have gone to the appointment yesterday. Feel like I'm going to have another panic attack.

The Goddesses kept different schedules. They posted and supported each other at all times of the day and night while they tended to their broods. It was something Claire loved: she so enjoyed waking up in the morning and catching up on this other timetable of care and chatter. She had not anticipated participating in the pre-dawn activity – not until the baby was here, anyway. Claire stayed sitting on the toilet seat. It was uncomfortable, but she was too scared to move. If she moved, she might dislodge something and intensify the bleeding.

> JessFromJersey: *Can you take a picture for us? How much blood is there, lovely? This happened to me with my baby girl quite a few times. But it all turned out OK! Baby girl is currently demanding a feed, greedy so and so!*
> DulwichGirl: *Oh it's good to know you had this too and you're OK. It's stopped now. It was like the end of a period, brownish.*

Claire wasn't sure if she wanted to capture the blood, its stark colour against the toilet paper. It felt too intimate, somehow, if it was what she feared. That the end could be documented and known by so many. Claire refreshed the group page with practised movements, dragging her thumb down the screen and holding it there. She liked the little whir her phone made while it scanned for any new activity. It made her phone feel like a living thing.

> JessFromJersey: *Oh, it's stopped? Well, that's a good sign. And a dark colour is fab news too. DM me if you need me, I'm sure I've got some pictures from the archives. Mine was like that*

too, especially in the first trimester. You're only just out of that, aren't you? Trust me on this one, it happens to loads of women. It's super common. Please take care and don't worry too much sweetheart.

Lucy_Loves_Life: *Hello DulwichGirl, it's me again. Don't be frightened. If it's as little as it sounds it's nothing to worry about. Hold tight and try not to get too worked up. It's the witching hour right now when all fears seem so much bigger. Remember what I said about stress hormones and getting all het up yesterday? And how you must do your utmost to minimise that toxicity? You've got this girlie.*

Outside, Claire could hear birds chirping. They sounded so cheerful. Claire wiped again and again, until it almost hurt. The toilet paper remained white, but she didn't feel reassured. These women's words seemed too positive compared to the visuals of that dark matter. She had felt something turn inside. And hadn't she instantly known that something wasn't right? When she went back to the bedroom, the duvet did little to warm her. She lay rigid on the bed, watching James's name on her phone screen, watching to see if his status would ever change to 'Online'.

DulwichGirl: *Ladies, I feel really strange. I think I need to speak to someone medical. I'm out of my mind with fear.*
Lucy_Loves_Life: *Oh, darling. It's stopped now, hasn't it? I know what you're thinking but they'll just tell you what we've said already. Many midwives aren't mothers, you know, and I'm not just talking about the men (I've always thought it's such a funny profession for a man, don't you agree?). The midwives don't know this as well as us. I promise you'll feel better in a few hours, just try and get some sleep. I've got a kicking monster inside and a*

screaming little one outside that I must tend to, but I'm always
here. Please get in touch if you ever need any more advice. I'm
only ever a message away.

Claire started crying then and found she couldn't stop. She had
been so strong until that point. She cried for the stupidity she
felt for missing yesterday's appointment, of missing the opportunity to have someone to check to see if all was right. She
cried because she was so afraid that the dream was over. All
she could think of was the blood. She checked her phone con-
stantly, swiping away fresh Goddess notifications. But the only
person she really wanted to hear from was her husband. She
couldn't call and wake her mam up in the middle of the night.

As soon as it turned 7 a.m., Claire dialled the doctor's surgery's out-of-hours line. She didn't feel up to speaking to the
midwife services yet; didn't want to have to explain why she
missed yesterday's appointment. That felt a very long time ago.
Pregnancy changes the timelines of things. The world shifts on
its axis so it revolves around the hope and the fear. Minutes
become days and yet somehow the weeks fly by.

She was connected to a female GP. Claire found herself wondering whether this woman had a child and whether the GP
was talking from experience or medical training. She tried
to discern it from the woman's voice, but it was inscrutable.
Claire didn't mention anything about missing the scan, only the
basics, which somehow became cloaked in new sobs.

Claire heard the GP take a sip of something, the noise clear
through the phone. Claire's device was gripped to her ear. She
wanted to hear every word.

'Right, well, this really is a question for your midwife. Their
number should be on the documents they gave you, no? The
blue notes? I would tell you to go to the early pregnancy unit,

but I suppose that's not right. If you're worried, you should go to A & E, you'll be seen fairly quickly, they're overly cautious about these things, but based on what you've told me I'm not too concerned. This kind of spotting happens to anywhere up to twenty per cent of women. If it had been red, on the other hand . . .'

When the call ended, Claire lay back on the bed and allowed herself to sink into its caress. She smiled for the first time that day, that already-long day. The women were right! Maybe she would be fine. Maybe this wasn't the end. The relief was almost overwhelming. More Goddesses had messaged, full of reassurance and kind words. She tried to respond to as many as possible before she showered away the chill that had crept up her body from the bathroom tiles and lodged itself in her bones. 'I just want this so much,' she said, many times over, when she replied to each comment on the group.

Claire was exhausted by the time she reached Soho. As she emerged from the Tube station, she squinted as she tried to adjust to the light. The day was fresh, the autumn sunshine surprisingly sharp. She was amazed by how many emotions she had already experienced that morning. Perhaps this was what it was like being a parent: you occupy far more of a day than before. She had a newfound respect for all the new mums and dads she'd ever worked with, who attended the same work meetings, responded to the same emails, and always expertly concealed their fatigue.

It was then that James called.

'James!' Claire said.

'Claire? Is everything OK?' he asked. 'Sorry, I've been dashing from meetings to drinks to dinner. I've not even had a chance to shower. And it's so muggy here! I feel like a sweating ham. I'm so sorry I missed your calls. I tried to ring back but I suppose you must've been underground. What's up? Nothing's wrong, is it? Is this about the scan?'

'I'm so tired too,' Claire said, and a yawn swept over her. She thought of what she would have to tell her husband if she mentioned the incident, and what he might say, and it seemed like an exceptionally bad idea to share the events of the last twenty-four hours now that everything was fine. 'I just had a rubbish night's sleep. I just miss you.'

'OK, phew. I've got to go, I only snuck out of this posho restaurant to check you're OK. I miss you too. Look after yourself, my lovely bear. Text me about the hospital!'

There was no further blood. Every time Claire went to the toilet, she gathered herself before checking the tissue paper, her heart thumping its way up to her throat. At the end of the day, she logged back on and provided the Goddesses with her final update. Flora apologised for missing everything, she'd been feeling too grim to even look at her phone, but she was so glad everything was OK. And Claire knew, she really knew, that she was doing the right thing. That she needn't doubt these wonderful women again.

Chapter 19

TheSecretGoddesses

Flora_Is_Free:

Hello lovely ladies.

Sorry for being a little AWOL recently. I'm so behind on all my DMs so I thought I'd post instead – please forgive my laziness.

I've officially reached that stage where everything bloody hurts and I've not been coping brilliantly. My feet look like two big sponges. Tom's started calling them my hooves, which is delightful. They're not helping me get about much, and when I do manage to hoist myself up, it's like I'm moving in slow motion. It's not ideal because this baby loves having a little stamp around on my bladder. It's like they're auditioning for *Riverdance.* At least I haven't needed to get the Doppler out at all recently – there's no doubting they're doing well!

I was just wondering, did anyone else feel peaky around the 36ish week mark (give or take a week or so – Tom and I weren't really keeping an eye on things and my cycles have always been a bit wonky)?

And related to the above, does anyone have any advice on how to power through this nausea? Ginger biscuits and sugary tea aren't doing the trick. I couldn't keep a pasta bake down last night. I'll spare you the details, but poor Tom had to put in a big cleaning shift.

This queasiness didn't happen with Freddie so I wasn't expecting to feel this rough. Thank God I'm a SAHM otherwise I'd need to take early maternity leave, and you all know how difficult employers can be about that. But as we always say, no two pregnancies are the same. A part of me wonders if maybe we're having a girl this time? I look awful and there's that old wives' tale that daughters like to steal their mother's beauty. Perhaps that explains why I'm bursting out of my biggest maternity knickers and have the complexion of a ghoul!

Anyway, I know I need to count my blessings and remember the baby is doing its wonderful thing and my body's supporting him or her in the best possible way. I just would like to, rather selfishly, fast forward this unexpectedly grim phase.

So, my gorgeous Goddesses, please share all your late third trimester anti-nausea tips.

Comments:

Lucy_Loves_Life: *Oh, you poor thing. I've been ever so lucky to never feel sick with any of mine. Have you tried thinking and saying aloud: 'I will not be nauseous today?' I really recommend giving it a go. Our minds are the most potent pharmacy. You can control so much with your thoughts.*

MrsSimms: *When I was 'on grid' with my first two, the midwives always found I had low iron/ferritin levels. Obviously not suggesting you get yourself to a clinic (ha ha!) but could you try having some spinach, steak or beans tonight and see if you've got a little more energy?*

Flora_Is_Free: *@MrsSimms Great idea about the food. I'll do my best to channel my inner Popeye!*

DulwichGirl: *You've got this! Sending you love.*

Chapter 20

James went straight from Heathrow to the office. Helen commissioned a fancy car to take them there, which Claire knew from checking the Holmesdown Capital team's various Instagram Stories. She'd discovered a tool online that allowed her to view their profiles anonymously, which was a godsend because Sally was too busy to keep stalking. Over text messages, Sally kept Claire updated on Rory's chicken pox: Sally had to Sellotape socks to the poor toddler's hands to stop his incessant scratching. Claire hoped she sounded sympathetic in her replies, and that she was offering actual comfort to her friend. She was running out of ways to say *Ah, that sounds really difficult.*

James arrived home later that day with an ashen face. When he rubbed his eyes, it made the dark circles even more prominent. He kissed Claire deeply. He smelled strange, like unwashed hair and wet cardboard.

'How was it?' Claire asked.

James unzipped his suitcase and started unloading its innards. 'Oh, it was champion,' he said, while flinging items in the general direction of the sofa. 'We need to go. I said to everyone how much you'd love it. The food, Claire. Oh my God, the food.

Even the street stalls have Michelin stars.' His face crumpled with a yawn. 'Sorry. I'm zonked. And how are you? What was it like, the hospital? I felt so bad, you know, not being there.'

Claire thought of the hospital incident and the bleeding scare. How she'd shouldered those alone. How it was important to just move forwards, think about the bigger goal. 'I'll tell you all about it tomorrow when you've had some sleep. Are you hungry? Want me to order something?'

'I'm totally done in,' James said, his face contorted as he struggled against another yawn. 'I don't think I'll be awake by the time anything arrives. And anyway, I could do with some time off eating.' He patted his flat stomach as he walked out of the room, leaving the mounds of unwashed clothes behind.

Claire tidied up, then heated a tin of soup she found in the back of the cupboard and defrosted some bread for dinner. All was quiet above. It's amazing how people stop questioning when they hear what they want to hear, Claire thought. To be safe, she read some more blogs about twelve-week scans, just in case he asked again. When she tiptoed up the stairs, tracing a well-worn track on the spots least likely to creak, she saw the lights were still on and James was drooling slightly on the pillowcase. He looked so peaceful. She gave him a gentle kiss before joining the Goddesses online.

One woman, who went only by the name BraveHearted, had just given birth on her bed. She was asking for advice in a post accompanied by a picture. The baby looked raw, unformed still, its face cracked in a scream.

BraveHearted:

Hey ladies, welcome beautiful Beau to the world! I'll do a full post on the experience, feeling a little worse for wear right now. Does anyone have any suggestions on what to do if you still haven't passed your placenta? I've fainted a few times (and been caught by my supportive, strong hubs, bless him!) but just looking for some help.

Comments:
Lucy_Loves_Life: *Have you tried talking to your uterus, darling? Works wonders.*

CharSays: *Congratulations to you and Beau and your wild pregnancy. I found Aesop's poo drops did the trick. Something about the natural oils helps draw everything out. Best of luck!*

SaskiasWorld: *My, what a beauty Beau is! I've heard that squatting can help? Or bearing down while by the loo?*

Claire pressed the like button on each of these responses. These women were so different compared to the people she normally encountered. She shook off doubts about whether BraveHearted should seek medical attention – she remembered reading something somewhere about the importance of passing the placenta – but she couldn't be sure, and really didn't want to be the voice of doom. After her flap earlier that week, Claire was all too conscious of her amateur status. And the ladies had all been so spot-on with their suggestions then, so what did she know?

Claire awoke the next morning to James sitting on the end of their bed. His cheeks still carried pillowcase impressions. She reached up to stroke his face but he jerked backwards. Something was wrong; Claire could tell.

'How did the scan go again?' he asked. His eyes were piercing in their directness.

'Good morning to you too!'

'I was so tired last night I don't remember what you said. I want to hear everything!'

'What, like a blow by blow?'

'That's a funny turn of phrase.'

'What's going on?' Claire asked. This manner of questioning wasn't normal for James.

James pulled a letter from his pyjama pocket. 'You tell me. I've been up since the crack of dawn and saw this when I checked the cubby hole downstairs. Took the liberty of opening it. I think it's you who should be telling me what's going on, Claire. Because from where I'm standing, it seems like you straight-up lied to me about going to the scan.'

'I. Well.'

'Yeah? Sorry, you're just going to have to think of something a bit better than that. You told me you went. You told me you saw our baby. I thought it was strange you didn't send any photos or details or anything, but no, it was because you lied, Claire.' James's voice was so measured that it made things even worse.

Claire hadn't come up with a James-friendly rationale for what happened while he was away. She didn't expect the truth would be exposed. Although, now, she realised just how stupid that was. She'd been too caught up in her new bubble to pre-pare. Claire wished she had more time. Why hadn't she listened to Flora's advice about getting James on board sooner?

'I – I didn't feel well,' she finally said. There was no other way she could placate him, tell him about what had happened, how the events of the last few days had solidified her beliefs that this was the best path for their baby. He was radiating such disdain, it would have to wait.

To Claire's relief, James's face softened. 'Was it morning sickness?'

'Mm.'

'You should have still gone, I'm sure they're used to it. You should have told me. I could have ordered you some – what is it that helps with sickness? Ginger? Oh, I wish you'd told me.'

Claire rearranged the covers and sat up straight. 'I would have gone if you were here.'

'But Bear, why didn't you say anything? I don't get it.'

'I don't know,' she started, before a current of something vicious ran through her. He *had* jetted off when she needed him. 'It was hard to get through when you were so busy having such a great time.'

'What?'

It was difficult for Claire to stop now. 'I don't get why you needed to brag about your trip so much. It felt like you were rubbing it in my face.'

'What? What are you suggesting?'

'I'm *suggesting* you shouldn't have gallivanted off. Everyone agrees: my mam, Sally—'

'What have they got to do with this? Do they know you didn't go to our scan?'

'Stop deflecting.'

'You're the one deflecting, Claire. Jesus! Come on, what's happening here? This isn't right. Why are you saying all this? I wanted to be there more than anything in the world. You know that, you know how excited I was.' His lip wobbled slightly, which turned Claire's stomach. It was too early for this much emotion. She wondered if she'd missed the chance to resolve everything with a hug. She wanted to say she was sorry, and she'd been so overwhelmed, and she seriously wanted to talk to him about birthing options and hospitals. But her mouth acted before she had time to start the reconciliation.

'Nothing's going on. It's all fine. I'm fine. The only thing that's not *fine* is the way you abandoned me.'

James stood up and made a move as if to leave the room. He turned round. 'OK, I wasn't going to say anything, but Lily got in touch. You know it's only a couple of weeks until she goes away? I said Singapore wasn't really her kind of place, so it's good she's not going there. But she's worried about you, said you've been acting strangely, and I thought she was just being a bit silly, nervous before her trip like, but Claire. Claire, can you please look at me when I'm talking to you? I'm worried too. What would you have done if I hadn't found that letter? What's next? You've rescheduled, right?'

'I don't know,' Claire said. And before James could answer, 'I need to shower, I'll be late otherwise.' She was desperate to leave the situation, this incessant questioning. She needed space.

He followed her into the bathroom but stayed silent as the steam crept up the shower door and separated their bodies. In a way, this was worse, his eyes on her, as if he could intuit all the ways she'd changed. She saw his mouth open and close, and wished, wished, this morning wasn't happening. She covered herself with a towel when she walked past and angled her body to avoid any form of touch. Everything about her husband suddenly felt so invasive. Why had he read that private letter from the midwife services?

'Claire,' he said, breaking the silence at last, when she finished getting ready and put on her coat. 'Please—'

But she shut the door and left before she could hear any more.

They barely spoke later that evening. The loudest noise in the flat was the sound of James's thumbs pattering away on his phone. He typed like an old man, always with a slight look of confusion on his face. Claire fought against the need to ask: Who are you talking to? Can I tell you what I've learned? Can we just make up? Please can you not do that underhand thing you've started doing and tell my mam about this? Her husband was within reaching distance, but he felt so far away.

Taya chose the worst time to remind Claire about the meal they'd scheduled for the following weekend. Taya said she finally had a spare evening among the recent chaos (four screaming-face emojis) and she was meal planning. Did she or James have any dietary requirements, and what was their favourite tipple? *I've missed you at the Darters sessions! We need to go for a trot soon! And how the bloody hell are you getting on with that little baby inside? I can't wait to hear everything!*

Claire almost mentioned the upcoming plan out loud. She got as far as walking towards the stove, but James shot her a glance that was so desperately sad, she pursed her lips and pretended to tidy away some pens on the windowsill instead. 'Want some?' James asked as he held out a saucepan full of spaghetti, and Claire shook her head. She regretted it instantly.

When James eventually left the suffocating awkwardness of the room, sighing and saying he wanted to talk as soon as she was ready, Claire stayed behind on the sofa and made herself a bowl of cereal. She wanted to escape for the evening; couldn't bear facing James just yet. Being the first to apologise had never been her way, James had even joked about it in his wedding speech. Instead, she loaded up the Goddess page on the laptop while googling the history of due dates on her phone: a blog told her they were invented by a man 250 years ago and now the maternity system claims women are at risk if they go over. It was all very interesting. Despite what she'd said to her husband, she never felt truly alone when she was online. She filled her mouth with that incredible combination of milk and sugary crunch and got stuck in.

Flora was the focus of that evening's chatter. The two friends hadn't spoken as much as normal, ever since Flora mentioned how she was really struggling with what she called the final countdown.

Flora uploaded a picture of her torso alongside her post. Her stomach was so distended it shone, each stretch mark a ripple of progress. She wanted the Goddesses' advice again, even though she'd only posted a few days before. Everything hurt more than she thought possible, Flora said, from her teeth to her hair. She had taken the group's advice: her partner Tom kept applying flannels to her stomach, and she was eating and drinking liquorice and masala chai lattes, but nothing was soothing the nausea or the pain.

The Goddesses were all resolute in their advice. Everyone said the same thing: *You've got this girl. You've come so far. So, so far. Keep up with the tantric breathing. Not long now, baby's just enjoying its last few weeks. You are so strong. Don't give up, don't panic, don't succumb.* Claire swallowed down a cluster of cereal that caught in her throat. She looked at the slight paunch that rested on her thighs. Still, no one would think she was pregnant. She just looked like she'd helped herself to too much lasagne.

She added to the conversation: *You're so amazing, Flora. I can't wait until I look like you.*

Chapter 21

Claire apologised to James the next morning. The hormones. They were the perfect get-out clause. She couldn't bear the atmosphere of their home, or the way James's face was fixed in a frown as he slept beside her, stuck in a dream almost as fraught as their current reality. She said she was sorry for not telling him what had happened. She didn't want to worry him while he was on his trip. When Claire said these words, she realised they were a version of the truth. James enveloped her in a hug. He had a plan, he said: they were going to call up the midwife service together to rearrange the appointment, and then they were going to turn off all their technology and spend the day just enjoying each other's company.

Claire leaned into James's arms and they rocked together, standing in the middle of the kitchen, until a car horn outside snapped them out of their rhythm. He would cook, he said. He might even dig out an ancient pack of cards and see if he was still the master of Gin Rummy. Claire wondered if her mother had been part of this midwife strategy. She'd been avoiding her mam. She'd allowed the calls and messages to build up, layers and layers of them, until it became exhausting to even consider coming up with a reason why she was doing it.

Claire went through the motions of following James's plan. The call with the receptionist at King's College Hospital's antenatal outpatients was a blur of suggested times and the sound of fingers clacking at a keyboard. They could fit her in right away, they said. James tried his hardest to look like he was interested in the contents of the fridge during the exchange, but as soon as she put the phone down he came over and whispered, 'I'm so proud of you.'

Claire forced herself to say 'Thanks.' She had to bite her tongue.

The following day, James sat Claire down and told her he'd established a hand-squeezing system to ensure he could provide the best possible support. One squeeze meant I'm OK, two: I'm not OK, three: I am having a very bad time, please talk on my behalf. He didn't allow a four: can we leave? 'I know you don't like hospitals, but it's going to be fine,' he said, which took Claire aback. Thankfully, the pre-hospital discussion was short. Claire found herself unable to say anything apart from 'OK,' or share how much dread was thundering through her body. Talking about it made it worse.

James reached for Claire as soon as they entered the hospital, his hand large and coarse. She let him tug her through the grey corridors and tried to only breathe through her mouth, like she did whenever she passed a butcher's. All hospitals smell the same. It's proof of the unifying fear of death.

The antenatal clinic was buzzing with expectation. She looked around for David and Ottie and was relieved when she couldn't see them. Women in varying degrees of pregnancy, bellies like waxing moons, sat or stood. There was a young girl sobbing in what sounded like Spanish in the corner by the water machine. Everyone made a big show of not paying this scene any attention, eyes turned to the bags of bottled urine by their feet. Claire wanted to put a hand around the girl's juddering back and ask if she was OK, but James nudged her away before she could muster the courage.

James found them a seat away from the main cluster of other people. 'Not long, I bet,' he said, and tapped his fingers against his knee, his knuckles pulsing like caterpillars. Claire resisted the urge to check her phone. James would be able to see and she knew what to expect: Flora was messaging frequently again, both privately and on the main forum. Everyone was encouraging Flora to remain home, remain calm, and do her absolute best to avoid medical interference. Claire felt like a fraud sitting on that blue-felt hospital chair. She hadn't responded to any of her friend's recent DMs or posted on the group since she'd made up with James the day before. It felt too disingenuous and wrong. There were two Claires: the real one online, and this shell who got herself into this hospital mess. She stared into space and allowed James to help her up when her name was finally called.

The room was dark and she was told to lie down. Claire's hands shook as she took off her shoes. James wasn't allowed to move his chair closer to the plastic bed. Claire felt the tissue that was laid beneath her start to dampen and stick to the exposed skin on her back. Without asking, the sonographer jerked down her underwear and exposed her pubic region before he slathered on gel. It felt so cold on the taut skin of Claire's stomach that she gasped. James was out of reach so she squeezed herself twice, hands held like she was back in the Sunday school choir. The screen was angled away, and for several excruciating moments she was sure that this meant something was wrong. She shut her eyes and tried to somehow not combust until James said 'Look,' and the sonographer had turned the screen round and there was a black-and-white *thing* throbbing before their eyes. Their three-inch, thirteen-week thing.

James walked over and his hand felt slightly damp as he applied pressure once. 'Bloody hell!' he whispered, in that irreverent way of his, and the sonographer told Claire to please try and stay still as she shook with giggles. It was mesmerising, watching the screen. Claire focused on it instead and tried to drown out the sonographer's instructions to a nurse sitting by a computer, saying things like 'Crown-rump length normal,' and 'Placenta visualised, anterior.' It was almost unbelievable to see there was something somersaulting, living, growing inside her.

James booked an Uber back home as a treat, and video-called both mams in quick succession. 'It looked just like an alien!' he said, twice. Only later did Claire realise her mam didn't ask any questions about why they'd been at the hospital again. She decided to park that thought somewhere far away.

James brought up the scan non-stop. Just before they went to sleep, in the middle of the working day (he sent endless variations of the alien emoji), or at home, when Claire just wanted to unwind. She had to agree that it was special, seeing their baby. She didn't deny that. But she didn't like the reminders of her duplicity.

'It feels so much more real now,' James said the following Saturday afternoon, and ran a finger gently in circles around Claire's stomach.

'James!' she said. 'That tickles!' She couldn't help but smile.

'Not too long until we know if the little sprog is a boy or a girl, right? Isn't it mad that we're going to find out? Mind-blowing, isn't it?'

'You know, we could check that ourselves,' she said. A recent Goddess thread had taught her everything she needed to know about this. They shared photos of bump positions and symptoms and how they were reliable indicators of sex. They were almost always right, they said.

'Ah OK. Sorry, remind me when you got your medical degree? Or was that a different Claire cramming Plato at 3 a.m. back in York?'

'I was reading about it. Loads of women do it themselves. There are YouTubes and blogs and stuff.' Claire wondered if James remembered his freebirthing shut-down. They'd never discussed that exchange.

'Right.'

'Seriously. I've done my research, James. I'm having to do enough for the two of us.'

James sighed deeply. 'I'm here for you,' he said, and it felt like someone else was guiding his words. When did he get so zen? Why couldn't he be real and raw?

Claire opened her mouth. She wanted to say how it felt like James, her mam, doctors, were pushing her to do something without asking about her feelings, like they were robbing her, the mother, of her choice. How it reminded her of her dad, who didn't want the final round of chemo that rendered him so weak and frail. But she didn't share any of those thoughts. Instead, she said, 'There's so much to think about. I'm just not sure.'

'You don't want to know if our baby is a boy or a girl? Bear, babies are all you've talked about for years. What are you on about?' He paused and blinked for longer than is natural. 'And what time do we need to be ready? Do you want me to get some posh wine from the shop?'

'I can change my mind, can't I?' Claire stopped herself before she said too much. If the conversation continued in this vein, all the work she'd put into repairing the fragile ecosystem of their togetherness would be thrown into disarray again. She forced her features into a smile. She had to bide her time. 'But let's not get into it now. We've got to leave in two hours exactly. And I've already got some nice wine.'

She kissed James on the lips to ensure his silence, and then left the room. They needed to prepare for dinner at Taya's. And she had nothing to wear. The maternity clothes she kept ordering were still a bit too big, her historic wardrobe uncomfortably tight.

James entered the bathroom while Claire was applying make-up. He was swearing so much that all the words blended into each other. Claire was looking at herself in the mirror: her face was puffy, but her lips were more pronounced than usual. She had just put on another layer of coral lipstick. She'd first spotted it on Holly. The colour made her eyes pop, the lady at the Clinique counter had been right.

'What is it?' she said. 'Oh God, does this make me look tacky?' Her skin was starting to improve, and she enjoyed how she could run her hand across her face now without wincing. People said this could happen during pregnancy. She was still waiting to experience the full effects of the pregnancy glow, however.

'Er, Bear.' James looked down. Claire noticed he was wearing a suit. 'I've just had a call from Helen. We've been called into the office for what she's called a war cabinet. The Singapore people have gone nuclear apparently and they're threatening to call off the partnership. I, well, I've got to go.'

Claire felt the sadness spread through her body. She had been looking forward to this for weeks. This was her first new friend in such a long time. Why did Helen have to ruin things again? 'That's such a shame,' she replied. When he kissed her, she left a greasy film of lipstick over his mouth. She didn't wipe it off. She wanted Helen, wretched Helen, to *know*.

In her pique, Claire forgot to tell Taya that James wasn't coming. She realised her mistake as she placed one hand on the carp-shaped brass knocker of number 34, Oglander Road. And *of course* Taya also had a stained-glass window. The effect was unbelievably stylish. Claire couldn't make out anything as she peered through. *I'm outside*, she messaged, *just me!* She used her phone camera to check she looked OK. The overhead lighting made her face look hollow. Taya opened the door and the smell of slow-roasted meat curled out into the evening.

'Claire!' Taya said. 'Come in, and no need to take your shoes off. And, um, is James joining us?'

'I'm so sorry,' Claire said, as she hugged her friend and handed over the wine. 'He had a work emergency. I've been so rushed I didn't think to tell you. Oh, would you look at this!'

The inside of Taya's house was as spectacular as its exterior.

'It's original Victorian,' Taya said, as Claire admired the wooden floors. 'I had a bit of a home renovation phase a few years ago.'

Claire just nodded. She was afraid she'd say something profoundly uncool. It was clear her friend had a real talent. Perhaps Taya could help her with the plans she had for the baby's bedroom? But Claire held back from mentioning the baby unprompted. She remembered how Sally always used to talk exclusively about her pregnancy and how much that hurt. How always hearing about milestones made her feel like her life was somehow less important and interesting than her friend's. She didn't want to inflict that on another childless woman. She didn't want to assume this was simply Taya's choice.

Taya led Claire into a room with a huge sofa, maroon walls full of tasteful art (no hang-up calendar, Claire noted), and a vintage drinks cabinet. Taya placed the wine there. 'I know, it's a bit silly, isn't it? But I saw it at the Battersea car boot sale a few years ago and fell in love. It must be the source of so many stories!' she said, as she poured Claire a large glass of sparkling grape juice and topped up her own drink. 'I've got this thing for sloe gin. God, I wish you could taste it. My friend Stew, he makes these huge batches every summer. It's like liquid English sunshine. Or is that an oxymoron? Sorry, I've already had one and it's gone to my head a bit!'

The two friends sat down next to each other and Taya put her arm on Claire's. 'Is everything OK? You've seemed distant recently. I know that's funny because I was thinking, we barely know each other, do we, but we've not run together in what feels like forever and I find myself really missing our sessions.'

Claire ran her tongue over her bottom lip. It felt dry and cakey from the lipstick. 'Oh, that's kind. I promise we'll go out together soon, I'm just always so tired at the moment. I'm so glad to be here, though. And sad James can't meet you!'

'If I hadn't seen many a picture of his handsome face, I'd think you've made this husband up.' Taya laughed. 'Is he looking after you? Is he cooking for three? I'm sorry to say I've totally cooked for about ten people tonight. I hope you're hungry. I know I wa—'

'I'm ravenous. This house smells amazing. Sorry, I just interrupted. You were?'

'I'm just going to give it a stir!' Taya hopped up and unrolled her top from where it had ridden just above her slim waist. Claire noticed a bruise the size of a plum to the left of Taya's belly button, the discolouration vivid, before it was hidden again by her clothes.

Taya wasn't lying. When she called Claire into the kitchen, Claire walked past a vat of lamb stew and an even bigger portion of couscous. The kitchen sink was bloody with pomegranate flesh. Claire pictured how long all this preparation must have taken and felt a fresh pang of irritation towards her husband. 'You'll have to take some back for James in Tupperware!' Taya said, and it was as if she could read Claire's mind.

As they ate, Taya shared stories from her life. Her upbringing in Dubai, her frenzied approach to studying, the mornings she would wake up to find herself still in the UCL Law Library, take out a face wipe and toothbrush and return, bug-eyed, to her laptop screen. Taya had always had a terrible habit of comparing herself to other women, she admitted, between long sips of her drink. In a way, she was thankful, because it got her to where she was today, but it had taken years of therapy to really notice the tendency.

Claire nodded sympathetically throughout. She didn't have it in her to say that evening alone, she had felt so envious of Taya's beautiful house, her impeccable decor, her evident wealth, even the way she cooked. She knew if she had done, Taya would have smiled and joked about how awful it is that women have competition drilled into them from childhood, and perhaps she would have shared things she wanted that Claire had. But Claire could not do that. She was too sober, for starters. Instead, she asked where the toilet was.

Claire opened Taya's bathroom cabinet after she washed her hands, just to see. It was impossible to resist peeping inside the holy grail of secrets. Behind some Le Labo toiletries that Claire knew collectively cost as much as a flight to the Caribbean, there was the familiar blue box of a pregnancy test. She picked it up. It was still sealed in its thin plastic. Claire was shocked by her surprise. She wasn't sure what made her feel most tender towards her friend: the dents that showed the box had been handled or the unbroken packaging. And then there, behind it, were the type of supplements Claire knew well. Had spent a small fortune on herself. Prenatal vitamins, maca root, folic acid. She leaned over and flushed the toilet again, just for good measure, before carefully returning the test to its original place.

'Your house is immaculate,' she said to Taya when she walked back into the kitchen.

Taya was propping her head up, her elbow on the table.

'We'll have to have you around, but oh my God, it is nothing compared to this.' She gestured around.

'You're so lovely,' Taya said, and hiccupped. It made her body jerk.

The two friends washed up together, settling into a comfortable rhythm of suds and tea towels. Taya hummed unselfconsciously as she put the various plates and pans away. Claire recognised the tune – some current chart song that occasionally blared in the office – and she joined in, not caring that her voice was often compared by her family to the sound of a strangled cat. Claire realised she hadn't thought about James since before they'd eaten. She'd missed the transportive power of friendship. She left in a fuss of hugs and commitments that she would join Taya for a mid-week run.

'Don't worry, you can run throughout a pregnancy,' Taya said, her eyes a little unfocused, the lids heavy, 'trust me.'

Claire found herself grinning as she walked up the steps into their flat, even though it looked so basic after an evening in Taya's personalised haven. Her cheeks hurt, the muscles unused for so long. 'James!' she shouted into the darkness, before the room lit up with the fridge. Taya had piled Tupperware after Tupperware into her arms as she stood on the doorstep. 'James!' she said again as she turned on the lights upstairs. The bedsheets in their room were still perfectly folded. She checked the spare room, even though neither of them had ever stayed there, even when they'd argued. Her instinct was right: as

Claire opened the door, she was greeted by the smell of old beer. James was snoring under the covers, surrounded by home decoration magazines and two cork pin boards tacked to the nines with Pinterest printouts. A small tub of pins was perched dangerously close to his arm. Claire sighed. She didn't wake her husband. *Yes, I'm home safe (happy emoji, kissing emoji), thank you so much for having me,* she replied to her friend, who was still such an enigma.

Chapter 22

TheSecretGoddesses

Flora_Is_Free:

Hi everyone,

Let the record state I officially feel better. I'm so sorry for wobbling. I've deleted some of my posts because I don't want my negativity lingering around this space. Thank you to the ladies who reminded me of our group's rules.

As I said to Tom, thank goodness it's the baby making me feel poorly rather than the other way around.

I'm determined to enjoy every last moment before we return to the sleepless nights and endless feeds. I keep thinking how we'll never get the opportunity to be a family of three again. We've all been talking about what we think the baby will be like. Freddie says he just wants a friend. All Tom and I hope is that they're healthy and happy.

The boys have done the most beautiful job preparing the baby's room. Freddie held my hand while giving me the tour (mainly pointing at things, misnaming them and grinning). He helped wash all the toys he so loved as a newborn and Tom surprised me by unveiling the cot he's repainted in the most beautiful sage-green colour.

There are a few things we still need to buy but I think I'm now up to doing a charity-shop sweep. And I will be making the most of Tom's newfound love of upcycling.

Our growing family has come at a strange time, truth be told. I think I've mentioned this a few times before but my lovely mum has early-onset dementia. I couldn't visit her when I started feeling ill (thank goodness for the kind people at the assisted living facility who helped my mum navigate phone calls) but I had enough energy to pop around yesterday. It's getting harder and harder for us to talk and I think the short time apart exacerbated things. I feel so guilty, ladies. I should have found a way to visit. My mum was taken aback by my bump at first and she got so frustrated with herself. It breaks my heart seeing her like this and I know it's only going to get more difficult. She was so supportive back when we had Freddie, including our decision to freebirth, but unfortunately those memories aren't accessible to her anymore. She kept making comments yesterday about doctors, which was strange given the incredible support she provided before, during and after Freddie's birth. I found it so startling. I'm not ashamed to say I cried the whole way home.

All this is to say I really don't know what I'd do without you ladies, you're truly my rock. My rocks!

Thanks to everyone who's kept me sane, stable and focused on providing baby two with the most special welcome into the world. And apologies for upsetting anyone when I was worrying. That was never my intention.

Love you all.

Comments:
Lucy_Loves_Life: *Flora darling, it's so nice to read such positivity. I've always thought words are spells of sorts, framing your reality. And I know your reality will be a gorgeous time with your boys now*

you've turned this corner. Quick question: are you based in the South? I was thinking it was high time we all met. We can celebrate your good health. I'm in Surrey and happy to drive wherever. I'm keen to do as much as I can before I start to nest – not long for me now either.

Flora_Is_Free: *@Lucy_Loves_Life I'm in East Sussex! Just chatted to Tom and he thinks this is an amazing idea! He can drive me! Can we do it soon, before this watermelon pops?*

MindFullOfLove: *Oh my gosh LADIES! Count me IN!*

MrsMellor: *Me too!!! I have wanted to meet you all forever. Let's get a separate thread going. All goddesses welcome, obviously!*

SanneHoward: *Lovely to hear from you, I've thought about you and your health often. I'm afraid I'm based in the West Mids so I can't make the social. I just have to say I was startled to hear your mother lives in an assisted facility. I've read countless horror stories about the drugs and treatments they force non-consenting residents into taking in those places. I'm sure you do this already but make sure you have full sight and sign-off of your mother's support plan. And please never forget that natural is always best. Have you tried intro-ducing Ginkgo supplements into your mother's diet? And cutting out all meat and dairy? There is almost never any need for synthetic drugs. Our earth is abundant.*

Chapter 23

James must have crept from one room to the other while it was still dark outside. The extra weight in the bed created the equilibrium Claire didn't know she needed. The last thing she thought before her body swept her into sleep was *Do not make this into a big deal*. While once she would have poked James and put her face close to his and said hey, what are you playing at, why did you try and sleep in the other room, now she wanted to remain silent. It was in everyone's interest that she channelled calm and rational thinking. Claire felt proud of herself for not slinking her phone out from under the pillow and checking Helen's Instagram to work out why her husband got himself into such a boozy state. Instead, she dozed back off.

They woke up entwined, James's large body curled around hers. Outside, rain tapped against the windows. It was as comfortable a moment as Claire could imagine, until she remembered James's strange behaviour the night before. Still, she lay there, ensconced.

'So, there's one thing we need to do today,' James said, his breath tickling her neck. Claire wondered if he was still drunk. 'We've got to talk about names. I've got you a present, I totally forgot to give it to you yesterday. Here, wait . . .' James crashed out of the bed and cackled. 'Oh my God. Those drinks. Helen made us do fireball whisky shots. It's like the room's rocking on water. Here, wait a minute.'

Claire heard her husband clatter around downstairs before stomping back up. *Whisky*, she thought, *but what about work?*

He held a book out. 'Look, I saw this on display. I was out for lunch and couldn't stop myself. Isn't it amazing?'

'Oh wow!' It was called *A Very British Suggestion of Baby Names*.

'Just look at the inside,' James said. He opened the book to M. 'It's cool, right?'

Margaret, Mark, May. Each suggestion was beautifully illustrated. *Monty is a pet form of the name Montgomery, meaning From the pointed hill,* was written into a watercolour rendering of a green peak. It was a gorgeous book. Claire sometimes felt like she was the only one who had wanted this pregnancy, this child. It was special to be reminded it wasn't a solo pursuit. They may have clashed on certain things, but here was James, planning for this little life. Being distracted from the present by glimpses of their future, just like her.

'Oh, this is so pretty,' Claire said, as she continued to leaf through. 'But we've already decided, right?' Jude. Or Emily. They'd discussed the topic almost to death, going back and forth over the list Claire had been building in the notes app on her phone for as long as she could remember. All the names had also been run past Sally, of course, to ensure there were no clashes later down the line, despite Sally's resolution she was one and done. Claire had read of friendships ruined by the race to claim names: two famous mummy bloggers were now sworn enemies.

'That was before, Bear! It's actually happening now. So, hear me out, what about something like Mildred for a girl?'

'Oh God no, I was in primary school with a Milly and she used to threaten people with her compass when the teacher's back was turned in maths. What if she found out we'd named our child after her? That would be so weird. Imagine if I'm back home and I see her and she's like, 'Oh, who's this?' and I have to say: My child has your name, you scary woman.'

James raised one eyebrow. 'Oh-kay!' he said. 'Not Mildred, then.'

The conversation continued when they left to get some food. It took time, but Claire managed to convince her husband to go for something a little more nutritious than McDonald's.

The brunch spot she decided on was close to Taya's house. Last night's feast sat heavily and she felt strangers' eyes flicker down to her middle when she passed people in the street. One woman caught Claire's eye and her face melted out of its haughtiness. 'Give way to the lovely lady, Cleo!' the stranger trilled to her daughter, who rolled behind her on a scooter. Claire smiled at them. Deep down, she hoped they were having a girl. She'd never really understood men.

Over shared plates of sweetcorn and avocado fritters and, on James's insistence, syrup-drenched cinnamon and pineapple pancakes, they reopened the book on S.

'I'll tell you one thing for free. No child of mine will ever be called Shirley.'

'Keep your voice down,' Claire said to James. He had a tendency to boom when he was hung-over. 'A Shirley might be able to hear!'

'Look around us, Bear,' James tried to quieten his voice, but it just made him over-enunciate, 'everyone's so young. Trust me; no one here is called that.'

Claire reached over the sticky, empty plates and play-punched his shoulder.

'It's strange you haven't had any cravings, isn't it?' James said, his head cocked to one side. 'I always pictured you as a crazy cravings kind of person.'

'Hey! What's that supposed to mean?' Truthfully, she kept craving avocados, which she didn't want to admit to anyone. It felt a bit embarrassing, do-goody.

'Claire, you once made me orange and tuna pasta. Your taste buds have always been . . . unconventional.'

'We'd run out of lemons! It was the only citrus in the house!'

'Ah, my Bear, the champion chef,' James said. 'I still can't look at tuna the same way.' He winked at her.

It was easy for Claire to forget her irritation with James when he was like this. She wondered if anyone could pick up on any lingering tension. She remembered how she used to feel seeing affectionate pregnant couples, and how it would make her crumple inside. She leaned over the table and found her husband's hand.

'What's that for?' he said, before running his thumb over hers.

Claire's mam kept messaging her links to things. *The Superfoods You Must Avoid During Pregnancy, This Pillow Mist Will Make You Wake Up Energised!, Top Tips For First-Time Grandparents.* Normally, she just clicked delete but the message that popped up as she refreshed her inbox during lunchtime caught her eye: *The One Trick to Stop You Worrying.*

Ration your worries, the quoted expert said. Only allow one hour a day to really feel your anxieties. Write them down, say them aloud, speak to yourself, whatever you have to do to make you feel better. But at any other time of day, cast the worries aside. Claire liked the idea in principle, but her mind was simply marbled with concern. *Thanks Mam,* she replied, *I'll give this a go.*

Surprisingly, though, Claire found she didn't even need an hour a day to decompress from her constant, ambient worries. Instead, she brushed as many things under the carpet as possible and hid them in corners of her mind. She didn't bring up the questions she had about James's work night out at any point, or mention her apprehensions or freebirth aspirations. She was proud of herself. Actions like this helped their relationship keep going, second by second, day by day. After all, she thought, every relationship involves some sort of compromise. It was all good. She just needed to slowly introduce the idea of freebirthing again at the right time. She was still waiting on the response from *Nature* about their study. That would be key.

Claire had six weeks, half a trimester, to nudge James in the right direction. Meanwhile, it was so nice to return to some semblance of normality, without the recent prickliness that had made home so tense. An automated letter arrived in the post with the date and time of their next scan. James had opened it, despite it being addressed to Claire, and marked the calendar with a picture of two stick figures smiling. To James, she found herself saying 'Yeah, sure, we'll see.' But to the ladies online, she reaffirmed her commitment that one scan was enough, and of course she wouldn't get the whooping cough vaccine. They were very specific about what a woman should and should not do when it comes to medical interference, and the dangers of any injections.

Claire's new Goddess routine involved checking the threads on the laptop whenever she got home from work. It inspired her to get through the Uno-filled day. She'd exchange small talk with Ali, keep an eye out for David, just in case that day would be the day he wanted to talk about their shared journey, then put her head down, beaver away quietly, and do everything she could to not attract any unnecessary attention. It was easier to read through the group on a bigger screen anyway.

That day's hot topic was about heel prick tests.

BumpyRoad: *I want to decline but they will ask why so what should I say?*

Lucy_Loves_Life: *You need to tell them your informed choice is a firm no.*

MindFullOfLove: *I'm with you ladies. It's something I've been thinking about too. My family has a history of lung issues but who knows where they would store my baby's blood. If it has Cystic Fibrosis, we will find out ourselves, as parents, rather than by some clinician.*

Claire was skipping from the chat to the NHS page on statutory maternity pay, reading about how she'd need a midwife form to qualify, when James surprised her with a tap. She'd been too engrossed to notice the sound of the door opening and closing. Normally she was so in tune with the sounds of her husband's return.

'I was on the seven thirty-eight last week and I spotted so many women wearing these. So I applied for one.' He held out a badge. *Baby on board*, it said. 'Now you'll always get a seat!'

Claire hadn't wanted to order this just in case. She stood up during her commute every day, dashing for an empty seat on the rare occasions one appeared. She shut the laptop and kissed her husband in one swift movement.

'It's that train, it's so rickety. I hate the thought of you being jostled around. I kept thinking: what if someone bashed into you. I sort of wanted to wear it home, just to see if anyone said anything. That would have been funny, wouldn't it?'

The earnest side of James reminded her so much of when they first started dating. He used to take the subject of learning about Claire's life incredibly seriously. Every time she said something new, she could see it register in his eyes, and understood this nugget would be stored away like a seed in a vault, where it would slowly grow into something bigger and be ready for instant recall. Somewhere along the years, when they'd learned everything there was to know about each other, his eyes would glaze when she mentioned how much she didn't like a certain new food she'd tried (papaya tasted like socks and anyone who said otherwise was pretending), or complain about a sassy email from a journalist at work. She liked the revival of this behaviour. She walked over and attached the badge to her biggest coat ready for tomorrow's commute. In the excitement of the gift, Claire forgot to clear the search history of the laptop, as she always did, and log out of the group.

Chapter 24

Claire decided to join the Goddess meet-up at the last minute. She'd followed the chatter as plans formed in front of her eyes. Every time a new venue was suggested, Claire hastily calculated the distance from Dulwich. When James kept murmuring about some football derby and 'super Sunday', Claire seized the window of opportunity. Late on Saturday evening, while James fiddled on his phone, she RSVP'd yes on the group. Lots of the women liked it. They expressed their pleasure through a button. It made Claire feel very secure, all this virtual liking.

Flora messaged minutes after Claire updated everyone.

From: Flora_Is_Free:

Claire, you've made my day. I couldn't be more excited to see you. I just started typing something silly about how you'll laugh when you clock the size of my bump but . . . can I tell you a secret? I keep thinking, am I maybe a little too big? I'm not so sure when we conceived and, as midwives loved to point out last time, my fundal measurements are skewed so there's no point in getting the tape measure out.

To be perfectly honest, I still don't feel brilliant, but I was

scared I was bringing the group's mood down. Don't tell the girls,
ha ha, especially after all their comments when I've been jabber-
ing on about my pain recently! I feel bad because I introduced you
to everyone and now I'm all over the place.

You won't say anything, will you?

DulwichGirl: *Ahh, Flora, your secrets are always safe with me.*
I'm sorry I've been so rubbish at replying. Please don't worry,
everyone says measurements are all guesstimates, don't they? My
friend Sally was told to expect a tiny baby and Rory turned out to
be in the 90th centile or something and he's still huge. Everyone
says babies will come in their own time, when they're ready. It will
be any moment now, I bet. I hope it's not tomorrow . . . Although
wouldn't that be funny?

Flora_Is_Free: *Ha ha, I'll make sure Tom's on standby.*

'I'm going shopping in town,' Claire said to James the next
morning. He made an 'mmm' noise and continued to dip his
hand in a bowl of dry cereal. She ignored her urge to move the
bowl away from the edge of the sofa and onto a more secure surface. Instead, she bent down, offered her cheek and accepted
a slightly distracted kiss while James focused on the action on
screen.

The noise coming from the TV was so loud that Claire could
hear it as she walked down the street. James loved to leave the
window open, no matter how cold it was outside, it was just
one of the habits she'd learned to live with. Claire hoped their
neighbours didn't think they were antisocial. It was strange
how she inhabited the same building as two other couples
but didn't even know their names. All she knew was their
hair colours, rough ages and the type of alcohol they enjoyed,

which she always noted when she put out the recycling. The edgy couple who occupied the garden-floor flat were into their crémant. Claire couldn't wait to try a bottle in five months' time. It sounded much more glamorous than Prosecco. She'd had to look up how to pronounce it.

When choosing what to wear, Claire opted for an outfit that emphasised her bump: a turtleneck that strained over her new bra size and a satin midi-skirt that hugged her stomach. It was the first time she'd really dressed with that intention. At work she opted for flowing tops that skimmed and flattened. Sometimes, she thought of conversations she might have with David, somewhere private, about how different it is for men and women. How she tried to hide her conspicuousness at Uno, while nothing physically changed for him, but he still enjoyed the exact same reward at the end. But these opportunities never came about. She deliberated over following him on Instagram or suggesting a lunch meet-up in his work calendar but always clicked away before pressing *add* or *send*.

Her skirt wasn't very accommodating. With every step, the material rode up and twisted, and Claire kept having to tug the waistband back round. Claire didn't mind the temporary discomfort. She'd had one of the youngest pregnancies out of anyone in the group and wanted to fit in. She'd already planned how she would pose if there were any pictures. It was all about exhaling at the right moment.

Claire's body was in a strange in-between place. She was showing, but only just. She'd tried to run recently but was spooked by the sensation she no longer had control. Every step was heavy and difficult and her pelvis hurt in a new way. She'd admitted defeat before she'd even reached the park and walked home, batting away beads of sweat, and messaged Taya to say she'd formally retired from running. Taya sent lots of thumbs-up emojis in response. *That's OK, we'll go for walks instead!* Taya replied.

This new body tired much more easily. Claire was glad the train chugging away from London was empty because she had the pick of seats. She took her planner out of her bag. The back pages contained each of the attending Goddess's details and she wanted to commit them to memory. It would be awful if she got their names wrong. Her revision was interrupted by the announcement the train was passing through a station called Berrylands, which sounded idyllic. A far cry from inner city names like Mudchute or Isle of Dogs, places James suggested visiting when they were first looking for flats. She looked up house prices as the carriage rattled away from London: Berrylands was far more affordable than Dulwich. She pictured herself telling people that was her address. It sounded perfect.

The group had agreed to meet in Guildford. It was close enough for Flora, who was venturing from her home in Sussex. Flora had uploaded photos of her bump bursting through the seat belt, as ripe and swollen as a watermelon, her partner grinning behind the steering wheel beside her. Claire stroked her stomach absentmindedly as she thought of James slouched in front of the TV at home. She couldn't wait to reach the later stages, to be on the brink of meeting whoever was nestling inside. Everything still felt so far away.

Green hills rolled in the background of Guildford high street when Claire got off the train. She stopped to take a picture before she remembered she was supposed to be in Central London. It was important, Claire knew, to be careful with her digital footprint. She hugged her coat against the gusts of wind and followed the map on her phone until she reached a café away from the main thrust of the town.

'I'm here for the, um, freebirthing event?' Claire said to the girl standing by the door, who looked barely older than a teenager. The girl's make-up seemed too intense for midday on a Sunday: her eyelids were painted like a sunset and her cheeks had two slashes of bronzer.

The girl furrowed her brows as she leafed through her rota, nails clinking together in the process.

'Do you mean the Belly Tots pregnancy group?' the girl asked, flicking page after page. 'There's nothing here about freebies.'

Claire noticed Flora's silhouette at the back of the room. 'Yes, sorry.' Her face flushed. She'd known that was the code. She was foolish for letting that slip. 'Do you mind if I go through?'

The group of five women occupied a large table in the corner of the café. Everyone but Flora rose to greet Claire. It was almost unbelievable to see the Goddess's avatars brought to life. They were real people, with actual smells and mannerisms and accents, and all so gloriously pregnant. Claire bent down to cuddle Flora.

'Claire, we meet at last! And look at you. How gorgeous are you?' Flora spoke with a gentle voice rather than the strident one Claire had pictured when reading her bold words online.

'It's so nice to finally see you,' Claire said. She tried to not let her pleasure at her friend's compliment show too much but her mouth kept slipping into a smile.

It was the first time Claire had been around multiple pregnant ladies, apart from the tense wait for the sonography appointment, and it felt amazing to be among people who just understood how she felt. She allowed herself to be carried by the flow of effortless conversation. The headaches, the boob aches, the fear of making a misstep. When one person spoke, they all listened.

Claire asked if anyone else was experiencing vivid dreams that startled them awake. All the ladies looked at one another and then at Claire and said, 'Yes.' Flora even winked as she laughed, her stomach bobbing up and down. Claire had forgotten how good this kind of validation felt.

A waitress came around and topped up everyone's tap water and the conversation dimmed. This had been one of the topics discussed in the build-up to the event: other people don't always 'get it', so they had to be careful.

Erin (MindFullOfLove) picked up the temporary lapse in chatter by commenting on Flora's phone background. It was a screenshot of a poem, a famous one apparently, although Claire had never heard of it. It said the greatest lesson a woman will ever learn is that she has everything she needs within herself. Erin asked Flora if she felt comfortable reading it out and she did, beautifully, in her soft voice.

'Women have always been punished for having opinions,' Erin said, 'and pregnancy is full of brutal judgement. Parenthood, too, of course. Do you remember that *Nature* article I found? That's the first time I've seen the system acknowledge that what we do is born out of love. We're still so far away from getting people to understand.'

'I like to look at the poem when I'm not feeling so good. It really helps,' Flora said.

There was a great amount of nodding and sighing.

As an act of solidarity, the other ladies set it as their background too. 'For Flora!' they said, and clinked phones across the table as if they were champagne flutes.

Flora was the real star of the show. Everyone marvelled at her largeness. Her partner Tom was so supportive, she said: he drove her here and was occupying himself in to town for a few hours. He was ready to be called and take her home at a moment's notice. 'I've been eating dates and drinking rasp-berry red leaf tea like they're going out of fashion,' Flora said. The group all said Flora's baby was clearly just relishing its time so much it needed a few more days inside. This made Flora smile until her gums appeared. A true smile, although Claire noticed Flora kept going pale and gripping the table. Above the crescent of her belly, her chest and face was slick. She glistened underneath the gentle café lighting. Claire tried not to stare.

A tall, pinched woman with a jutting ridge of a bump com-mandeered conversation whenever Flora looked particularly peaky. This was Lucy (Lucy_Loves_Life) one of the group's most prolific posters. Lucy told the group to not be shy around her bump, as it was already very sociable. Claire found herself having to say hello to the woman's stomach. 'Their womb name is Pip,' Lucy said. 'Go on, they love meeting new people, just like their mum.' Claire wished she could tell James this story. He'd find the thought of a womb name so entertaining.

Lucy asked the ladies if any of them had any difficulties con-ceiving. Claire felt her heart flutter in the memory of her fifteen months of failure. Lucy didn't allow anyone to respond before she launched into a loud confession that when she was trying for her first, she used to find other women's bumps upsetting. It once got to a point, Lucy boomed, that her old hairdresser stopped answering her calls and the receptionist refused to take her bookings. Lucy recently found out it was because the hairdresser had become pregnant: she spotted the former friend hand-in-hand with a toddler in town and put two and two together.

'That's so hurtful, don't you think?' Lucy asked. 'To conceal that from me just because she knew I was trying so hard? So hurtful. And you should have seen me back then: my hair never looked worse. It was a double injustice.'

183

Claire put an arm on Lucy's bony shoulder to support her. It was interesting to see someone who seemed so unflappable online express their emotions. Lucy was always stoic and consistent with her advice on the group. Claire thought the hairdresser's behaviour was considerate, truth be told. While Claire always adored updates on Rory, sometimes Sally had unintentionally shared a picture at the most painful moments. An image of Rory with his angelic face covered in mashed potato, just as Claire reached for a hot-water bottle to calm treacherous cramps. She often needed some time alone in the car after leaving the happy chaos of Sally and Conor's home, time to decompress before they returned to their pristine, sterile flat. But even though she thought this, she said, 'That sounds awful,' and the other ladies murmured similar niceties.

Claire noticed Flora wipe her forehead with a napkin before she agreed. 'Awful,' Flora said.

'Hey, are you OK?' Claire asked her friend over the table. She kept her voice low. She didn't want Flora to feel uncomfortable.

'Yeah, it's nothing, really,' Flora said. She was only just audible over the group's babbling. She held one hand to her middle.

'You sure?'

'It's just – the baby, it's not moving so much. I don't think it's moving so much.'

Claire's stomach dropped. 'Flora? What do you mean?' Claire looked around the room. She wondered if she should try and get the others' attention, ask if Flora needed to see someone. Not a doctor, God forbid, but a midwife, perhaps? A doula? Although – in an emergency, would a doctor be the best person? Claire didn't know what to think.

'Do you mind coming with me to the loo?' Flora said, extra quietly.

Claire walked over, careful to focus on the ground so she

wouldn't catch any of the other Goddess's eyes, and helped her friend up.

'We'll just be a minute, she's not feeling so great,' Claire said to the now-silent group of ladies, and she was relieved when they resumed their chatter. She allowed Flora to shuffle ahead.

'What's happened? Is the baby OK?' Claire whispered, after she closed the door of the disabled toilet behind them.

Flora's eyes seemed unfocused. 'I think I just need some sugar, or something. I feel – I feel a bit funny. I think it was maybe too much coming today.'

'And the baby? Is the baby moving?'

Flora shook her head. 'We're both just tired, I'm sure of it. Probably too much tea this morning. The baby must be sleeping. Do you mind helping me get down?'

Claire held her friend's hand again as she lowered Flora onto the seat. 'I'll turn round,' she said, and stared at the door as she heard the removal of clothes, the urine, the flush. She wanted to ask more questions but was wary of spooking Flora. Could she ask to feel her stomach, reassure her? Sally had often guided Claire's hand so she could feel Rory's kicks and somersaults. Claire could still remember how strange it was, the reminder that her friend's body supported another life and all of its squirming potential. She waited for Flora to say something else, something that would allow her to spring into action. Why was Flora not speaking? Claire hadn't felt anything resembling a kick yet but she knew she'd be feral with fear if her baby stopped moving. The panic that Claire felt build with every silent second seemed to make the dingy bathroom walls throb. It felt like she was playing a part in a film.

Finally, she heard Flora move. 'Right, I'm up. Let's go back. Sorry about that. I'm going to order a hot chocolate and it'll all be OK. Baby really loves sugar.'

'Are you sure?' This situation felt surreal.

'They'll get going again soon.' Flora rubbed her middle. 'Won't you, bubby?' Her face was so waxy that her cheeks looked glazed.

Claire looked her friend up and down. This woman was so different to the feisty figure presented online. 'You said in your message you'd been feeling unwell?'

'I'm fine now. Sorry, I didn't mean to worry you. You're so lovely, Claire. Thank you. Really, thank you. But we're better now, aren't we, bubby?' Again, Flora caressed her belly.

The desire to tell Flora to speak to someone returned with even greater force. Claire found herself wanting to put her hands on Flora's shoulders and suggest she get another opinion. But Flora had already unlocked the door and, in her own gentle way, she'd indicated that she didn't need Claire meddling. Claire walked slowly behind her friend, one step in front of the other like a funeral procession.

Lucy lent over and cackled when they sat back down. Flora had declined Claire's offer to lower her, and Claire tried not to notice Flora wipe her forehead with a new napkin. 'Oh, ladies, look at your faces! What do I keep on saying? Hang tight, it'll all happen in good time. Now, Flora, Flora, eyes over here, darling, you're going to be just fine. Just remember how well you did with Freddie. This one's going to appear so soon, I can just feel it. And everyone says I have a sixth sense about these things. Mark my words.'

'Sorry about that,' Flora said, her voice a little louder now. 'I'm fine, of course I'm fine.'

It was so easy for Claire to be carried away from her concern and absorbed by the never-ending stream of mutual under-standing that existed between these women. They discussed Epsom salt baths, ambient lighting, the best music to push to:

wonderful things that Claire hadn't been able to talk about with anyone in person. She didn't want to say anything that might alienate such invigorating and inspiring company. These women had all experienced childbirth already, all five of them, whereas she had not. And Flora was an experienced mum, wasn't she? Claire vowed that she'd do something if Flora said anything else, but whenever she looked across to her friend, she seemed to be doing OK.

When the time came, Claire didn't want to leave. This had been an afternoon of pure joy and comfort, the upset with Flora a clear misunderstanding on her part. She hugged each of the women as tightly as their protuberances allowed. She had to bend down for Flora and kiss her moist cheek. 'Good luck,' she whispered in her friend's ear. 'You are so strong.'

The network was alive with chatter as Claire journeyed home. So many people expressed how jealous they were because they couldn't make it. Lucy had taken a picture of the six of them, their faces crammed together on screen. For once, Claire looked truly, transcendentally happy. She even looked pretty. She could see that on herself. She wished she could show this image to James. He loved it when she smiled with her teeth, and not with her mouth pursed together to disguise the discolouration she was convinced everyone must find unsightly. Maybe this was what NCT was like? A supportive network of like-minded women. Her mam kept texting her to sign up before the local class sold out.

'Get anything nice?' James shouted when Claire unlocked the door.

Claire could still hear the aggressive jeer of crowds. How many games had he sat through? She was frustrated to see he had left the beautiful artisan sourdough loaf she'd picked up yesterday out on the counter unprotected. It would be stale.

He never thought of these things. 'Not really,' she replied, and headed straight upstairs so she could resume the conversations uninterrupted. She changed her phone's background from the poem to the usual picture of her and James. They were grinning into the camera, eyes squinting under the Cretan sun. Their last overseas holiday felt like a distant memory now. They'd laughed and explored all week, enjoying the simple pleasure of just being together. They'd been so happy back then.

Chapter 25

TheSecretGoddesses

Lucy_Loves_Life:

Ladies, it was magical meeting so many fellow Goddesses last Sunday. It really nourished my soul. Pip's soul too. Like I said, they just love hearing new voices. They wiggled away so merrily for the rest of the afternoon – and evening too! Really put on quite a show. Pip's been transverse for several weeks and the excitement of our rendezvous meant they managed to jive their way head down. I can put aside all the peppermint oil and Pulsatilla remedy now, thank you all.

We must do it again. Hopefully soon, otherwise I'll be bedded down in newborn bliss. My body is simply bursting with the desire to breastfeed again. I can't wait to lock eyes with Pip, knowing I provide everything they could ever want.

But I'm getting ahead of myself. You all know what I'm like when I get talking about La Leche.

Two questions for you all: one, has anyone got a recommendation for a birth photographer?

And secondly, has anyone heard from our darling Flora? Do we think our little group may have multiplied? I've got a real feeling something has happened.

Comments:

MindFullOfLove: *You've beaten me to posting. I was just thinking how our meet-up has been the highlight of my pregnancy. Isn't it electrifying to be around like-minded women?*

How exciting about Pip turning, hopefully they'll start engaging soon.

I've not heard from Flora, no. Flora (and please don't be cross when you see this, F) did seem jumpy. I do hope she hasn't considered . . . you know what . . .

Lucy_Loves_Life: *@MindFullOfLove Oh Erin, don't be unkind, don't you remember how drained you felt when you were at that final stage of bloom, providing your child with every last droplet of your energy? I'm sure we'll hear from her. I just love a birth story.*

Marigold_Goldie: *I think it's all good, Flora's been on/off for weeks. I don't want to sound preachy, but I think we all forget that we don't owe everyone updates. Speaking of which . . . Lucy, I'm going to share my birth story this week. Marlowe was born last Saturday. Here's a pic of the little man. We didn't have a photographer, I'm afraid. My eldest captured this photo.*

SanneHoward: *@Marigold_Goldie, what a dear name, and what an alert face! @All, Flora's baby will come when they're ready. I've delivered at 43+4 before and it was the most ecstatic birth experience. The later, the better, in my opinion.*

MrsMellor: *I thought Flora seemed in excellent spirits. May her strength inspire us all.*

Lucy, I'll send you the details of the photographer we used. She's had three wild pregnancies herself and she really understands how sacred the experience is. When I roared, she roared. You'll love her.

DulwichGirl: *Hey ladies! LOVED last Sunday. I've just checked and Flora took a while to update everyone after Freddie was born. I bet she's nestling down with a gorgeous newborn and we'll hear all about it shortly.*

@Marigold_Goldie oh my gosh I can't wait to read and soak up every single word. Please don't spare any details.

@Flora_Is_Free hopefully hear from you soon!

MindFullOfLove: *@Flora_Is_Free, when you see this, I can't seem to edit my first comment so would like to apologise. I'm in a foul mood today. The health visitor for my youngest is completely on my case and making all sorts of threats because I won't open the door to them. I shouldn't have said that, of course you wouldn't have done anything so silly as engage with the system.*

MamaMartha: *Ladies, I'm detecting a worried energy from some of you regarding Flora. Can I ask that instead of low-vibration worry, we send her high-vibration love? We really don't want anything to negatively transfer onto her child, in or out of utero. We must all remember there is no rush. All babies will come out and it's much better to empower them with the ability to choose their own time. There's less risk of complications that way. Many thanks.*

TheTruthFairy: *Hey all, just prepping final bits. Hubby's starting to panic. Can anyone suggest the normal timing for baby to transition to oxygen after birth? We want to be fully prepared.*

MrsMellor: *@TheTruthFairy, You've got the wrong thread, lovely. Both my unassisted babes took approximately 60 seconds to breathe and cry. But many mammas here have reported it taking several minutes. If the placenta and cord are pulsing and your instincts say baby is OK, you're absolutely fine. DM me if you'd like to know more.*

Chapter 26

'Oh, not again,' James shouted, when the doorbell rang for the second time that afternoon. 'Claire, another one, seriously?'

Claire could hear James from her position in the shower. The latest haul must have arrived. She had always loved online shopping, but the behaviour had ramped up recently. It was so easy, and Amazon and Instagram somehow always knew what she wanted. The Internet was so clever in that way. All she had to do was click *swipe up* or *buy now* and the next day something would just arrive. She hadn't checked their bank account in a while. It was better to not know these things, she reasoned.

She hummed to herself – plausible deniability – and continued to watch the little rivers slide off her stomach. At the meet-up the weekend before, the Goddesses warned Claire about the rapid decline of their mobility, sharing stories from their various pregnancies. Flora, in particular, had encouraged Claire to enjoy every opportunity to see her toes. This advice had been taken literally. Every day since Guildford, Claire ran a long shower. Today's was the luxurious type that allowed her to fully relax: she'd shampooed twice, scrubbed her body using a Laura Mercier travel sample she saved for special occasions, and was in the process of shaving her legs.

'I'm in here!' she said as she re-lathered the foam. 'Just a minute!'

When Claire stepped out and wrapped herself in a towel, she thought about the recent speculation about Flora. Claire hadn't heard from her friend since the group message confirming a safe return home last Sunday – with no signs of labour. But Claire knew what this silence meant: she would have to do even more online browsing, send the baby a gift. Maybe some books. Flora had mentioned how her partner Tom loved reading *Winnie the Pooh* stories to her bump, and how it danced to the sound of Tom's special Eeyore voice. Yes, books would make a perfect present. Perhaps a little Pooh hat too.

Claire wandered into the second bedroom, the centre of James's sudden passion for DIY. Over the last few weeks, when he wasn't watching football, James had developed a keen interest in constructing as many parts of the baby's room as possible. After work, she'd find James looking at YouTube videos from accounts with names like Bodge It Yourself or The Crafty Dad. Whenever Claire saw this, she felt her heart run faster. Somehow, James's excitement made it all feel more real, this still-intangible imminent change.

James recently framed their scan and fixed it to the wall using one of the daddy blogger techniques. Claire was shocked to see it there. She had no memory of the sonographer printing it out or how it came to be in their home. The experience had been so laden with anxiety and guilt that she wondered what else she'd forgotten. She didn't mention this to James, and instead said, 'Lovely,' when he unveiled it one evening. The only part of the scan Claire really liked was the name at the top: Hansen. She'd always loved a sense of ownership. She stood in front of it and watched her breath mist the frame. That scan was alive and inside her. That was their baby.

James walked upstairs, arms loaded with cardboard boxes. 'What did you order, an elephant?' he asked and pretended to stagger.

They unwrapped the latest order together: a white wooden cot, a miniscule mattress cover and a play gym, so the baby could look up and wrap its miniscule hands around the tentacles of jellyfish or clutch on to the barnacled midriffs of whales. Claire started laying the pieces out on the floor alongside her husband.

'Isn't it gorgeous?' she said. She loved this part, creating this oasis within their home, a room with such unparalleled potential.

'Bear, do we need to talk about how much this all costs? Shahnaz, this girl on my team, said they got everything second-hand on various marketplace sites. Shouldn't we be doing that?'

'Second-hand? But how would we know it's safe?' It frustrated Claire how James didn't think about these things. Perhaps it was because he grew up without either a sibling or a pet. He'd never had to look after someone who depended on him. She'd already welcomed Sally's offer of Rory's hand-me-down clothes, but a cot? That seemed like a step too far.

'OK, but – ah, where's the screwdriver? Have you tidied it away again?' James started huffing around the room, peering under various objects, before clopping downstairs. His tools were an assembly of unwanted Christmas cracker gifts pocketed over the years.

Claire sat and admired the room while James clattered around. She was so lucky. Everything was falling into place.

When James finally reappeared, he looked sheepish. 'I can't

find that screwdriver anywhere. Can we go to B & Q? I promise it won't take long,' he said.

Claire agreed, but only because it was exciting to have James so on board with this side of the planning. It was an excellent step, she thought to herself. Soon, she would be able to re-broach the essential freebirthing conversation.

They took the bus to West Norwood and held hands while it chugged along its leafy route. South London was full of con-tradictions: brutal concrete buildings loomed behind terraced Victorian houses with two Land Rovers parked in their front gardens. The engine's vibrations made their way to Claire's bladder. She unlocked her phone to track the distance between the bus and B & Q. It was a dangerous move: any new Goddess comment might ping its way into James's eyeline, before he was ready to engage. But it was essential. Only three minutes left, the screen said, before it warned of heavy traffic ahead. Claire shifted her legs to try and distract herself.

The bus came to a halt by the empty front of a primary school. Ofsted: Outstanding, it claimed. She had to tug James's arm to stop him from reading more about the school's specialism in computer sciences. 'Come on, not now,' she said. Thankfully, the toilets were located by the hardware shop's entrance. James scuttled ahead, his long legs nearly tripping over themselves in anticipation.

Claire found her husband staring at shelves. He rocked slowly back and forth on his heels as he took in the wallful of options. He didn't react when Claire wrapped an arm around his middle.

'Oh, hey,' he said, distractedly. 'Look, what about these for wall mounts? I thought they could work for storing the toys, maybe. It's like that picture you showed me. What do you reckon?'

Claire didn't think James had been very interested when

she showed him her nursery vision board. She gave him a hug, there and then, her bump nestling between them. 'That sounds perfect,' she said.

They wore their matching York University t-shirts during the DIY session later that afternoon. The tops had once been a speckled grey, but years of love and mixed-load washing had faded their colour to off-white. James procured a spirit level he claimed he'd owned for years but Claire was certain was fresh out of its packaging. 'I'm sure the landlord won't mind,' he said, as he bashed a nail into the rented walls, 'we can just fill it with that tube stuff, he'll never know.' A small piece of wall landed by Claire's foot and crumbled when she prodded it with her big toe. This was a James problem, she decided, as she felt her stress levels rise.

James turned his head round. 'Ah,' he said, more of an exhale than a word. 'You look lovely, you know.'

'James, this top is genuinely about three wears away from giving up the ghost. And I doubt I'll fit into it much longer.'

'I think I always knew we'd have a baby.'

'You what?' Claire had known she wanted to be with James from their first date. She used to mouth *I love you, I love you, I love you* into his thin, single spare pillow when he was asleep, just so she could get it out of her body and not say it too soon, scare him away. But when they left university and tried to live adult lives together, Claire always led conversations about children. James never made comments about others' babies or bumps, never really cooed over Rory. Claire always felt like her husband would have been happy either way.

'Yeah, I always pictured us growing older, starting a family. Is that weird?'

Claire felt herself beam. He'd never spoken like this before. Maybe he was absorbing more than DIY advice from all the

YouTube dads. She pulled the limited fabric at the back to emphasise her bump. 'No, not at all weird. Hey, can you take a picture?'

James snapped back to the wall. 'Not if it's for those Internet people you're always talking to.'

She froze. What had he seen? Surely nothing. She forced herself to not react, maintain the smile. 'Oh, come on. It's for my mam. She keeps asking for updates.' This lie came so easily she almost believed it herself.

'Claire, my hands are covered in dust. I couldn't take a picture even if I wanted to. Can this wait until later?'

'Fine,' Claire muttered, but James didn't seem to hear.

He still wasn't looking at her. He brushed away the little splinters of their building with his fingers.

Claire went into their bedroom and stood by the window, where the late afternoon sun burnished her face with the kind of glow that she could never achieve even when she put in the hours on a beach lounger. The light made her eyes look alive; their brown highlighted by flecks of copper. 'Your eyes are the same colour as mud,' an ex-boyfriend once said, and then acted outraged when she got upset. She angled her phone and puffed her belly out to make sure its dome was the best, smoothest kind of round. It still didn't look right. She tried again, this time placing one palm against her stomach. She wondered when she'd feel the first movements she'd read so much about. They should start any day now, and the thought was thrilling. Claire rubbed her bump while waiting for Lily to confirm which picture looked best. After five minutes with no response from her sister, she opted for the photo where she looked slightly over-awed by her body, her gaze cast downwards, drawing the viewer's attention to the surprising newness she contained. She uploaded it.

The other Goddesses loved it. When James called her into the baby's room her phone screen shone through her pyjama pocket. The rest of the room was dark. James was testing the new rabbit-shaped lamp he'd assembled.

'Someone's popular!' James said, when it lit up again.

Claire wondered if he'd make another comment like earlier, but his barb seemed to have faded as quickly as it was issued. Her husband was correct. Claire was popular, more popular than she'd ever been in her life. Not even their wedding photos got this kind of online engagement. It felt like every single Goddess had commented. It's different when you're complimented by another woman. It means more. The new notifications were especially electrifying because she knew these women now. They'd crossed the parapet and were true, actual friends. After feeling so lonely, Claire couldn't believe how far she'd come, and how very glad she was for this online outlet.

James was asleep when Claire refreshed the group in bed, her final check of the day. She'd spent a significant part of the evening researching new children's books – she was sure Flora must have all the classics. She'd built a sizable wish list, but nothing could be ordered until she spoke to Flora about her address. It was high time she got her friend's number. Their bond may have been forged because of the forum but it somehow already felt bigger than the Goddesses. It was Flora, after all, who'd introduced her to this incredible community. Claire was sure she'd hear from her friend soon. She couldn't wait.

Chapter 27

TheSecretGoddesses

Flora_Is_Free:

Ladies, it was so nice to see some of you last week. I'm sure you're all wondering where I've been. I've received so many DMs and haven't had the time or the strength to respond separately, so I'm sorry to everyone who must think I've been so wrapped up in happiness I haven't bothered to reply. How I wish that might have been the case. The reality is, right now, I'm struggling to see the keyboard through my tears.

I started leaking a dark fluid two days after I met some of you kind souls. It came out of me like tar. I knew you would all be angry, so I didn't update you when we made the decision to drive to the hospital. My temperature was sky-high, I couldn't remember the last movement I felt, and although I could hear something on the Doppler, it seemed slower than usual. It was Tom who persuaded me, who said we should just get the darkness looked at, then leave. Tom narrowly avoided a speeding ticket, we drove so fast. The fluid seeped through the car seat.

I will never forget the doctor's face when she said there was nothing they could do. Our baby was gone. It didn't make sense, I said. We just heard their heart. But the doctor just shook her head.

But the worst part, ladies, was for my safety, they said, they needed to remove my son. He was a son. We were going to call him Barney. I've always loved names beginning with B. I think I'd known it would be a he, because we always just know, don't we, as mothers.

He was so big, so perfect. They gave me a steady stream of pills to start contractions. They were desperate to get him out of me, take away all his traces and his love. All I have left is the scar from my tear and the scar in my heart.

I delivered Barney without any form of relief, as I did his brother. But they forced my hand afterwards and carted me to the theatre. Said repairing a fourth-degree tear without anything could lead to dangerous shocks on my system. I wanted to feel everything, I wanted to be present for it all. But they numbed me before sewing me up.

Here is a picture of my beautiful son. You can see how peaceful he looks. He was nearly 11 pounds and he had so much hair. Black, you see, like his dad's.

I have been through a lot of challenges in life, but I've never felt more like I could just explode from sadness and anger as I did when the doctor muttered to a colleague that maybe we should be supervised while we said our final goodbyes. At least one midwife had the decency to sit with us, cry with us, during those terrible days in the 'butterfly room'.

Before we left, I had to sign a form to confirm I'd refused earlier intervention by not booking or attending any appointments. I was told to expect a debrief and Tom was sure he heard someone say something about social workers, as if Freddie isn't the most loved and cherished big brother in the world. We are all right to stay away. They do not have our best interests at heart. I failed my beloved Barney by taking him there. If only this could have happened at home. The Doppler showed some activity, so how can they explain his passing? What did they do to him? We've made a record of everyone's names for our complaint. There's so much more I can't bring myself to share today.

All I think about is what could have been with my darling boy. I'm going to try not to visit this site for a while as I have to focus on planning his memorial. The hospital refused to release his little body until we could confirm arrangements and we were in no fit state to do that. So, if you don't hear much from me, I wish you all the best in your journeys. There's truly nothing like the blessing of motherhood.

Be strong, be free, and keep Barney and me in your thoughts. He's up there somewhere.

Flora

Chapter 28

Somehow, Claire made it to the bathroom. The guilt charged through her oesophagus and splashed downwards. She wasn't aware she was screaming until James slammed the light on and scooped up a chunk of her hair from where it hung inside the toilet bowl and held it while he said, 'Claire! Claire! What's going on? Are you in pain?' The noises her body made were feral and wild. Her whole frame shook involuntarily as she retched. James crouched down and stroked her back in steady, heavy movements. The bathroom wasn't big enough for two people, really. Claire tried to focus on what was in front of her rather than the images swarming behind her eyelids. The hidden white underbelly of the toilet needed cleaning. There is always something that needs cleaning.

'What's happening? What can I get you?' James asked.

Claire couldn't muster a single syllable.

'I'm going to get some water, OK?' James slipped his hand over Claire's and tugged off her hairband in one quick movement.

Claire felt the tight pull of inexperience as James tried to tie her hair up. It hurt. She didn't say anything. She didn't drink from the cup James put by her side. When the surges subsided

into hiccups, James led her back into the bedroom. She reluctantly accepted the guidance; her body was incapable of inde-
pendent movement.

'Is it morning sickness? Can you tell the baby that one a.m. is
a little too early, please? We want to use these months to catch
up on as much sleep as possible!'

Claire stayed silent.

James rubbed Claire's arm. 'Talk to me, please talk to me. Are
you unwell? Is it the baby? Is it making you poorly? Claire, will
you please tell me what's going on?'

Claire caught a waft of sick as she flopped onto the bed. She
felt her insides tighten and coil. 'I can't,' was all she managed
in response.

'Please, Bear, please talk to me,' he said.

When the room filled with the gentle rise and fall of James's
breath, she played out a confession in her head. How would
James ever love her once he knew what she'd done. She'd
ignored her gut instinct that Flora should have sought help;
she'd encouraged her friend to ignore her body, ignore signals,
instead of doing right by poor, innocent Barney. She'd enabled
a baby's death. Hadn't she known, really known, when she'd
been in the bathroom of that Guildford café, that something
was wrong? Why hadn't she done anything? She clamped a
hand over her mouth to stop any sounds from coming out.

Muscle memory guided Claire to the group when finally she
unlocked her phone. It was impossible to avoid the comments on
the page. Lucy, bold, shrill Lucy, had petitioned for the post to
be removed. Lucy led the charge for calling Flora weak. That she
should never have gone into hospital. Almost everyone agreed.

Claire had to close her phone. She lay staring at the ceiling
instead, nauseous and wide awake. Her teeth felt crumbly from
the acid she'd unearthed from deep inside. The horror was

present every time she closed her eyes, but she deserved it. All she could see was the picture Flora uploaded of Barney, his dark tufts of hair carefully flattened, his eyes permanently closed. How had everyone else managed to switch off their conscience? How did they not also feel these great hulking pangs of guilt? She did her best to keep her eyes open. Think beautiful things, her dad always used to say. There was no beauty anymore. She'd seen to that.

'Come on,' James's voice came from above. He loomed over Claire. 'It's midday, I thought you might need a lie-in. Want to walk to Greenwich and get a roast? Looks like a smashing day outside.'

The thought of meat and fatty gravy was too much. Claire tried to outrun the rising bile but she didn't make it to the bathroom. She fell onto her knees with a thud. The carpet did little to cushion the impact.

'Oh Bear! You're really not OK!' James sounded surprised.

'Something's happened.'

'Yeah, you've got morning sickness! I was talking to everyone at work about how great it's been for you – no sickness at all – and they did say it can come on later for some people. Helen said that happened to her friend, so sick from sixteen weeks onwards. And you're past that now, aren't you? OK, let me just clean this up. And then Lucozade. I think that's what she said. Lucozade, yeah. The pink one. I can run out in a bit.' James was blathering. He always did this when he was nervous.

Claire looked up and saw James pacing. She knew how bad she must look. She didn't even care about the mention of Helen. 'No. I've . . . Can you get my phone?' There was no other way she could imagine going forward. It was time.

'I'm going to make you a cup of tea first. You need something. You're shaking.'

Claire tried to stem the tears that had already sprung. 'Please.'

Claire directed James when he returned with her phone, a rattling can of carpet cleaner and a tub of baking soda that hadn't been touched since they'd moved here. He helped her up and she doused the area with the powder while she gave out instructions. It was amazing that she was able to speak and guide him. Her PIN, the app, the group's name, Flora, Barney. Claire stared at the floor as the white grains soaked up the smell. She couldn't look at her husband while he operated Claire's phone and took in the horror of the situation, realised what his wife had become.

'Claire, what is this?' James said, at last. 'Do you know these people? Did you know this family?'

Claire nodded.

'This is. It's. Sorry, I need a minute?' Claire heard him walk up and down the corridor. 'Oh God,' she heard him say, over and over. 'That poor baby, oh God, oh God, oh God.'

She wanted to join him, grieve the loss of Barney with him, but she couldn't move.

After an eternity, James came back. 'I'm going to go out. I think I need some fresh air. I really think I need some fresh air,' he said.

Claire said nothing. She heard the door slam.

Claire traced the decline of the day from the way the light was sucked out of the room. When it darkened, she felt a slight relief. She had coped, lived, for almost twenty-four hours now. James had her phone and all the awful secrets it contained. There was no hiding. Every time she heard a noise, her heart leapt, thinking James might have returned. She wanted to try and explain, but how could she ever justify this outcome. When she heard the unmistakable sound of the key turning the latch, every hair stood on end.

James knocked on the door and switched on the light. He carried a tray wobbling with greasy food in one shaky hand. 'Breakfast for dinner. Remember?' Claire tried to smile, and she felt her bottom lip crack in the process. Her body was dry. All the tears had robbed her of her life-force.

James sat at the end of the bed and took her phone out of his trouser pocket. 'I didn't mean to take this. But, do – do you want me to keep it?' he asked.

Claire shook her head and he handed it back. He waited for Claire to eat, but the poached eggs bulged and throbbed as James adjusted his body on the bed. She sucked in as much of the room's air as possible and tried to keep it in her lungs. Thankfully, she was able to both manoeuvre the tray off the bed so it didn't spill everywhere and make it to the toilet in time. Her body forced out orange lumps that made her weep in agony.

'When did this all happen, Claire? I mean, I knew you were part of something that keeps you glued to that phone all times of day and night, but I had no idea it was this – this . . .' James's voice tailed off as he guided Claire into the shower. He remained clothed, the water splashing his grey tracksuit bottoms.

She had to sit down because she felt too dizzy. She couldn't find the energy to apply any shampoo or body wash but instead allowed herself to be soaked. She didn't answer James's questions.

James was waiting with a towel in their cramped bathroom and he covered her with it. 'Claire,' he said into her wet scalp, 'I can't stop thinking about that baby, that poor baby. What those women do should be illegal. But Claire, Claire, we're going to get through this.' His words sounded rehearsed.

'It's my fault, isn't it? I killed him,' Claire said. She saw James had a vein bulging down his forehead, the one that always appeared when he was stressed.

James sighed. 'No. No, you didn't.'

'I did.'

'Oh, that little baby. Jesus.' His voice started to waver. 'You just got carried away trying to fit in. These people aren't well, Claire. That woman, what's her name, Flora? She'll have to live with her choices for the rest of her life. What happened is beyond awful. It's so, so awful. Why didn't you tell me this was going on? I saw something on my laptop the other day but I didn't pry. I don't understand, Claire. I don't understand any of it.'

Claire just looked at her husband, and wondered what else he wanted to say, and where he'd just been, and how he could ever learn to forgive her. When she crawled onto the bed, which still carried the faint smell of egg, she could only think of the overgrown child hammering inside his mother, trapped, exhausted, desperate, while Flora sat smiling at her screen, ignoring all the signs. She saw Flora exposing her beautiful teeth to her phone as she read through all the encouragement. She pictured her friend's waxen face under the lights of that café's bathroom. Would Barney have survived if Claire had convinced Flora to go to hospital there and then? Could she have saved that child? No matter what James said, it was impossible to believe she could ever get through this. The truth was, it was a series of small decisions that amounted to an avoidable tragedy, and she doubted her husband would ever be able to see her in the same way again.

Chapter 29

James left a fresh tray with now-cold toast and chamomile tea on the bedside table the next morning. Claire slept through his whole pre-work ritual. When she checked the time on her phone, she was confronted with hundreds of notifications from the Goddesses. She dismissed the page as quickly as possible. James had messaged: *I've contacted Uno to say you're under the weather. Please, please try and eat. Can you try and eat for the baby?* Claire managed three claggy bites. The butter had split into grease and fat on the plate.

All Claire had the energy to do was watch TV. Reality stars' squawks and squabbles filled the room with a chaos that drowned out Claire's stomach rumbling, the sobs that kept coming, or the thought of baby Barney. She tried to not look at her phone too much, but it was difficult to break what felt like a lifetime of habit. At lunchtime, she saw Holly had messaged. Holly hoped Claire would get better soon but could she urgently (this was both in red and capitals) provide a full and thorough (these were bolded) handover at the soonest. Over the next hour, Holly emailed three more times. The last one just said *Bump!* Holly marked it as high importance.

Claire started typing a reply, but a Goddess notification appeared, caught her off guard. She flicked it away, but it was impossible to avoid the last sentence.

MamaMartha: . . . *Flora clearly lacked the commitment, allowed the system to get its claws into her and Barney. If only she'd held firm.*

Claire felt bile rise again. She couldn't respond to Holly. She had to, but she physically couldn't. She turned her phone off, fingers scrabbling at the button so much that her screen asked if she needed emergency services. This is an emergency, Claire thought. This is an emergency, but no one can help. Barney's already gone.

Claire started walking around the room. When did this space get so cluttered, so filthy? She hoiked her sleeves up and grabbed her supplies from under the sink. She got to work with the dustpan and brush, collecting the disgusting crumbs that had accumulated on the floor. It felt good to focus on something productive, to remedy the chaos she left in her wake. On her hands and knees, she reached as far under the sofa as possible, hearing the blood pound in her head with each scrape of the floor. A wave of wooziness hit her. She lent backwards and caught her breath. She tried again but it returned immediately, slamming into her brain. Sit, it felt like her body was saying, you've got to sit.

Reluctantly, Claire covered herself with a blanket on the sofa and tried to concentrate on the TV. She noticed she was sweating. Her face was damp, her pyjamas sticking to her, the buttons around her stomach starting to gape a little. She held one hand where her baby must be, but it offered no calm. A thought festered: what would Holly do if she didn't send a handover? But when she tried to pick up her phone again, she found it impossible. It was radioactive with hatred, with reminders.

On the TV, women shouted at each other with a new type of viciousness. It was no longer distracting. This was unbridled loathing. They had all turned on one lady, who was sobbing, left to defend herself, staring at the fingers jabbed towards her in accusation. How had she ever found this entertaining? Claire pressed the remote.

The house was so quiet Claire could hear her thoughts ringing, amplifying, bouncing off all the surfaces. She tried again to put her hands to her belly, to breathe, try and stem the rising cortisol that was so bad for this pure life inside. But she felt nothing, no usual connection or surge of love. This baby knew that its mother had done something terrible. She had to get out. She had to go somewhere. Where? She ran upstairs, almost enjoying the way the dizziness offered distraction. She changed into the first clothes she saw, skidded down the stairs and pulled on her coat.

Outside, everything seemed normal. There was nothing to mark the way Claire's life had changed. How Barney's life had ended. Children were playing on the swings in the park Claire passed, the park on her way to the station. Her legs were carrying her to the station. Yes, she realised. She needed to speak to Holly in person. Give her a full handover verbally, because she couldn't turn on her phone now, no way. She'd have to get James to delete the apps. She would speak to Holly, make sure she didn't need to keep checking her phone for work messages, then come home. It was a good plan.

On the train, Claire realised she hadn't washed her face or brushed her teeth in – she couldn't remember now. When she reached to adjust her ponytail, she felt matted clumps. Claire avoided her reflection in the train window. She didn't want to see how the loss of Barney had etched itself on her face.

Transitioning to the Tube, Claire felt as if she was floating.

It was comforting to follow the routine her body had become so accustomed to. Nice to be carried away by the movement of other people, have her thoughts dulled as she looked at the adverts, other passengers, the way they all jerked together as they pulled out of stations. She found herself above ground. Soho was beautiful, crisp and cold. The streets were vibrant with noise.

'I didn't expect to see you here,' Holly said, when Claire arrived at her desk. The tiredness had evolved into something that felt like normality.

'Hi,' Claire squeaked. She found that her voice wasn't working properly.

Claire felt her boss's eyes burn into her. 'Let's get a room, shall we? Ali. Ali? Can you help here? We've got a situation.'

Claire stood still, unsure if she should sit down. The overhead lighting flickered and she noticed she had a headache. How long had that pain been there? When she blinked, her eyes wanted to stay closed. The burst of energy that propelled her into Central London had expired.

'Let's go this way,' Holly said. 'Ali! That email can wait.'

'Can you just give me one second?' Ali said.

Claire had never heard Ali sound frustrated before.

'Claire!' Ali said, when she got up to greet her, arms twitching slightly. 'Sorry about Holly. She's really on one today,' Ali whispered as they followed Holly into the only meeting room without glass walls. 'Hey, do you want to borrow something? I've got a sports bra in my locker that should fit.'

'Oh, thanks,' Claire managed. She looked down. Her coat was undone. She tried to fasten it but her fingers felt so big, the buttons so small. She hugged it close to her body.

'First things first, why are you here, Claire?' Holly said.

Claire pulled the sides of her coat harder. 'My handover?'

Holly exhaled loudly. 'You need to go home. Before anyone else sees you. Before I have to file a report. What's going on? Look around. Can you see anyone else looking like they're hot off a bender? Have you been drinking?'

'What? No! I'm pregnant, I can't drink!'

'You need to go. Honestly, Claire, can you be normal for once? Send an email, work from home, not do – whatever this is. Christ, I don't have time for this today. Ali, come on, action stations, can you help Claire out please. Claire, nine a.m. tomorrow, we're going to go through whatever's going on. I can't be dealing with this right now.'

Claire allowed these words to wash over her. She smiled and felt the split of her lip widen. Where was her lip balm, she wondered. She wanted to look around in her bag but also knew she should try and maintain eye contact. This had been a mistake; it was obvious now. The skin of her mouth felt taut. Could they tell, Holly and Ali, that she felt so empty? They were both staring. 'OK. But do you want me to go through my handover?'

'No, Claire, you need to leave and get over whatever is going on right now. Ali, do you mind?'

'Here, Claire,' Ali said, and extended the crook of her arm. She lowered her voice. 'Do you want me to call a cab for you? Do you have an app?'

Claire handed over her phone. She was distracted by the way Holly stomped away, the swish of her boss's hair.

'Oh, this is off. Is it out of battery? Hey, are you all right? You can talk to me, you know.'

'Can I have that back,' Claire said. 'Please, can you give that back? My phone.'

Ali passed the device over, her eyes wide. 'OK, don't worry. I'll get you one. What's your address? Do you want to type it in?'

Ali's phone glared at her. 'No,' Claire said. 'No, I'll get the Tube.'

Claire noticed smudges of mascara that had crept into her colleague's waterline. 'Want me to come downstairs with you?' Ali opened the door for her and stood in front of it. 'Will you let me know when you get home OK, though?'

'I just wanted to go through my handover,' Claire said.

Ali looked down at her phone. Frowned a little, her young skin barely crinkling. 'Holly says – no, nothing. Hope you're OK, Claire. See you tomorrow, OK? If you walk past a Holland and Barrett, they sell an amazing sleepy tea.'

'OK,' Claire said.

She floated down the stairs, to the Tube, on the train, to home. Everything felt light and far away. Her mouth was so dry that when she yawned, she heard the inside of her cheeks clack together. It revolted her. Perhaps, she thought, this was the way to cope, to move forward. To be so tired that she would blink and find her legs had carried her to the next place.

When she got home and lay back on the sofa, embarrassment started to creep in. What had she done? Why had she left the confines of her home, let her grief outpour in this way? 'No,' she screamed to the walls. 'No, no, no.' She let herself wail until she had to choose between breathing or screaming and opted for the latter, her throat closing, her lungs burning with furious guilt.

Time moved differently now. Claire found herself on the sofa, looking at her dead phone, turning it over and over in her hands. She'd stopped shouting. The blank screen had turned into a terrible mirror. Her eyes seemed uglier. Darker, crueller, capable of terrible things. She stared into it as she pressed the on button.

There it was, as expected, the slew of Goddess notifications.

The sight made Claire shiver in revulsion. She closed the app as quickly as her fingers allowed. It provided no relief. No matter how many times she shut it down, they'd be there still, all talking about Flora and innocent Barney. Or worse, talking about their futures. Futures completely untainted by what had happened, as if Barney had never died.

Claire's hands were already shaking when her work emails sprang into action. *Urgent ahead of tomorrow,* Holly's subject said.

Claire, today was unacceptable. As per the employee hand-book (please see attached as reading is mandatory . . . I did mention this in your induction), any sick leave must be requested by the employee before 9 a.m. on the day of leave. Not only did your husband message us, you stumbled into HQ at 2 p.m. in completely inappropriate clothing. I've never heard of an employee entering the office in such an unfit state. I expect to see you at your desk first thing tomorrow. We can touch base on next steps then. Need I remind you that you are employed as a manager? Please see page 43 – promotions and demotions – for our policy when colleagues are perform-ing above or significantly below their responsibilities.

Claire read the email once, twice, again, again until every word became meaningless. When James got home, because somehow more hours had passed by, she looked at her husband, guided him to the sofa with her eyes.

'I went into the office,' she said, before he could say any-thing. Her voice was croaky.

'Pardon?'

'I tried to tell my manager my handover. I don't know. It felt like the right thing to do.'

Claire followed her husband's gaze. There was nothing he could comment on, nothing that could distract him from this situation. 'But why did you do that? You went into town? Oh, Claire, look at you. You look haunted.'

Claire ignored the comment. She handed her phone over.

'Oh no,' he said, as his eyes skimmed from left to right.

This was it, Claire thought. James would see what her boss was really like. There was no point in maintaining the illusion that she was happy or liked at Uno, that she was doing well.

'OK,' James said after he read. 'OK. I'm not sure exactly what happened today but tomorrow you can just go in and explain.'

'About Barney?'

'Well, yes. You could say someone you know lost their child, and the news has torn you apart. I mean, I could barely concentrate on anything today. Your head's all over the place, isn't it?'

Claire nodded. How did he do that, her husband? Despite their recent distance, he could still manage to make these kinds of earth-shattering situations so much easier to bear. 'Yes,' she said.

'And what's this?'

James turned the phone round. Another Goddess had commented on the bump selfie. She watched as he clicked. Hadn't she closed it earlier? How had it popped up, exposed itself yet again. It felt so strange for James to see it now and read all the comments underneath. Two days felt like a lifetime ago.

'Who are all these messages from? Do you know them?'

'They are . . .' Claire stopped and took a breath, her heart suddenly tripping over itself. 'They were my friends.'

'But who are they?'

'Women online have always just . . . been there.' Claire hated how small this seemed. How the support could be reduced in such a way.

James reddened. 'I've been here too, haven't I?'

'No, you have, but . . .'

'But what?'

Claire scrabbled to find the right words. She could see her husband's face starting to warp. Was it her tiredness that made his eyes seem to look at her with such fresh disgust? Was he stepping back slightly or was it a new wave of dizziness? Her voice came out so weak that it made her cringe. 'But they always wanted to know. Every single thing, every single day.'

'Right.'

'And it was nice to have people to speak to.'

'People like Barney's mam?'

Claire shuddered, an involuntary response. 'No, that was later. This was before, back when we were still trying.'

There was no mistaking it now. James's eyes had lost all warmth. 'What else did you tell strangers?'

She was so very tired. She couldn't hide anything anymore. 'Well, they were the first to find out we were pregnant.'

'What? What do you mean? No they weren't. It was that morning, you made me breakfast. It was the best breakfast of my life.'

'No.'

'What do you mean, no?'

'No, James. I told them the night before. You were out, so I posted first.'

James's cheeks flared even more. 'No, no you didn't. Ah, Christ.' He opened his mouth, as if to say something, and Claire braced herself. Instead, he clenched one hand so tight that his thumb made a grotesque click. 'Why did you have to do that?' he said, his eyes two pleading pools.

Claire wanted to shout, like the women on TV earlier: Because

I was so lonely! You were out, and it didn't mean anything! But she stayed quiet instead.

They ate bowls of plain microwaved rice in silence. James told her she had to do it, had to fuel both her body and the baby's. The three minutes on the timer felt excruciatingly long. They stood and watched the packets turn round and round inside. Claire caught their reflection in the machine: two blank faces trying not to fall apart. James didn't comment when Claire sloped off upstairs and lay in bed. She placed her hands on her stomach and willed it to move. She pictured Barney inside and it was as if she'd been electrocuted, her whole body reverberated in revulsion. *Please be OK, little one,* she said under her breath, *please.*

Claire heard James use the broad Geordie accent he reserved for their own, its lilts reaching up through the walls separating upstairs from downstairs, and wondered who he might be speaking to. She realised their voices had changed since they'd moved here. So much had changed.

'Claire, this is serious. I'm not just talking about today or the weekend. It's everything. These groups. It's gone too far. I don't think I recognise you anymore. You need to see a specialist, the GP, anyone,' he said, when he eventually came into the bedroom. He stood as far away from the bed as possible, his back brushing against the photo of them on their wedding day. It made the photo hang askew. 'And I can't believe that so many random women knew about the baby before me. Were they the ones who told you to join the other group? No, don't answer that. I need some time to think about it all and I really think you need help.'

Claire was too numb to say anything. The tears came at once. When James asked, in a clipped voice, if she'd like him to schedule an email to Uno for tomorrow morning on her behalf explaining she needed some more days off, she moved her head up and down so quickly her brain rattled. He sat beside her in silence, his shoulders hunched over, while she continued to sob. 'There,' he said, once he'd finished typing, 'and please don't go in. I need you, we need you, to try and get back to your old self.' He left the bedroom then and didn't return.

Lying alone, Claire felt the ceiling sway above her. It seemed like the whole world was asleep. There were no cars purring up and down the road, no mewling foxes raiding the bins, no sounds coming from James in the next room. She so wanted to hear something, anything, that might suggest her husband would come back. She burned with sorrow and shame. For what had happened to her relationship, but mostly for her role in Barney's avoidable death. She noticed a glass of water on her bedside table. When had James put that there? She downed it, the liquid rushing down her throat, almost choking her.

The thought was overwhelming, but she knew she would need to face her fears and re-engage with the system, with the dismissive doctors and midwives. She couldn't end up like her friend. She wouldn't be able to live with herself if that happened to her child, because she had been too stubborn, too deluded. *I'm so sorry,* she said to her unresponsive stomach, *I'll try my best to make this right.*

As the sky began to lighten from behind the blinds, Claire finally sent the message to Flora she had been drafting in her head. She apologised for not helping sooner, for spurring her on, for not being there to hold and grieve with her that very moment. The words, the sentiment, rushed out. She was so tired that the text swam on the screen. Claire put down her phone and mourned for baby Barney anew.

Part 2

Chapter 30

Flora couldn't move. She called for Tom but he was outside in the garden with Freddie. Even though the curtains and windows were closed, she could hear them playing together. Her voice was still so hoarse, maybe that's why Tom wasn't responding. She'd rolled over on the bed and there was no way of turning back over. Her body had seized up again. The painkillers were still in their paper bag in the corner of the room. Flora wouldn't touch them; she wanted, needed, to experience every bit of hurt. Her milk still hadn't come in. She was thankful, in a way, that her body had spared her that small cruelty so far.

Flora's phone was out of reach so she couldn't message Tom. It was lying, silent as ever, on the bedside table. She'd dropped it when sedated at the hospital and it had smashed. Little fragments kept catching her fingers when she typed, drawing blood. Mainly texting Tom, to ask for things like more water or for assistance getting up off the rubber ring she had to sit on. Flora hadn't really contacted many people in the last week, ever since they drove back from the hospital in silence and picked up a confused Freddie from their neighbour. Online, Flora let people think she spent her evenings with friends but truthfully, over the years, they'd become their own isolated family bubble. And they'd been so content that way.

'Tom!' she said again.

Eventually, after an indeterminable time, Freddie burst into the room.

'Mummy!' he squealed. 'We found this!' He jumped onto the bed. The movement of the mattress was terrible against her body. She was so tender. He pressed a conker into her hand. It was late in the season. Flora used to collect conkers when she was a child, get her dad to drill holes into them and tie string through. Everyone fought with them in the school breaks, smashing glossy seeds until one cracked. Freddie was too young to know about those kinds of games. They'd received a letter saying he'd need to be registered for school for the next academic year. Flora had taught him everything he knew so far. And the new baby was going to help him with his interpersonal skills. She'd read up on it.

'Oh wow,' she managed, before her little boy ran out, chuntering to himself. 'Can you tell Daddy to come upstairs please?' But Freddie was already too far away.

By some miracle, Freddie hadn't absorbed the sadness that seemed to have permeated every part of their home. Flora had noticed new things while in bed. The black freckles of mould in the corner of the ceiling or the way her body soured a room, only perceptible when she shuffled (with Tom's support) to and from the bathroom. But somehow Freddie continued to create light and laughter, crashing around with his toys and his imagination. Maybe he was overcompensating, Flora thought, shoving all his worries far away somewhere that would haunt him for years to come. He was normally such a sensitive child, bristling if he heard raised voices, his lovely eyes moony with worry over the dinner table, looking from Mum to Dad. They'd become much better at defusing arguments since they'd had Freddie. Resolving them immediately so they didn't curdle. Flora hated being trapped here in bed, but she couldn't think of a way out. She was consumed by the millions of ways this would affect her family, not just right now but in the future. They were now all members of a club no one wants to be part of.

'Flor?' she eventually heard. 'Tea?'

'Help,' she said.

'Flor? Last orders! I'm making Fredster a cocoa.'

Please come up, please come up, Flora thought.

Tom entered the room. Flora raised her head. 'Could you not hear me?' she said. 'The ring's fallen off again.'

Tom gently propped her up with pillows and turned her so she was back on her raised seat. 'I think you need to take those meds, love,' he said. 'This is the, what, third, fourth time now?'

'There's no way. I can't do that,' and her voice started to crumble.

'I know. I know. How about I get you a cocoa, eh. And let's get you on the sofa downstairs. Remember what they said about moving around.'

'I need to stay up here.'

'OK, love,' he said, and placed his nose against hers. She opened her eyes and she was so close to him, she could see the hurt carved into his face, the very make-up of his irises. But she couldn't help him. She couldn't do anything but keep breathing, wipe the tears that were running down her face, collecting on her chin like stalactites. She didn't have the strength to do more than exist here in the darkened room.

'Let me in!' Freddie squealed. She hadn't heard him come in again. He wriggled his perfect, living body beside her, and Flora didn't mind the flames of pain that burst through her. They stayed there for a while, the three of them, and Flora wondered if Freddie could tell that both his parents were crying. They'd been handed a leaflet on how to talk about death with children. Tom had pocketed it, but they simply couldn't broach this conversation with their beloved boy. How could they do that to him? How could they show their son that lives aren't always long, and nothing, absolutely nothing, is guaranteed. That the sage-green cot he'd helped paint had already been taken up into the attic.

'Shall we give Mummy some space, Freds? She's very tired,' Tom said.

He returned carrying a mug of hot chocolate. Little marshmallows had pooled on top, Flora's favourite, and Tom had given her a spoon so she could syphon the molten sweetness off. He'd stuck a Post-it note, normally reserved for updating shopping lists on the fridge, on the mug. *I love you always and forever,* his message said.

When they got home that first awful night, Flora turned to Tom and asked if they could try again, as soon as the bleeding stopped. She needed to know that he would give it a go, that they would do whatever possible to fill the gaping hole ripped into their lives. But he had bowed his head and said, 'It's too soon to talk about these things, my love, you need to focus on getting better.' Did Tom really love her if he wouldn't at least promise they could, at a moment in time?

Flora realised she was crying again. When she drank the hot chocolate, it was too hot, but she kept going, felt the liquid race down her oesophagus.

Flora's phone rang and she straightened in a painful jolt. She could reach it, now she'd been repositioned. It was her mum. She didn't answer. She couldn't have the same conversation again. She couldn't repeat what she'd heard Tom say down the line just the day before, that there was no new grandchild to meet. And that Flora had to have surgery and was trying to recover, but as soon as they could they would come and visit. And no, no, there was just Freddie here, the other baby had passed away. No, they weren't doing any tests. On and on in that circular reminder of the great tragedy.

She checked the group to see if any of her friends had messaged. She knew it had been a mistake posting without a trigger warning. She just hadn't been thinking. There was Claire's message, her offer, and a few condolences from other women she'd never met, but nothing yet from the long-haulers. They would get in touch, Flora knew. They must be aghast, reeling, just like her. Why, why, why, had they gone in?

Apart from the Goddesses and her mum, Flora hadn't told anyone else their news. She knew Tom had spoken to his colleagues because people kept dropping frozen lasagnes at their doorstep. And their neighbour, a middle-aged single woman called Sinead, the one who so kindly looked after Freddie, knocked most days. Flora had heard Sinead offer to give the house a clean, do the food shop. Flora wanted to screech from bed: We don't want anything apart from our Barney back! She wanted to tell this to everyone she'd ever met, so they would know that she was no longer the Flora she was before, the Flora that lived in their memories. But how could she just start conversations with connections that had faded away over time? She wanted to update her Facebook to get it out of the way, but then she'd risk losing everyone in one fell swoop. She'd not done things the right way with the Goddesses. And what good would it do, telling people anyway?

Flora placed the phone next to the mug, wincing as her torso torqued, and took one of Tom's pillows. She screamed into it until she left a brown print of her hot-chocolated mouth. She gasped out of pain and sadness. For the smallest fraction of a second, she felt better.

Chapter 31

The knock on the bedroom door confused Claire. It wasn't like James to announce his presence. He had tiptoed around her for days now. He normally walked in, placed a tray of food and drink by the door, and left as quickly as possible. He had slept in the baby's room ever since he found out the forums were the first to know about the pregnancy. Claire didn't understand why that seemed to have been the final straw.

'Claire?' the voice on the other side of the door was unexpectedly soft. She hadn't realised how much she needed to hear it.

Another day had passed with Claire sitting on top of the bed while thoughts raced through her head with such violence that she was left slumped against the pillows. She was like a sea anemone, melded to one place, while wave after wave of regret pummelled her from above. She imagined that James was afraid to touch her, afraid she'd suck him in deeper, try and drown him too. From time to time, she would muster the strength to check her phone, before placing it face-down again. She saw a message from the research team behind the freebirthing study in *Nature*, but clicked delete without hesitation. No part of her was curious about the outcomes anymore. All she could do was remain lying down and allow the day to pass, hope that time would heal in the clichéd way everyone claims. She felt drained, deficient, eating the plates James left out without pleasure, gagging the cold food down to support the mysterious life inside. But this voice filled her with a sudden energy.

'Lily? Oh my God, Lily! Come here. Ah, get in here!'

Claire's sister clambered onto the bed. 'Are you poorly?' Lily asked, her face so close the words tickled Claire's face. 'James said you're poorly.'

Claire inhaled. Her sister smelled of the shampoo she'd always used, apples and peaches. She tried to push some of the thoughts about Barney aside but they remained there, gnawing at her ability to focus on anything else. Some of Lily's peroxide had grown out. The shortness of her sister's hair was still so unexpected. 'This is such a surprise!' Claire eventually managed.

Lily blinked. 'What do you mean? I'm flying on Sunday, remember?'

'Of course. Sorry. It's just . . . I've been a bit out of it. Why didn't you text?'

'James said you were tired so I thought I shouldn't message. I'm sorry.' Lily shrugged away from their closeness and played with the longer strands of hair at the front, twisting her fingers in an endless loop. Claire watched as her sister looked around, took in the crumbs that suddenly seemed so stark against the sheets, the box of tissues that James must have replaced at some point, 'Should I – should I not have come?'

Claire heaved herself upwards. When had she last washed? she wondered. 'No, no, this is the best thing that's happened to me all week. Come back here.'

They hugged for a long time, until James entered the room.

'Ah,' he said. He lingered by the door. 'So she was awake, you were right. Anyone for some tea? We've got some of that herbal stuff you love, Lil.' He must have been downstairs for a while in order to have let Lily in. Claire hadn't heard him get home, heard any kind of chatter between the two of them. She felt very out of touch with her life.

'I'll do it,' Lily offered, and sprung off the bed.

'But Lil, you don't know where anything is!' Claire tried to shout, but her sister had already padded away. 'I wish you'd said something,' Claire whispered to her husband, who remained by the door. She gestured at her pyjamas, the greasy fronds of her hair. 'Why didn't you?'

James didn't respond, he just pursed his mouth until his lips were no longer visible, and stepped back so Claire wouldn't touch him when she walked past.

When James appeared downstairs, he told Claire and Lily he would leave them to catch up; he'd go and get something nice for dinner. And yes, he knew Lily was dairy-free now, he'd received all her messages. His toothy smile was too bright to be real. Claire saw right through it. She felt sorry for Lily, who was now stuck in this dense, treacly tension. Her sister didn't belong here.

'Are you sure you're OK?' Lily asked after Claire threw the old blanket over both of their legs. Lily's arms were peppered with bumps.

'I'm going to be fine. I've just had some horrible news. Maybe James filled you in?'

Lily reached for her front tufts of hair, her nervous tic. She knew.

'But I don't want to talk about that. I want you to open that bag and show me what you've packed for the adventure of a lifetime.' Claire forced her mouth into a smile. It was important she assumed her normal role in front of her sister and did what she could to make up for the mess of their bedroom meeting.

Lily unzipped the rucksack and showed the mass of empty canvas inside. It was clear Lily wanted to perform her usual role too. 'I'm not done yet! I want to go to Shoreditch. Are we anywhere near? London's so confusing.'

'Oh, it's not too far. I'll show you on the map. So, what's the final route? I want to know every detail.' Claire couldn't believe she'd forgotten about this visit. She should have counted down in her planner and on the wall calendar, met Lily at the station, made a lovely scene of it.

Lily loaded up Google Maps on her phone. She'd added digital pins to one side of the world, jumping over oceans until they stopped at New Zealand. Lily had signed up to a group tour for the first five weeks, to ease her into solo travel. She described the itinerary: cookery classes in the paddies of north-eastern Vietnam, a moped trip winding through the country until they took boats to secluded, palm-fringed beaches in Cambodia, and Claire was relieved to feel genuine happiness for her sister's getaway. She had wondered if it was possible to experience that emotion anymore. Just as Lily was explaining the final fortnight island-hopping in Thailand, her face started to crumple. She blinked several times.

'Sorry,' she said. 'I'm just a bit worried. I know it sounds stupid.' She pawed at her eye. 'I know I'm lucky. Argh, this keeps happening.'

Claire pulled out a wad of tissues from her pyjama pocket. Some were already shrivelled with use. It didn't matter. All that mattered was helping her sister.

'I keep having these funny moments,' Lily said, after dabbing at her eyes again.

'What? When?'

'Just when I think about the holidays, I think of all the bad things that might happen. Like, do you remember whenever Mam or Dad would be late from work and I'd get into a tizz? You'd tell me I was overreacting, and they were fine. It's like that but, anyway, I nearly didn't come here. I wanted to call the whole trip off. It all just seemed so – so crazy, when I thought about it. Mam made me get on the train. She drove me to the station herself.'

'Why didn't you call me, Lils?' Claire could see now. The bruised bags under her sister's eyes, the extra sharpness of her collarbones, the way her faded summertime freckles were stretched over her cheeks. What else had she missed?

'You've been kind of hard to reach.' Lily shrugged. 'And I didn't want to stress you out. Or the baby.'

Claire felt her throat thicken. She'd promised her dad she'd look after Lily, and she'd stuck to her word for so long. But there was no part of her life that was under control anymore. She couldn't let this show, so she pulled her in for another huge hug. She'd managed to put a stopper on the great dam of grief on Lily's behalf before, when their dad died, and she would do it again now. She could rise to this, be the second parent that was so clearly needed. The hug was just the start.

'I'm here now, Lils, I'm here,' she said.

When James came home with arms full of thali from the new Indian restaurant by the park, he found them bundled together, flicking through Lily's dating apps and laughing at some of the awful one-liners in people's profiles. It had felt like a big moment when Lily offered Claire a glimpse into her love life. Claire couldn't stop herself from saying 'Oh!' when both men and women appeared on the screen. She felt so proud of Lily for living her truth. She was desperate to communicate this new information to her husband, but he was too busy pretending to be normal in front of their guest. The three watched

230

an inoffensive romcom while they ate and it was almost like old times, when Lily would enjoy the warmth of their place in Gateshead. The façade came down when Claire and James went back upstairs and he only said, 'I've got you stuff to make pancakes tomorrow,' before he turned away and made noises that surely couldn't be the real sounds of sleep.

Lily banged Claire awake the following morning by rapping on the door. She brought a package into Claire's bedroom and flung back the curtains. 'Oh my God, Claire, how could you sleep through that? He was ringing like a madman. I had to work out how to buzz him in.' She handed over a large bouquet of flowers and bounced slightly as she sat on the end of the bed. A thorn snagged Claire's thumb and made it bleed on the white sheets. Claire sucked it to make it stop. It was always strange to taste yourself. To imagine the metal coursing through you.

Claire found the dropped card by the landing later, when she paused a romcom (she couldn't handle any more reality TV) and got them both glasses of orange squash, their childhood staple. *Thinking of you*, the card read. *I found your address on the system.*

'Is that from your boss? The bitchy one?' Lily asked. She had snuck up behind Claire.

'Maybe,' Claire said, but there was simply no way. The number of messages from Holly marked 'urgent' were overwhelming. Her boss had not taken kindly to Claire's morning emails calling in sick. In between Holly's wall of texts and rescheduled catch-up meetings, was something from David with the subject *Monday/ are you OK?* Ali's name popped up frequently too. She didn't open any of these. She didn't feel anything when seeing either of their names, the people whose companionship she previously craved. The flowers must be from one of them, but

231

the thought carried no interest for her exhausted brain.

Claire liked how Lily didn't question her further on why she wasn't at work. Her sister didn't press the matter when Claire said she didn't feel up to going charity shopping on Dulwich High Street. She didn't move the whole time Lily was away, and was surprised when she heard the key turn in the door. 'Rich people throw away some amazing stuff,' Lily said upon her return, the weight of the plastic bags leaving red marks on her forearms.

'Let's show Mam,' Claire said. She wanted to keep Lily distracted.

Their mother was delighted when they summoned her via video chat: 'My darlings, back together,' she said, and made Lily hold the phone so Claire could twist and turn for the camera and show the new roundness of her middle.

'Eee, would you look at that,' her mother said, while Claire forced herself not to say something like: Help me, what am I doing?

Their mam was abnormally gentle with her questioning. Claire was now certain James had told everyone. For a few minutes, the image of Barney faded, but as soon as the sisters hung up, the picture of him, huge and pale, returned and she had to say she needed the toilet. She sat on top of the seat and tried to remember how to breathe, but it felt like her mouth was closing itself off. The episode passed and when she returned to the sofa, she put one arm around her sister and squeezed her sharp, lovely shoulders.

This was not the first time Claire had been unable to leave the house. As Lily slept in the baby's room and James remained out at what the wall calendar said was work drinks, she remembered what James called her lost year. The time after graduation had been a perfect storm of grief, a jobs market decimated by the recession, and the unshakeable sense that Claire would never be able to find a way to move on from the place where the carpets were spattered with tears and seeped in her dad's smell.

That year was especially difficult because Sally had no problems after the thrill of graduation wore off. Sally went straight on to a PGCE and enjoyed another turn of the wheel at fresher's week and new teacher friends. Claire would log on to Facebook and see a stream of pictures of Sally with shots or cocktails or a soggy bag of takeaway in her hands. James was in his first accountancy role, living back with his mam, studying every evening. He'd try so hard to feign positivity whenever Claire showed him yet another rejection email. 'Let's give it one more go,' he'd say, and open a new word document and start yet another cover letter. 'It's a numbers game, we'll get there.'

Lily had been in year 10 then and would sneak into the house smelling of the cheapest possible spirits with a mad glint in her eye. Sometimes she would slither into Claire's bed while it was still dark outside and tell her she really loved her, her words soaked in booze and belief, while Claire just said, 'Sh, sh, sh, you're home now.' Claire never told their mam about Lily's behaviour. She didn't want to add to her mam's suffering and from Claire's regular checks of her sister's bag and marked-up homework, Lily's grades didn't appear to be significantly lowered. Whenever Claire would wake up, her sister would be at school and her mam would be at work, so she'd sit at the wooden table in the kitchen and go online and see how everyone else was out there living their lives. After a while, Claire stopped applying for jobs, stopped engaging with Lily's increasingly infrequent visits and stopped being able to pretend to match James's optimism. She would just scroll, scroll, scroll, her hand bent like a witch's around the worn black mouse.

We got through that period, we'll get through this, Claire said to herself when James fell into the bed and started sputtering with snores. All she ever wanted was the type of family she so adored growing up: both parents, healthy and happy, so visibly in love with each other and their lives. She looked at her husband as she ran her hands over her stomach. She'd still had no sense of a quickening. Every day without movements increased her concern. She wondered whether the stress had had an impact, how much she'd already hurt her baby. She looked over to her husband. He was frowning in his sleep. *We have to get through this. There's no other option.*

Chapter 32

Taya appeared on Claire's doorstep on Friday afternoon. Claire couldn't believe it when she saw her friend's petite frame through the intercom camera. She'd never experienced so many unexpected visitors before. 'Shit,' Claire muttered, as she looked down and around. Suddenly she wished she was wearing something other than faded pyjamas and one of James's hoodies.

Taya's skin was shiny and raw, as if one layer had been peeled away, when Claire opened the door. 'I hope you don't mind me popping over,' Taya said, 'I started to get worried when you didn't reply to any of my texts. I found your husband online and he told me you were under the weather.' She held out a plastic container that sloshed. 'My mum's famous chicken soup. The ultimate panacea. This has cured everything from heartbreak to heartburn.'

Claire was so taken aback by the sight of Taya that she clung on to her friend's embrace for a little too long. Finally, someone who had no idea what had happened, what she had done.

'Should I put this in your fridge?' Taya said, after a while.

'Please. Please come in,' Claire said.

Thankfully, Lily was out, armed with her final must-buy list.

Claire had noticed a change in Lily over the last few days: she seemed bolder, as if to compensate for her sister and brother-in-law's cowardice. James still couldn't meet Claire's eye. Whenever they closed the bedroom door, silence descended. Claire found herself suppressing coughs, trying her hardest to go back to sleep if she woke up needing the toilet. Somehow, suddenly, it felt so awkward to just exist alongside her husband.

The afternoon had been spent pacing and planning, free from the need to maintain a sense of normalcy for Lily's sake. Claire knew the responsibility to salvage what remained of her marriage lay with her. She had to tell her husband how and why the Goddesses became so central to her life. The support they provided, the guidance through the bleeding scare when she'd been alone, the knowledge that radiated from each post. And how she had had no idea of the potential danger, she really didn't. But it wasn't as simple as that. How could she broach the real fear – that they were drifting apart, that they were different people now, when they were responsible for a child coming into the world? She'd tried writing out what to say on an old Uno notepad, but ripped the pathetic sentences into shreds. Claire had attempted recording herself on her phone, but knew within seconds of starting that it sounded completely wrong. She would wait until Lily left and hope inspiration and courage struck by then. The pretence they were maintaining for her sister was so flimsy and exhausting. She tried to summon the energy to smile for her friend.

'Your flat is so you,' Taya said, as she turned on her heels and took in the image of the duvet and blanket on the sofa, the heap of teabags by the kitchen sink. 'It's so modern – you wouldn't expect it from street level, would you? God, my place is a shambles compared to this!' Taya had no idea just how wrong she was. Claire had spent hours looking for a drinks caddy like

Taya's. She had a Pinterest board of maroon walls, all inspired by her friend's beautiful home. She'd recently re-read their rental contract to see if painting was possible. They'd already taken liberties with James's DIY habit.

'So, how is the second trimester treating you?' Taya said, after Claire rushed the duvet upstairs and shooed some stubborn sofa crumbs into her hands. She declined a drink of anything. 'Are you feeling better?'

'I've just had an awful week. I'm . . .' Claire thought about inventing an explanation, and how easy that would be, but Taya looked so sincere. She recalled James's advice, before the breaking point of his discovery. 'Well, a friend lost their baby.'

'Oh.' Claire noticed Taya's hand jerked towards her own stomach, perhaps out of innate maternal horror.

Now she had started, Claire couldn't stop. 'I gave her some very bad advice. I feel like it's my fault.'

'Oh, Claire! Oh, that's just the worst news. And of course it wasn't your fault. You know what I've always thought about you? You take the world's problems on your shoulders. How old was she, if you don't mind me asking?'

'Flora? She was. Sorry, my brain's blank. I can't think.' Claire hoped Taya couldn't see her panic. She didn't even know her friend's age.

'No, I shouldn't have said anything. I'm sorry. Poor woman. Gosh, this must have been particularly difficult news for you to handle. I hope you're getting lots of love and help. I can see you've been beating yourself up. Has your work been understanding? James mentioned you'd been off.'

Claire didn't dare say anything else. The flowers from Uno loomed in the background, their careful presentation so out of kilter with the disarray of the room. Her friend would be so confused if she learned about the office visit. Claire regretted it all. Sadness brimmed under her eyelids. The year had been defined by so much crying. She hated that. But they poured out in defiance of her wishes.

Taya reached for Claire's hand. 'You know, I saw one of those silly quotes on Instagram the other day. It said something about grief being like the ocean in a storm: it might feel impossible to imagine being out of its eye, but with time, the furious waves will become calm.'

Claire took a deep breath, steeling herself to respond.

'I just thought it was nonsense. Nothing makes grief easier. It's always there, lapping away. Sometimes I'll go on WhatsApp and see the last moment a loved one was online, or a song will remind me of someone who is no longer here, or didn't make it. It's just so unfair. I bet your friend is in the thick of it right now. I bet she'll find she can't look or see or touch certain things.'

Claire opened her mouth, but her mind was racing too much. She thought of Barney and Flora, and of topping up her dad's old mobile every three months, just so she could hear his voice on his answerphone message. She thought of the tiny beacon of hope inside of her. She nodded instead.

'People treat grief like it's this short spell of horror and it'll get better, or that ocean rubbish, as if there's any beauty in it. But the reality is, I often feel like someone's taken my heart out of my body and stamped on it. And oh, I'm sorry, I'm absolutely all over the place. I am so sorry.'

Claire tried to make a sound, something that showed she was listening, but it came out as a whimper.

'My definition is this,' Taya said, when she was able to control her voice again, 'and I hope I don't sound like one of those stupid Instagram posts, but I'm sure grief is the awful barter we make for the chance to love. And love is what gives me the reason to keep trying, keep going, you know?'

Claire looked at her friend, took in her sore, blotchy face. 'Thank you,' she said, barely louder than a whisper.

'I promise you tomorrow will be a little bit easier. It always is. Please take care of yourself. And tell your friend I'm thinking of her. I'll light a candle for her baby. I light one every Sunday anyway. Now, I'm going to have to go home before I embarrass myself any further. You'll text me when you're feeling up to it? Please.'

When Claire cleaned up, she realised she hadn't asked Taya how she was doing, or when she had experienced so much grief, or asked for more information about her Sunday ritual. But that wasn't the done thing. Taya would have offered information, Claire was sure, if she had wanted to discuss it further. Claire messaged Taya to check she was OK. *Don't be silly, it's you I'm worried about!* her friend replied within seconds. As soon as Lily arrived back home, beaming and ready to parade her new purchases, thoughts of Taya's visit were subsumed by Lily's infectious giddiness.

It was only in the departures lounge of Heathrow Airport on Sunday, when Lily admitted she had heard the encounter from the street, that Claire realised she should have pushed the matter with Taya further. The two sisters passed a bottle of water between them while James paid for parking. 'Was everything OK with your friend by the way?' her sister said, 'I was waiting outside. She sounded really . . . broken.'

Claire hated how she kept doing the wrong thing; why hadn't she enquired further, made sure her friend was OK? Nothing felt natural anymore. Even being outside, the first time she'd left the house in nearly a week, felt strange. She opened her phone to start drafting a message to Taya but was distracted by the announcement that Lily's check-in desk was opening, and the draft was left half finished. James carried the bags, solemn and drawn, until they reached the point where they'd have to say goodbye, and the matter was forgotten once again.

Lily left in a burst of hugs that were so tight they hurt, and promised to come home to meet her niece or nephew as soon as possible. Lily looked so small, walking away, the ends of her trousers frayed in a way that only twenty-five-year-olds can pull off. Claire felt so proud of her sister. She would never have the courage to book a one-way flight halfway round the world. James and Claire walked to the car park in silence. Claire wished she could hold her husband's hand without the fear of him jerking away.

There's something desperately sad about going to an airport and returning home while planes and their passengers smile down from above. Airports promise transformation and the ability to leave normality for a while. And yet, there they were, stuck in their terrible reality. When James unlocked the car and immediately turned on the radio to fill the emptiness of their relationship, Claire felt choked.

She was shocked when James placed his hand on her thigh, startling her out of her thoughts. James kept his eyes fixed forwards on the road, but Claire felt her body relax into the seat. The baby, she knew, was now the size of a turnip, her least favourite vegetable. It still hadn't moved. She hoped it was more resilient than its mother. That it could protect itself against the fear, anxiety and self-loathing that coursed through her veins.

After a week of miserable eating, Claire's appetite had returned with a furious rush. They stopped off at two service stations on the drive home, even though it added an extra half an hour to the journey, already thick with traffic.

'You're turning our baby into a fast-food monster!' James said, and looked Claire in the eyes for the first time in so long.

He pecked Claire's cheek as he handed her the second brown paper package of fried, salty goodness.

Our baby, she thought.

Chapter 33

TheSecretGoddesses

CrunchyMumma:

Evening, lovelies. It's come to my attention that a certain member is trying to post on this page again.

So, the question for today: should we let Flora back in? I'm opening the floor here and will go with what the majority vote.

First, I want to provide some context that may impact your judgement. As both a moderator and a mother, I've always found great value in learning what led women to join our path.

As legacy members of the group know, Blossom was snatched out (sadly, I can't say 'birthed', as Caesareans don't count) following a minor car accident when I was 37 weeks. Never again, I vowed to my partner, my body, my future children. And Indy, Echo and Olive are testament to the fact that it is possible to heal and experience a perfect passage to motherhood if you truly commit.

So many Goddesses have experienced the poison of medical births. To ban someone permanently based on this fact alone would mean many of us would be barred from the page.

I'd like everyone to bear this in mind when they share thoughts on whether Flora should be allowed to continue to be able to access

242

our insights. In the meantime, I've set up an auto-delete on anything she shares, and she'll be unable to see this post.

I don't want anyone to feel like I'm minimising their trauma by considering sanctioning Flora's return. Our community was deeply upset by her story and understandably very angry that she'd endanger her child in such a way. There's a tragic lesson to be learned from this mistake.

Please be free and be wise.

Comments:

MrsSimms: *Oh goodness, I hate the idea of anyone being excluded. That being said, I can only imagine how devastating her update must have been for all you pregnant ladies. No trigger warning as well . . .*

Mandy_Sturgis: *Hmm I don't think it's right. I hate hypocrites and she was always telling people how special and perfect freebirths are. At times, it was like she was judging anyone who'd done otherwise to begin with?*

SanneHoward: *Everyone makes mistakes. Let's try and practise compassion and let her back in. I lost one of my children and there's no pain in this world that compares.*

MindFullOfLove: *I KNEW something was up. Didn't I say? And everyone told me I was being cynical.*

Lucy_Loves_Life: *Is this definitely private?*

CrunchyMumma: *@Lucy_Loves_Life Yes, dear.*

Lucy_Loves_Life: *Well, I have to say, I was the biggest advocate for Flora's post being deleted but I do believe in second chances.*

Flora been messaging me non-stop and she is frankly desperate to return. Maybe it's my hormones (I'm currently harvesting colostrum and awash with delicious oxytocin) but I think we should allow her back in. I've not responded so far but think the gesture from her community, from us, would be particularly special right now. And maybe she'll stop these incessant DMs ha ha. Between Flora and my mother-in-law asking if the baby's arrived, I can't get a moment's peace!
@MrsSimms Thank you for your considerate comment. We needed a trigger warning and Flora should have known better.

TheTruthFairy: *I'm not comfortable with this woman being readmitted. We all made a promise. If she's in, I'm out.*

DulwichGirl: *I can't believe what I'm reading. Flora's baby died. Barney died, and you're all talking about yourselves. Has anyone stopped for a moment and thought about how she must be feeling? Lucy, you've ignored her messages? It's shocking that most of you don't seem to care there's a woman out there who lost her son.*

CrunchyMamma: *Don't worry, Goddesses. I've banned DulwichGirl. Please all take some extra time to care for yourselves today and this week. This entire episode has been so distressing for us all.*

Chapter 34

The most difficult thing, Flora found, was the quietness of the day. She'd been in dialogue with Barney ever since she realised it had been a long time since her period, the test she'd taken before popping into the shower, the stomach-flipping moment when she turned it over, called Tom's name, the room full of steam and love, and saw a line so strong it had stolen all the dye from the control. Now, she was alone. Every day, her stomach was a little flatter, her lochia lighter. When she got up to use the toilet, there was no familiar response from Barney, the wiggles she'd come to anticipate and adore. Twice, she'd expressed her engorged, excruciating boobs, but that was it. The milk was being reabsorbed, she read. Her body was slowly acknowledging the grotesque truth of her recovery.

Tom was back at work two days a week, an offer from his company to help stagger the paternity package which they said would still be offered in full. On the days he was out, the house rarely heard conversation. Flora would place Freddie, her lovely boy, in front of the TV almost all day. She'd reheat meals for him, and he would eat so neatly and quietly, take his little plate over to the sink for her, that she would be flooded with a gratitude that was impossible to share with a toddler. Flora wasn't sure how these days managed to pass. Freddie would wait by the door as soon as it started to get dark, in time for Tom getting back in. Flora didn't dwell on what this meant for their relationship. She wanted to sit right there with her son on the stairs. Sometimes she did, and Tom would rush in and scoop one under each arm.

Sinead the neighbour was going to look after Freddie when they attended their debrief meeting. They'd received a letter with the date and time almost as soon as they were discharged. The letter mentioned a senior midwife would be in attendance along with the consultant obstetrician. When Tom put Freddie to bed, they would talk about what to say. The injustices they'd faced. The Doppler had shown a heartbeat, Tom had heard it too. Something had happened under their regime. They were still in the process of their formal complaint, but Tom said they should wait until after this meeting.

When Flora looked online, she couldn't find anything about their specific situation. It seemed like other people were offered debriefs much later, not after just a few weeks. She tried posting in The Secret Goddesses to see if anyone had any advice but the system must have glitched because when she went back and checked for comments, it had disappeared. She hadn't updated HomeBirthHeroes on what had happened, so didn't bother writing anything there. Tom was her only confidant.

On the day of the meeting, Freddie was awake before Flora went into his room. She knelt by his bed and inhaled the precious smell of his scalp. Bending still hurt a little, and she hoped the darkness concealed her grimace. 'Mummy's going to get better soon,' she said to her first-born. 'You're such a big, brave boy.' He squirmed, half kicking the duvet off. She tucked him back in, said Daddy would make him any breakfast he wanted that morning.

'Anything?' Freddie said, his face peeking over the cover. 'Really?'

Freddie held both of their hands as they dropped him at Sinead's. He'd barely touched the pancakes Tom made and had dark circles under his eyes. Flora felt her heart wrench as she waved goodbye to her son, who she loved with every single speck of her being, but whom looked so much like Barney, the spitting image, that it was difficult to look at him, talk to him. She promised herself that when they picked him up later that day, she would shower him with all the extra kisses and love she had inside, now her heart had expanded to accommodate three instead of two. But it was just so hard.

'You holding up OK?' Tom said as they drove. A friend of a friend who worked at the local mechanics had cleaned up the car, no questions asked. Flora had inspected the seat carefully; they'd done a brilliant job. It hadn't gone unnoticed that they were in the same positions, on the same route, as last time.

'Not really.'

'What are you thinking about?'

'I felt him move this morning. I know I didn't, but I felt it.'

'Who? Fredster?'

'Barney, after breakfast.'

'Oh, Flor.'

Tom turned the radio down slightly. 'I'd put my hand out but I don't dare risk it. I can barely think straight.'

'I know,' Flora said.

Flora waited in the car while Tom paid for parking. It was a beautiful day and the sun warmed her face through the window. It was the type of day that normally made her want to stay outside, go on a walk, lap up the vitamin D.

Tom opened the passenger door. 'Come on,' he said. 'Let's get this over and done with, shall we?' He reached over and unclipped her seatbelt.

It was awful being back. This wasn't just Barney's place of birth; it also was where they'd had Freddie's short-lived antenatal appointments. At the check-in desk, Flora kept her head down, even though there was no one else around. The letter mentioned it had been scheduled outside of usual clinic times, but she couldn't bear the idea of seeing another woman's body in bloom. Tom signed in on their behalf. Almost as soon as they sat down, a midwife scuttled over.

'Please, you can wait in the rainbow room,' she said. 'Come this way.'

'That's good of them, isn't it,' Tom whispered in her ear.

The room they were led to could have been anywhere were it not for the sink and the bright yellow clinical waste bin. They sat on a well-worn sofa and faced the door. The box of tissues on the table looked empty.

A man and a woman walked into the room, each carrying a crisp cardboard folder.

'Miss Whyman, Mr Bradley, thank you for coming in today,' the man said. His name badge said he was a senior consultant obstetrician. His face was grizzly, his chin prickled with overgrown hair.

'Now, do you know why you're here?' the woman asked, as she perched on the chair opposite them. Her voice was sickly sweet. Flora felt like she recognised her, but couldn't be sure. Perhaps she'd been there in the hazy days after Barney's birth.

'We do,' Tom said. 'We got your letter.'

'I have here that you didn't consent to a post-mortem analysis,' the midwife continued. 'Or any testing? Typically, these meetings take place once results come in, which can take

248

several months, but we understand you wanted to speak to a team about what happened to your son.'

'That's right,' Tom said. 'That's what we said before we left.'

Flora tried to pour herself a glass of water, but it splashed on the table. She fished inside the box of tissues, but it was empty.

'Barney,' Flora said, after she put the box down, her hands still shaking. 'Our son's name was Barney.'

'Well, what we will do today is talk about what happened to Barney. And my colleague Sam is just held up, but she'll be joining us too. She's the specialist bereavement midwife. I'm here to talk you through the care decisions made when you arrived and what we can do to support you now. And Dr Moran here can answer any questions you have specifically about your surgery and recovery. Sam will be able to advise on the next steps for both Barney and yourselves, and how she can help facilitate those.'

'Should we wait for her, then?' Flora asked. She took in the midwife's face, her thin-lipped smile, her badge. She was called Kamini. She seemed far too upbeat for this kind of meeting.

'Let me just pop out,' Kamini said. 'Won't be a minute.'

Tom reached his hand out to her lap. She held it. Both of their palms were moist. 'You OK?' he said so only she could hear. The middle of the table was still splotched with water. Her throat was so parched.

'Sorry about that,' Kamini said, when she returned with another woman.

'I'm Sam. We briefly met when you were with your little boy saying your goodbyes. I'm sorry that we're having this meeting. I'm so sorry, both of you.'

Flora had no idea who this person was.

'Our records indicate that upon arrival, two midwives performed a CTG which detected no foetal heart,' Dr Moran started.

249

'That's right. And they wouldn't tell us what was going on,' Tom said.

There was a rustling of paper as the doctor opened his file. 'At eleven minutes past midnight, two scans from the obstetrics team also recorded no heart activity.'

'That's what you said. But Flora used her Doppler just before we left. I saw it. I saw the reading. His heart was beating. I just said we should come here to check what the fluid was.'

The doctor moved as if to crick his neck. 'Well, we advise against at-home Doppler use for this very reason. Our notes show that Flora was told this several years ago during her routine antenatal appointments. Without training, you can misinterpret placental blood flow or the mother's heartbeat.'

'And on that note, Flora, just looking here, it says you hadn't booked in with us. Were you under care elsewhere?' Kamini asked.

'No,' she said.

'As is our legal right,' Tom added.

'We understand that Flora was greatly distressed when presented with induction options to support Barney's delivery,' Dr Moran said.

'Wouldn't you be, doctor?' Tom spat.

'Do you have any concerns that you weren't provided with adequate information before taking mifepristone?'

'We do,' Tom said.

'The on-call consultant, registrar and midwives all spoke to Flora throughout the administration, and subsequent misoprostol and IV antibiotics.'

'Yes, but . . .' Flora said. She wanted to get up, there and then. Questions were coming from so many angles. It reminded her of the appointments with Freddie, the sly accusations that accompanied each comment.

'Yes?' Dr Moran stared right at her.

'But we came here so you could help Barney.' Flora heard her voice falter. 'And you didn't.'

Dr Moran nodded. Flora had read up on body language betraying the truth. So he agreed, she thought. 'Sam, would you mind stepping outside please?' he said.

When they left and Flora and Tom sat with just the midwife and the crushing weight of their child's death, Kamini pretended to notice the spilled water for the first time. 'I'll get something to clear that up. And would you like a hot drink? Tea? Coffee?'

Flora and Tom both shook their heads. Flora was thirsty, so, so thirsty, but she wanted nothing Kamini could provide.

The way Kamini cleaned the table was so over the top, Flora had to look at her lap.

'Let me take this somewhere,' she said, holding up the damp blue tissues before leaving the room again.

'It's like Piccadilly Circus in here, what are they playing at?' Tom said.

Flora didn't respond. She thought of the plan she'd made with Tom, how they'd been forced to be on the defensive yet again. This place brought out the worst in everyone.

Only Sam returned.

'Flora, Tom, I've had a word with the doctor. We think the best thing to do is to arrange this meeting for another time. We're not getting anywhere, and we can see you're both getting upset. I can only apologise: I think we've jumped the gun here on our side. I believe they explained the standard procedure is to set one of these up after several months. Flora, I'm also going to arrange for a counselling referral at the soonest, and I can sit in on that, if you'd like me to. You don't have to decide now. But we've agreed the best thing is to allow some time for you all to process what's happened.'

'We have a list of questions to ask you all,' Tom said.

'And I will be there to hear them and help you process them at the next session, so will Dr Moran or one of his team.'

'But what do we do now?' Tom asked, and Flora turned and saw her partner, her life partner, her love, looking totally lost. 'How can we make a complaint?'

'The most important thing is for you to make plans for Barney's memorial. I've got a leaflet here on the next steps. And Flora, I've written my number on the front. I can help with the planning too. Then we can talk about the complaints process after that. How does that sound?'

Late foetal IUD, the leaflet said. *Intra-uterine death.*

'Just before we go, Flora, can I confirm that you do not want any testing of Barney? Many families find that it provides closure.'

'Don't let anyone touch our son,' Tom said. 'Don't let them do one more thing to him.'

'Flora, Tom, I am here to support you. I'm not sure if you remember, but the doctors said that the level of meconium on Barney's skin indicated he'd passed at least a day, maybe two, before he was delivered. I know the team mentioned safeguarding issues before you were discharged, and that Barney may have required medical attention before he came in, but that is not my area. I am only focused on allowing you to process and grieve everything that's happened.'

'What is wrong with you all?' Tom said. 'How many times do we have to repeat ourselves?' Tom's face was mottled. Tiny flecks of his spit landed on the table.

'I'm so sorry, Tom, Flora. In this job, I've unfortunately worked with many parents in the inexplicably awful situation you're in now. Some people find it comforting to hear they're not alone in going through this. Now, please, Flora, here's my information, here's everything you need, and please, you can call this number and if I'm not available or on-call, it will go to another member of the bereavement team.'

'OK,' Flora said, as her heart caved in on itself.

Tom and Flora drove back in a silence broken only by Tom saying, 'We'll get our answers, Flor. We'll get them. Bunch of arse-covering fuckers.'

She waited for the tears to come, but for some reason, her face remained dry. All she could think about was the fact she should be sitting in the back of the car, observing Barney in the new seat they'd bought, making sure their son was safe as he was taxied about. That was all they wanted, to keep their children so safe. They would start the formal complaint procedure later, once they'd digested the day. The time delivering and leaving Barney was so difficult to remember. Flora felt blindsided still. Staggered by the way she withered in those sterile clinic rooms. She'd had a fever, they told her in the immediate aftermath, and again in the letter. She'd been experiencing delirium, required cannula after cannula of medication. But Tom had been there, lucid and desolate. He'd seen it all while their son lay in the cold cot beside them in the butterfly room.

Tom's hand automatically found hers when they parked, walked towards Sinead's door. He kissed her cheek before he pressed the doorbell.

When the door opened, Freddie ran towards them. Flora crouched down out there on the porch and held her arms out.

'I love you so much,' she said into the wild clusters of his curls. She didn't care that this was out in the open, that people might walk past. 'I love you, Freddie, I love you, I love you, I love you.'

She stood back up, using Tom's body to keep her steady.

'He's been such a good boy,' Sinead said to both of them. 'We've had a lovely time, haven't we?'

Freddie buried his head in the folds of Flora's dress. She allowed the pain to sear through her skin, her bones, every part of her body. She was there, outside someone's house, with her son, with her partner, without her baby. But this was her world now. These people were her world.

Chapter 35

Claire lingered outside the entrance of Uno Energy's headquarters and braced herself. She checked her phone one last time to see if Holly had responded to the message she'd sent apologising for everything: her behaviour, her absence. There was still no reply.

Claire hadn't come up with an excuse for her absence last week. She'd hoped to find the right moment to get James's advice, but the previous afternoon had been close to perfect. When they got home after the airport they went straight to their bedroom and just held each other, and enjoyed the sort of silence that exudes comfort not crisis in a relationship. They lay there until it darkened, and James assembled plates of snacks and leftovers that they ate upstairs, their laps covered by the shared duvet. Together, they'd gone on the Goddesses page. Claire showed James her defence of Flora in the latest revolting thread. She'd been banned from posting any more. Afterwards, she purged her device of all Goddess remnants – images, messages, contacts, groups. At no point did Claire want to disturb this new harmony, the fledgling hope that they could get over this experience, by reminding her husband of her strange Uno visit. Her plan was to just wing it at work.

Claire was the first at her desk. She'd planned it this way, set her alarm so she was up before James, out the door just as he started brushing his teeth, his eyes still half closed while foam collected in the corners of his mouth. It was better to be at Uno when others arrived instead of conspicuously announcing her arrival, she decided. The sight of five hundred unread emails felt less daunting when the office was only starting to show signs of life. She started clicking through everything she'd missed, grateful for the distraction as the team pod got busier. The backlog gave her a valid excuse to keep her eyes on the screen.

'Claire! You're back!'

Claire turned her chair round to greet Ali.

'Glad to be back,' she said, and hoped it sounded convincing.

Ali presented a cup. 'Here, I got you a coffee, just in case. My backup was to just neck it if you were still off.' She lowered her voice. 'Last week was hell. I hope you're OK?'

Claire took a sip of the offered drink, to be polite. 'Thank you,' she said. She would bet anything that it was caffeinated. She wasn't sure how she could ever communicate the importance of decaf to Ali if their coffee-buying became a legitimate *thing*. This development was both confusing and exciting. She would reciprocate, as she had before, but what next? Would they be able to get lunch together? Would they ever speak outside of work? Claire didn't have anyone from Uno's number saved. All she knew about Ali was gleaned from their shallow small talk or the snippets of social media she could access. Younger people were so good with their privacy settings.

'At last, she returns,' Holly said as she approached.

'Here I am,' Claire said, as she adjusted herself in her seat. She wished she'd come up with something wittier.

'We need to talk,' Holly said.

When Claire locked eyes with Ali, she thought she could sense real compassion. 'Good luck,' Ali mouthed.

Holly led Claire to the quiet spot near the printer.

'Right. You'll have seen my calendar invite. It's a back-to-work necessity. Look, I didn't tell them about Monday. Somehow, probably because HR are useless, they don't know about your *visit*. Seriously, what inspired you to come here in that kind of state? You know what? I don't think I even want to know. But you can thank me by never pulling that kind of trick ever again.'

Claire thought of Barney, the way loss still clutched at her heart. How she'd do everything in her capacity to avoid being in that kind of situation again. 'Thank you. No, never.'

'And I've put time in for weekly one-to-ones. Clearly I'm going to have to be a bit more hands-on for the rest of your time with us. We need you focused, not frazzled.'

Claire inhaled deeply. She would endure this, do whatever it took to get through the day. 'Of course.'

'I'm just fed up of people coming here and tapping out the second they get pregnant. It was like this with Caro, although I have to say she never rocked up looking like she'd been electrocuted.'

Claire did her best to try and look neutral, to not let the scorch of anger show. This wasn't right. She tried to change the subject. 'Holly, do you want children?'

'Claire, I couldn't think of anything I'd like less right now. What is it about pregnant people thinking everyone wants to be just like them? From what I've seen, it really does a number on your . . .' she looked Claire up and down, scanning her slowly – 'health.'

They walked back to their desks in silence.

As a back-to-work treat, Claire ordered a slice of pizza at lunchtime instead of her typical soup and a roll combination. She perched on her usual window seat of her favourite café. The windows misted up as her breath mixed with the other office workers of Soho. She picked up her phone for something to do. After her Goddess cleanse, the phone was far less explosive, but also lonelier. The constant company had been blocked for good and Claire was on her own again.

Claire was about to text Lily, to see if her sister might be free to FaceTime, when someone knocked on the window, startling her.

'Claire!' David said, and rapped again. He did a thumbs-up. 'You good?' he shouted.

Claire nodded.

He walked in. 'You don't mind if I . . .?' he said, and took the stool next to hers.

Claire looked at him, his arms, the way the ink danced. Meeting at last, she thought. So much had changed in such a short time. She tried to smile.

David pulled a chair out and joined her, looking out over the busy lunchtime concourse. 'So, you're feeling better now? The girls seemed a bit worried.'

'Yes, thanks.' She didn't want to bring up the conversation with Holly.

'And did you get the flowers? Hope you don't mind. I just – well, I was just concerned something might be wrong.'

'No, we're good,' Claire said. She desperately wanted this conversation to go well, but her brain and mouth were experiencing real disconnect. It was difficult for her to really think about the previous Monday. 'And how's your . . . wife?'

'Ottie? She's good. She's swelling already. Makes me massage her ankles every night.'

Claire found herself looking down at her own, encased in thick black tights. It was almost impossible not to compare, always.

'It's weird they'll be due at the same time, isn't it? Do you know what you're having? We went for a private scan last week to find out. We got a real eyeful. I said, that's my son, he's taking after his father, if you know what I mean. Ottie didn't seem to find it too funny.'

'Ah, right. No, we don't know anything like that yet.' She tried to imagine James making that kind of joke. He'd taken everything so seriously.

David pulled out his phone, made a face at it. 'Right, I've got an all-hands-on-deck situation now. Shall we do this another time? And you must be local, right? We're by Sydenham Hill. I should put you in touch with Ots, shouldn't I?'

'Definitely,' Claire said.

'Glad you're better!' David said, a little too loudly, before he shut the door of the café.

Claire thought about the David encounter as she walked back. What it might mean. How funny it was that the second she stopped trying, the friendships blossomed.

For the second time that day, she paused outside of the imposing office exterior. She forced herself to straighten. Keep your shoulders up, she said to herself, don't let anyone see.

The back-to-work interview was painless. No, Claire didn't have a doctor's note, yes, she was feeling better, yes, she understood company policy, and yes, she was aware that best practice was to go to HR directly about pregnancy – although she didn't have to officially tell them for another month. While she went through the motions, she thought of the initial disappointment of seeing that GP, Dr Faulkner, and the way he'd made her feel like she'd wasted his time. How nothing met her expectations

259

of pregnancy. For over a third of her life, she'd planned for this experience. The family with James, the shiny home that hosted friends, the job that allowed her to switch off in the evening and enjoy what mattered. The telling-off from stern-faced Trisha was certainly not part of that dream, neither was the week indoors, or Barney. It all came back to Barney.

'Do you have anything to add?' Holly asked, when Trisha made her sign a form to confirm she was au fait with Uno's sick-leave requirements.

Claire thought about asking Holly whether it's appropriate to discriminate against pregnant women, make snide comments, run secret reports on Internet activity, and actively and con-stantly encourage people to feel inferior. But what was the point? She couldn't risk rubbing Holly the wrong way, have her manager mention her office episode. The great embarrassment of her appearance. 'No, nothing,' she said.

'Suit yourself. So, next steps. We'll schedule another meeting about your *situation*, and we'll need one of those Mat-B forms, won't we, Trisha?' Holly said. 'Maternity policy details are on the intranet.'

'Are you sure there's nothing else you'd like to add? We've got this room booked for another twenty minutes,' Trisha said.

Claire shook her head. Under the table, she rubbed her stomach, her thumbs trembling. She'd spent so long waiting for her life to mean something. Waiting and hoping. She never expected for it to take her here. To her great surprise, the baby responded. An unmistakable thump deep within that she knew, she just knew, could only be from her child. Claire managed to contain herself while she remained in the room, but inside, she burst with something that felt like fulfilment.

At her desk, while everyone typed emails with thunderous force, she stroked her stomach. She was pregnant and the baby was alive. That was all that mattered. Not Holly's politics, not Ali's friendship, not this potential new connection with David.

Claire thought about this as she sat on the toilet and messaged James to say that she could feel the baby moving, she loved him, and yes, they would talk tonight, and of course he could try and feel it too. Claire was ready to share it all. To talk about her hopes for pregnancy, and birth, and the rest of their lives together as a growing family, and what she would do to make sure their baby arrived as well as possible. It was time to tell James absolutely everything. She would expose her raw, true self. Talk about her childhood experiences in hospital, her dad withering away, the fear that surrounded that 'h' word, and how she required James's absolute support now, more than ever.

The baby kicked once more in approval.

Chapter 36

Claire led the way to the appointment. The thin layer of her jacket did little to protect against the cold and her teeth refused to stop chattering. James had one arm linked with hers: he was worried she might slip and fall. 'Are you sure it's down here?' he asked, as they trod down a street full of mulchy leaves. All the vibrancy of the city had suddenly disappeared. The pavements were slippery, the transport frantic, and thick fog had eaten the twinkle of tall buildings. Earlier that week, Claire's train had been delayed because a tree fell on the track. It felt like everything was giving up.

As they trudged on, Claire thought of the stream of pictures she had woken up to that morning. Snapshots of joy: Lily holding a coconut to the camera, her eyes creased and gums exposed in a true grin. Lily looking at a monkey sprawled in front of a temple. Lily's tanned arms raised in the air while the sun flashed its last embers. As Claire scrolled through the images in bed, she felt real pleasure at the delight on her sister's face. Every time Lily messaged from a new location, Claire added the place to her weather app. It made Claire feel like her sister was closer, even though she was half a world away.

'Careful!' James said, as she reached into her pocket for her phone. She stumbled slightly on the kerb as she rummaged. 'Claire!' he almost shouted, 'You've got to pay attention.'

'Sorry.' She kept her head down. She didn't want to see what kind of facial expression matched his tone.

'Just, please, try and concentrate? You need to watch out. What if you hurt yourself, hurt the both of you?'

'I was only checking to see if Lily had sent anything else,' she said.

He sighed.

'It's just up here, James, here, on the left.'

They walked the remaining few steps to the children's centre without speaking. Little incidents like these kept happening. James kept flashing with a panic that seemed to take them both by surprise. And Claire knew she'd triggered it. She'd triggered the man who once refused to wear shoes while driving them on a moped around Crete, who would backflip off boats and rocks without ever checking water depth, who had never been the type of person to feel nervous about physical safety.

It was still too early for the centre to be busy with chatter. Claire led them to the seat she'd sat in last time, when she first encountered David outside of the office. She was pleased there was no chance of a meeting today. It would just add extra pressure. She'd spoken to David while he made them matching mugs of lemon and ginger tea in the Uno kitchen, and he'd tilted his head to the side and said Ottie had this appointment weeks ago, it was strange how she was so behind. Claire had sipped her tea and done her best to move the conversation on swiftly.

Being back in this building didn't feel good. She was nervous the midwife would comment on how late this appointment was, and how she'd failed, yet again, to respond to their voicemails or letters until she finally got back in touch last week. Claire put a finger on the point where her wrist met her hand, something she'd read online that made people feel calmer. She wondered how long she'd have to do it to feel any kind of effect. James was too busy to notice. He was flicking through leaflets, fanning a chosen few out on his thigh. 'Have you seen these?' he turned to Claire at last, and she removed her finger from its position. 'Should we be reading them?'

Claire looked, nodded.

He pulled one out. 'Maybe we can go through this together?' *Prenatal anxiety: symptoms and support*, it read.

At the weekend, after Claire had survived five full days at Uno with Holly constantly bringing up her episode, James initiated another deep conversation. He sat next to Claire on the sofa, put his arm around her shoulders and gently stroked the part of her forearm that always made her shiver. He said he hadn't quite realised how much time she spent online before, but he understood now he knew how lonely she'd been. Claire had just looked at the way he brushed her arm, that intimate gesture she'd loved for so many years, as he asked if she'd been able to book a GP appointment yet, and if not, if she'd like him to be there when she called up. He spoke so reasonably that Claire simply had to say yes, yes she would get in touch with the doctor, she'd do it that week, and no, she could do it alone. Afterwards, James placed one hand on her stomach and they talked about the midwife appointment. He'd researched what to expect in the session, he said. He looked relieved when Claire said she no longer wanted a home birth, not after everything that had happened. She hoped the more she said things like this, the easier it would get. Anything to try and move their relationship in the right direction. And that included this new leaflet.

Claire's voice wavered. 'OK,' she said. She heard James fold it together, stuff it in his pocket.

The midwife, when she came to greet them, was another stranger. She was older than the others, with a kind, crumpled kind of face. 'Claire Hansen? James Hansen?' she asked. Her name badge said Bonnie. She ushered them into a cell of a room: sparse walls and a single table. 'Sorry, it's not much, is it? We should start bringing some nice cushions in for these clinics, I keep saying that. Now, before I go full Laurence Llewelyn-Bowen on you, do you have your notes? Shall we start there?'

'I didn't realise I was supposed to bring them,' Claire said. They were somewhere at home, stashed in anger and shame after the first visit.

James chose that moment to cough. The timing made Claire wince. 'Sorry,' he whispered.

Bonnie was only looking at Claire. 'No worries. People forget all the time. More often than not, actually. So, why don't you fill me in and we can get a fresh set of records sorted before your next scan.' She waved the pastel-blue paper at them. This woman was well practised, Claire could tell.

'OK.'

'That must be in just a few days, mustn't it? I bet you're both so excited.'

'Er, no, I don't think we've got a date, have we, Claire?' James said.

'How strange. Well, let me just check for you both here, give me a mo . . .'

Claire concentrated on removing tiny bits of fluff from her tights while Bonnie typed at her laptop.

'Here we go, you're in for twenty-one weeks, three days, which is a little late. Would you like me to see if it could be brought forward? I'm not quite sure why this appointment's so delayed either. Did you have to reschedule? I'm sorry about that. We're so understaffed at the minute that things must have slipped.'

James responded first. 'No, no, all good. Let's stick with that slot please.'

Claire focused on breathing. She had to do this.

'Good idea,' Bonnie said. 'So, have you two discussed where you're giving birth?'

'We know what we're definitely not doing, don't we?' James said.

Claire felt the familiar tingle of her face pinkening. There was nothing she could do to stop it. 'Yes, at King's, but, I was just wondering, can we talk about it again?' She wasn't sure who she was addressing.

'Of course we can, love, that's a great idea,' Bonnie said. Claire was thankful that it was Bonnie who had replied.

Bonnie encouraged them to agree to a plan in time for their next meeting. They had to decide between a midwife-only ward or one staffed by doctors. 'I always say to parents: this is your choice,' Bonnie said, and ran a hand over the creases gathering in the lap of her tunic. 'It's like bungee jumping. If you read the health and safety forms properly, you'd never do it. But we're all adults. I'm not going to lecture someone on bungee jumping's associated risks. I assume you have read up on it and I'm here to support you. And your baby.'

'I just think it might be better to have doctors on hand. Just in case, right?' James said.

'Let's talk about it, definitely. That's OK, isn't it, Bonnie?'

'Oh, you've got plenty of time, loves,' the midwife said.

Claire wished there was a way James could just know that she was trying, she really was, but she was still herself, and all that raw fear hadn't disappeared overnight. 'I'm just a bit worried,' she said. She thought of the leaflet in James's pocket. She cleared her throat. 'Actually, no, I'm petrified.'

'Ah,' Bonnie said. 'Well, that's what I'm here for. And between us three, I'd be far more concerned if you said you *weren't* worried about becoming a mummy. Now, would you say you're able to manage these worries? Do they feel under control?'

Claire looked at her husband again. She turned to Bonnie and shook her head.

'Well, I can refer you to a specialist team who are experts at making you feel as comfortable and supported as possible for the next twenty weeks. They take mental health in pregnancy very seriously, so if I refer you now then you will be assessed within the next few weeks. How does that sound?'

'Perfect,' James said, a little too quickly.

'Um, I think that would help,' she said. She had to show her husband she was willing to re-engage. Keep doing what she could to repair the shattered fragments of trust.

'And you know what else I can do? I can also put in a request that I remain your midwife for the rest of your care. As part of that, I'll give you my work number so you can contact me any time. If you're ever feeling at all concerned about anything, just message.'

When the appointment ended, Claire really wanted to hug Bonnie: she gave the impression of a woman who doled out spectacular hugs. Instead, Claire felt at the air around James's hand until she finally collided with his fingers. They stepped out of the room into the sudden chaos of the children's centre, palms and pulses together. A play group was taking place and the space was transformed. Ashen-faced parents sat and observed from the spot Claire and James had just waited in. They saw their future.

Before they walked back onto the street, Claire sent smiley emojis to her mam and Sally. 'All good with the midwife,' she messaged one, then copied to the other. She wanted to prove to everyone that she was able to do this.

Taya had also texted, asking if they could meet if Claire was feeling better. Somehow, it is easier to be honest to someone who hasn't seen you hiccup out vodka in the back of a taxi, or accidentally walked into the bathroom when you're shaving, or picked up calls only to listen to half an hour of incomprehensible sobs. Taya only knew Claire as she was now, after all the years of work she'd put into crafting a veneer of composure.

I'm not sure, she messaged her friend. *But I'd love to see you soon*.

Taya arranged a date to meet, and Claire and James walked back to the flat in silence, the air damp with pre-winter chill, the sky stretching interminably grey in front of them.

When their front door was in sight, James turned and said, 'I think that went well? Right, Bear?' His voice cracked a little, a sound that would usually make Claire laugh but now filled her with sadness.

Chapter 37

The warmth of the place Taya chose made Claire's face overheat. As she entered the crowded bar, she tried to wipe her upper lip discreetly. It was full of beautiful people who didn't realise how lucky they were to still be in their twenties. They were a hipster crowd, drawn to the type of venue that had the cocktail list and menu scrawled on chalkboard walls. Claire had to squint to read what the wall said. From what she could make out, everything seemed wildly overpriced. She wondered why Taya wanted to meet here when the new Scandinavian bakery was just across the road. It was obvious they didn't belong.

Claire looked around for Taya and found her towards the back, sitting at a picnic-style table. They both waved at the same time, further signalling their lack of cool.

'Oh, look at you!' Taya said when Claire squeezed herself between the two hard surfaces of the table.

Claire felt her face get even hotter.

'You don't mind, do you?' Taya gestured at the two glasses and picked up the one with some wine left in it. She rolled the liquid around before taking a deep swig. The corners of her lips were stained purple.

It was still light outside, a rare day without any rain. Claire opened her mouth to comment on the weather, because her mind was suddenly empty. Taya got there first.

'You must think I'm loopy. I've had the most horrendous week and got here a bit early and thought why not? I didn't finish work until three last night. Or morning. I always get that wrong. You know when you're so tired your brain feels numb? That's me right now. You could hit me over the head and I wouldn't feel it, I reckon.'

'God, really?' Claire examined her friend's face. This version of Taya wasn't what she had expected. Claire started rubbing the corners of her mouth and to her relief, Taya also wiped. Claire was glad her friend picked up the subconscious cue. She didn't know Taya well enough to mention the wine remnants outright.

'You know we have sleep pods at the office? Some of the juniors were told to bring in suitcases this week. Their faces, you know, when they rolled those things past everyone. I've been there. I've tried to help, but wow, what a week.' Taya pulled at the skin on her face and slumped forwards.

From this angle, Claire could see the sizing label of Taya's jumper. An extra small. She could have guessed that.

Claire thought: it's difficult, when you've been stressed all your life, to be reminded there are people who go through infinitely more testing circumstances and continue to put on a brave face. The latest Claire had ever worked was 9 p.m. and she'd made sure everyone in her pre-Uno office knew about it, referencing it for weeks afterwards. Meanwhile, Taya must have been sleeping by her desk, and the whole world kept on going thanks to the many others who started overnight shifts, kept working, smoothed things over. Claire felt ashamed for her recent days in bed, her moping. The fact Taya had seen her in such a state.

'That's so tough,' she said, when Taya looked up.

Taya slouched further onto the picnic table, her head heavy on her thin wrists. She looked fragile.

'I'm sure you've noticed something is up, and it's not just work. That's been the real icing on the cake,' Taya said. Her teeth had a dark glaze. 'I feel so bad. I've not seen you so much recently, have I? And we'd got into such a good routine! I've been all over the place, really. I just wanted to tell you, because I think I owe it to you. When I came over to your place . . .' Taya drained the remainder of the wine. 'When I came over, I'd just found out my application for more treatment in Greece was declined. They told me I don't have enough follicles, that I don't respond to any stimulation, and discharged me from their care. Can you believe it? I was born with all my chances and now they're just gone.' She tried to drink out of the empty glass. She didn't seem to realise there was nothing left inside.

Claire gasped. 'I'm so sorry,' she said. 'I am so, so, sorry.' She didn't need her friend to explain. She was an expert in the clinical language of babies. Taya had been denied the opportunity to continue IVF. Claire didn't know how to arrange her face in response to the news. How could she make her features convey the right kind of horror, of sympathy, show that she understood the difficulty of talking about the combined taboo topics of grief and gynaecology? She felt dizzy with it all.

Taya's words started to lose their definition. The tiredness or the wine or the wretched unfairness meant they took on a blurry quality. 'Oh, you know what, it's fine. It has to be fine, doesn't it? I'm thirty-nine, I'm single, I've got a hostile environment inside of me. That's what they said. Hostile. It's why none of the embryos ever took, why I should never do the typical IVF thing of assume I'm pregnant until proven otherwise. But I always did, every cycle. And there are so many prohibitive rules and logistics if you're single and want to try here, you know. Such intense processes around donors. I don't understand why. I look at unhappy families sometimes and I just think why can't I . . .'

Claire gestured for the waiter and pointed at Taya's glass.

He wrote in his pad and walked away.

Claire found herself still utterly lost for words. There were so many common phrases she could use, like 'Everything happens for a reason', or 'You can look after our baby any time', or start a sentence with 'At least . . .' But when Claire opened her mouth to say one of these platitudes, she realised they would almost certainly make her friend feel worse. Much worse. Instead, she rooted around in her handbag for her lip balm. Just to have something to do. Just to stop herself from making a terrible situation even more awful. Claire wished there was something, anything, that might help.

Claire offered the little tub. 'Would you like any?'

Taya snorted a little. 'You know what's funny? The day after you told me you were pregnant, I sat in a car on the way to a meeting and I just made the decision. I made the decision to be happy for you. Because you're my friend and I don't want what's happening to me to affect things between us, between me and anyone, really. I've been so sad, though, Claire, so incredibly sad. But please don't think I'm not glad to see you and make sure you're OK. I'm so relieved you and your baby are well. I really, truly am.'

Somehow, Claire managed to keep her voice together when the waiter returned with a new glass for Taya and they ordered. She didn't taste the food when it arrived, only noticed that it wasn't that warm, but that was perfect because she could focus on filling herself with something other than self-loathing. She hadn't really noticed anything different about Taya because she was selfish and horrible and didn't deserve this friendship.

She managed to not put one hand on her bump, even though the baby suddenly squirmed with such newfound force that she had to force herself not to react, not to show the woman sitting opposite that she had something so painfully, acutely coveted. *Not now, baby,* she tried to communicate inside, *please not now.*

'Are you feeling better?' Taya asked, once their plates had been cleared. Taya's eyes were unfocused. Her left one kept blinking for a fraction longer than the other. 'And your friend, how is she doing?'

'Oh, well, she's – she's not really in contact.' Flora hadn't replied to her recent messages. Claire had tracked the read receipts. She would message again later that afternoon. She had to be the one to keep reaching out, to atone, to support.

'I bet she appreciates you getting in touch.'

'I'm not so sure. Sometimes there are just no words, you know?' Claire said.

'I know.'

Claire opened her messaging app on the walk home, after she'd hugged Taya so tightly that it was almost uncomfortable. She asked Flora whether the memorial had happened yet, and if she could visit, cook, bring something over. Claire still wanted to scream at the awfulness of it all.

Claire didn't have the strength to greet James when she finally made it to their apartment. She heaved herself upstairs and straight into bed. The sadness of Taya's news had settled on her skin, seeped inside her bones, left her chilled. She googled *Greece IVF single woman* but shut her phone when her screen showed a page full of hope and success. The sobs were caught in her throat. Taya was right. It was so unfair that we are born with all our opportunities to procreate. It was sick, actually, when she thought about it, and she couldn't stop thinking about it. The tears, when they came, flowed without interruption.

Claire took her time composing a message to Taya. She chose each word with care. She couldn't let her friend go through this horror alone. *Whenever you need to talk, I'm here. Thank you for telling me. Day or night, I'm a message or call away.*

Claire didn't move her phone when James crawled into bed and kissed the top of her head. He wiped her face with his thumb and pulled her into a hug, her body spooned into his, and his arms around her bump. Their hearts beat in unison, chests rose and fell, rose and fell, while Claire thought of her stoic friend Taya and the cruelty of bodies revolting against their owner's wishes. She thought of how Flora should be at home with two sons, not one.

'It's going to be OK,' James said, and kissed her on the back of her neck. 'I've got you, Bear. It's going to be OK.'

Claire allowed herself to be wrapped in his embrace. She didn't tell him Taya's terrible update. Perhaps he might see something appear if Taya replied. Either way, he wouldn't understand. He'd always had a limited view of what makes a family. He wouldn't be able to comprehend Taya's strength. He wouldn't agree with what Claire knew as fact: Taya would be a far better mother than her.

Chapter 38

Flora decided to only invite family in the end. It was easier that way, keeping the funeral to the smallest possible circle. With Tom's consent, she blocked the bereavement midwife, who kept offering to arrange a service on behalf of the hospital. They wanted nothing to do with the team there, especially not this token of their guilt. Instead, her mum and two in-laws came to the cemetery for the ceremony they arranged themselves, the product of a series of decisions that haunt any parent's worst nightmares. Tom's sister was in Australia and claimed she couldn't get last-minute time off. She sent a *Thinking of you* card in the post.

The memorial was the second most difficult day of Flora's life. She wasn't sure how she managed to dress herself, let alone keep herself together. The size of the casket, ordered over the phone, left her breathless when she saw it. It was an object so small it shouldn't have to exist. An object sold to them at a great discount, full of apologies. Tom had arranged for the funeral director to collect their son from the hospital. They would never visit that place again.

Flora's partner had been a beacon of strength, taking the

lead and organising everything. Calling the families to confirm the date when she could not. But she would never forget the way Tom howled when he was unable to finish his reading, the animal sound that tore through her in response. The looks his parents didn't try to disguise when her mother expressed her confusion, gasps, cries, like clockwork. As if his parents were better people, just because they'd yet to be touched by dementia. Flora linked arms with her mum throughout. She wanted to be held and cared for. She wanted to be told it would be all right. She wanted her mum back, fully back, just for this day.

'No parent should outlive a child,' her mum said, in a rare moment of clarity, as they walked back to the two cars, still arm-in-arm. 'Ever.'

Afterwards, when they dropped her mum off at the facility and collected Freddie from Sinead's, Tom's parents sat in their front room and sipped endless cups of tea. They had never fully accepted their son's partnership, Flora knew. For the first year of their relationship, so long ago now, his mum kept forgetting her name, calling her Fiona, Florence, Laura. It took a call from Tom to ensure the slip-ups miraculously never happened again. They had a similar attitude towards being grandparents, always keeping Freddie at a distance. Sending near-empty birthday and Christmas cards where only the to and from sections were personalised. On the sofa, Freddie clung to Tom's mother, so excited to be reunited, while she intermittently patted his head. Flora had to stop herself from screaming: cuddle him! He's the only child you've got! But rather than saying anything, adding more friction to the horrendous day, Flora offered everyone another round of tea and biscuits. She found that it was better to keep moving, have a constant to-do list. That helped her progress from one minute to the next.

'It's a terrible, terrible shame,' Tom's mum said on the

doorstep at the end of the day. His dad was already in the car. 'And I'm sorry but I can't help but think, if you'd admitted yourself sooner, not wanted this—'

Flora was relieved when Tom closed the door and said, 'Bye Mum,' before his mother could finish her sentence.

Meeting up with Claire reminded Flora that she'd made the right decision to keep things intimate. Flora hadn't quite realised how easily flustered Claire got, or the obvious tells of her discomfort: her bitten, chapped lips, the way she kept fiddling with the back of her left earring. Had Claire been like this in Guildford? Flora couldn't remember, could only recall Claire's skittishness when they'd been in the toilet together. She had no doubts that Claire wouldn't have been able to handle the miasma of horror that surrounded the funeral day. The dense, crushing sadness that defined their circumstances. And it wouldn't have been fair to share that with a pregnant person, despite Claire's offer. After all, one of the founding principles of The Secret Goddesses was to only surround yourself with positive stories.

Flora decided to meet Claire in the Costa Coffee by Eastbourne station. Her friend had travelled over an hour to get there, so Flora didn't want to add to any inconvenience, not when Claire was well into her second trimester. The visit was a lovely gesture, a sign that some of the community was still there for her. Flora was giving the other ladies time before she got properly back in touch. She'd started re-engaging with certain posts, though, and several members had liked a few of her comments, which flooded her with relief. Flora didn't think Tom needed to know exactly what was going on with the Goddesses, the narrow margin of the vote that allowed her back in, but he had been told all about Claire's trip and was thrilled. Flora suspected he was beginning to worry about how much time she was spending on her own.

As soon as Flora stepped into the Costa, she realised her mistake. It was bitterly cold outside, the wind lashing people with drops of icy seawater, and families had flocked indoors, drawn in by the reliable comfort of overpriced milky drinks. She'd been avoiding busy places for this very reason. It seemed like everyone had at least two, three, children with them. At least, she thought, there weren't any babies. That would have been unbearable.

Flora had intended to dig out her brush to go through the build-up of tangles before she met Claire. She gave up in a matter of seconds. She couldn't stand the image that confronted her when she looked in the mirror. She needn't have worried about her appearance, as Claire arrived looking similarly exhausted. Claire's hair had been matted by the drizzle outside, fronds sticking up around her face. As they went through all the pleasantries, Flora noted her friend's baggy clothing, unconcealed blemishes, and how different Claire seemed to the dressed-up person in a skin-tight skirt she'd met back in Guildford. Her friend's bump was impossible to ignore now, and Flora hated how there must have been an attempt to hide it away. She wanted to ask Claire if she could touch it. She wanted to feel the sensation of the pulse of life underneath the abdominal skin, just for a second. Imagine it was still happening to her. The request was on the tip of her tongue as they went through the motions of conversation.

'I'm still in maternity jeans,' Flora said, as she tried her hardest to keep her eyes on Claire's drawn face and not her stomach. 'They're the only things that fit.'

'Oh,' Claire said.

'I'd offer to lend you all my bits but, gosh, you're so neat still, aren't you.' Flora wasn't sure why she was saying this. Not only were they very different sizes, but she wanted to keep all her maternity wardrobe. She would wear it all again soon, hopefully. As soon as Tom allowed. She'd bought some ashwagandha tablets online to try and get her cycle to restart.

'Ah, right, that's so kind of you though. It's all so expensive, isn't it?'

'Extortionate. I wanted to ask: have you bought a pram yet? We're past the point where we can take Barney's pram back now so you could borrow it if you want? We'd like it back, you know, as soon as we're blessed again, but it seems like a shame for it to just be unused. We live right by here, if you want to come and get it after we finish these drinks? I've got some other bits I'd love to show you too.'

'That's so kind, Flora, but I can't, I can't do that.'

She didn't understand why Claire was being so evasive. Flora had always jumped at offers to save money, scouring second-hand sites, visiting charity shops, hunting down the best bargains. The pram had been one of the few brand-new purchases they'd made. Freddie's one – an online marketplace steal – started to develop suspension issues, so they decided to splurge. Flora had taken so many photos of Tom testing all the buggies out, his head thrown back in an exaggerated version of the excitement they both felt. They'd felt like first-time parents again.

'How are you doing? Really?' Claire said, and Flora wondered how long she'd been reminiscing for.

Flora wasn't sure what she should say. That she would never forget the image of Barney lying there, his chest so still. That Freddie had suddenly turned and would only eat cereal and scream if offered anything else. That, despite the ashwagandha, she was still bleeding.

'I think I'll get there, someday,' Flora said. She had hope, she really did. She would never be the same Flora as before. She'd read that foetal cells stay in a mother's body for decades after birth, and this comforted her. Barney would forever be a part of her DNA. She imagined the cells combining, hugging each other, helping to heal all the shattered tissues inside. Perhaps, one day, she'd wake up and feel a little less broken.

'I'll never forgive myself. I just want you to know that. I meant everything I said in my message.'

This comment grated. Flora shut her eyes. 'Claire, please.'

'And I'm so sorry for not sticking up for you more when people were being cruel. I really regret not saying more. I should have been there for you. It must have been awful, seeing some of those comments.'

Flora wasn't quite sure what Claire was talking about. She'd seen a few posts that suggested the Goddesses had been disappointed. But rightly so. There was no word she could think of that could contain her own phenomenal despair. 'It's fine,' she said.

'Right, sorry. I'm just so sorry.'

Flora didn't want this response. Claire seemed to think she was to blame for what happened at the hospital. It all seemed very self-involved and strange. It was like Claire couldn't hear Flora's comments about the hospital's failings, their responsibility, the update on their complaint. 'I'm trying to focus on healing, preparing, before we try again. And we'll do it properly this time.'

'I see,' Claire said. But Flora could tell she didn't. Perhaps she'd misjudged this woman when she introduced her to the Goddesses. Online, Claire always seemed so open-minded. But the person in front of her didn't seem to take in anything she was saying, hellbent instead on apologising over and over again.

Claire couldn't seem to stay still. Her leg kept knocking against the table, making their coffee cups shiver. Flora wanted to ask her to please stop jiggling, please, but she didn't want to add to the already strained feeling of this second meeting. It would have been rude.

Later, after Claire insisted on paying for some dry pastries, Flora tried to ask if her friend was still in touch with anyone in the group. She'd tuned in to Lucy's livestream of her birth. When the recording cut out, Flora feared the worst, the kind of thoughts she'd never had before Barney's tragedy, until she checked and saw Lucy's explanation of technical issues, and the beautiful picture of baby Cressida. The bath, the set-up, it was so like Freddie's arrival all those years ago. Did Claire watch it too? Wasn't it just beautiful?

Claire seemed to wince. And when Flora asked about Claire's birth plan – was it still like they'd discussed all those times over their messages? – the face on the other side of the table drained of all colour. It made no sense. Claire always used to ask so many questions about Freddie's birth story, giving her the chance to recall every lovely detail. But the woman in front of her refused to meet her eye.

Flora thought about saying something, addressing the thick layer of awkwardness. Death, she knew, made most people uncomfortable. She was building up the courage when suddenly, Claire mentioned needing to catch the next train, and the opportunity passed. When they hugged, Flora closed her eyes and imagined that Claire's stomach, Claire's baby, was inside her own body. For the briefest moment it almost felt real.

The end of their meeting was so rushed that Flora didn't invite her friend back to see the box she'd created, the one with all Barney's memories. She'd assembled it over the last week, finally piecing together all the things that lay in different rooms.

It became increasingly important to Flora that someone beyond the family could engage with, feel, mourn the very real things Barney had left behind. He existed, and he would never move away from the centre of her world. Flora had been so sure that Claire would want to come over that she'd ordered a special online delivery of bits she thought Claire might like: nice biscuits, posh mint tea. But Claire seemed to only want forgiveness rather than learn about the boy Flora birthed. A terrible thought flickered as she walked back: if Claire truly felt that guilty, maybe she could hand over her baby. Flora managed to shut this down quickly. Perhaps, she reasoned, it was for the best that Claire dashed off. She scared herself sometimes.

When Flora returned home alone, she went into the bedroom and removed the little wooden box from its position under the bed. She opened it up, smelled it.

Freddie wandered in, his face already screwed up, raring for an excuse to explode. This was his way now, and Flora knew she had to just allow it.

'Want to come here, Fredster?' Flora asked, and patted the spot next to her.

He came and sat by her, face still puckered.

Flora gently took out all the things she'd collected: the newborn outfit she'd washed in non-bio organic detergent, the muslin with a *Winnie the Pooh* pattern Tom had found, the picture of Barney they'd taken on Tom's phone that she'd printed off at home on a piece of paper that was getting more and more crumpled by the day. She'd have to print off another one soon. Or look into laminating it.

'These belonged to your brother, Freddie. We loved him,' Flora said.

Freddie looked at the box, then at Flora, and flung his little body into his mother's arms.

Chapter 39

Claire and James discussed names again on the way to the hospital. It was still one of Claire's favourite things to do. On the weekend, he'd looked up from his fantasy football app and asked if Harry or Phil might work. Claire blinked one, two, three times, until he got the point. Claire wanted something memorable, classic. James said Claire's new suggestions were either too pretentious or sounded like they belonged to old codgers.

'So, I've been reading, and you'll like this,' James said, his eyes glinting extra green. 'If we can't decide after the baby's born then we've got a certain amount of time until they get a government-issued name.'

'Pardon?' Their hands were intertwined and swinging with each step. It felt natural. Finally, they had a reason to be cheerful again. Claire focused on the body attached to that happy hand instead of their destination. They were united once more. They were a tiny family already.

'I think it's forty-something days. Then His Majesty's Government swoops in. No, stop laughing, I'm telling the absolute truth here.'

'But how?'

'I think someone in some office just goes: We are your governors and this is your name.'

'That's a bit authoritarian, isn't it?'

'Yeah, so we'd better get cracking. We should look at that book I got you again. And I've told you: I like Billy.'

'Like Billie Piper?'

'Is that the only Billy reference you can think of? I like it for a boy or a girl. Billy Hansen.'

'Hm,' Claire said, then giggled again. 'Government-issued name. But for me, it's still between Jude or Emily.' She placed one palm against her bump, the other comfortable in her husband's clasp.

It was natural, now, for her hand to just gravitate there, regardless of whether she was outside or at home. James had felt his first kick a few days before as they lay in bed. Claire had finished a rare cup of caffeinated coffee, a special treat, and the baby responded with gusto. 'Was that?' James asked, before her stomach bounced a little again. 'No way, no way!'

After a long period of nine-to-five silence from James, he resumed his messaging throughout the working day to see if there had been any further movement. He texted; he knew not to email, not with Holly hovering over Claire, her eyes lingering on the screen, her scent forcing its way down Claire's throat. But every day in the Uno office was easier now she had David for company. There was a sweetener in the form of actual conversation: by her desk, by his desk, sometimes over lunch. It was platonic, of course, but Claire did enjoy the way David's acceptance, his attractiveness, made her seem a little more appealing by proxy. She'd noticed Ali listening in to their conversations, trying to join in – and Claire always obliged. She never wanted anyone to feel the way she used to in this workplace. She had hopes that one day, Ali might detach herself from Holly and join her and David at their now-regular table at the café around the corner.

Most days, James nudged her to check the maternity policy. Claire was still building up to this. His work was generous with shared parental leave, but Claire had a feeling that Uno wouldn't be so generous. She didn't want to ask Holly or HR just yet and disturb the temporary peace. She told James she'd do it in time.

James seemed happier to be kept slightly out of the loop now. His appetite for answers had calmed down. The meeting with Flora in Eastbourne was never discussed. Claire hadn't felt much like talking when she got home, but if James had probed, she would have mentioned Flora's lingering stare at her bump, the haunted expression on Flora's face, the ongoing references to another chance at a freebirth that she found genuinely shocking. She regretted not saying something there and then, like: This is very wrong, you've got this all wrong. How could you possibly put another child's life at risk?

Flora had messaged her afterwards with some photos of Barney's clothes and another image of her son. Flora asked if she would honour Barney and promise to learn from her mistakes and never, ever enter a hospital. Claire had still not found a way to respond. She was glad the request was made digitally so she had time to think. She needed to say something, but how could she break her friend even further? There would be nothing left.

Claire tried her best not to think about Flora's wishes as they walked to King's, her hand rushing forwards alongside James's, swinging with each step. Her favourite thing as a child was holding one of each parent's hand and allowing herself to be hurtled up into the air. The feeling of total trust and freedom. James didn't seem to notice how Claire tried to slow down. She wanted to eke this all out, this good bit, before they had to go inside.

Claire and James paused outside the hospital. They were early. Emergency vehicles were lined up, ready to shriek away.

Claire turned to her husband. She could tell he saw deep inside her, that he was ready to move on. 'I think we should go home soon. We could see the mams, do some Christmas shopping, see the sea. I think it would help. I want to get better, James, I do.'

A grin burst across James's face. 'I couldn't think of anything I'd like to do more. I've been thinking for a while that we should go back.'

'OK, but I've got one condition: you have to drive up. I don't think I'll be able to fit behind a steering wheel soon,' she said. She had suddenly popped. James kept poking at her belly button, which was rising further with each day.

'And Bear, hear me out, but what about if we look at this place I found?'

'What?'

He flashed his phone. 'It's an actual house, look.'

'I don't get it?'

'I was thinking we could talk about – well, think about – moving back. We could be near our families again. Wouldn't that be great? And before you say anything, I could take the train down once a week. They'd let me work from home, I asked. And I know how you feel about Uno, so you could just find a new job nearby once you're ready to work again. It's just an idea, but don't you think it's a good one? We could go for a viewing?'

Claire felt blindsided. She couldn't process this information on top of everything she was about to face. 'Can we talk about it later?'

'All right, let's go, then, let's meet the bairn,' James said, and started walking.

Claire stood still. She just needed a few more seconds. She unlocked her phone. Nothing from her mam, Lily, Sally. No apps to check. *Good luck,* Taya had messaged. Claire responded with a series of hearts. Earlier that week, Claire sent flowers. She'd deliberated for too long over which bouquet best conveyed her feelings: sorrow, love, hope. The Internet helped her decide on sunflowers. Perhaps they hadn't arrived yet. She was certain that Taya was the type of person to say thank you.

James turned round, 'Come on, Claire, I don't think I can wait any longer!' He took out his mobile, shoved it back in his pocket. He looked older, in that moment. She could picture him doing this same routine in the future: cross before a train journey, hurrying their child along. 'Claire? What if we're late?'

Claire shuffled towards her husband. They still had plenty of time. He was always a stickler for punctuality. Claire checked her phone once more, willing the universe to provide a distraction. It all seemed so imposing and real. She just needed a few more breaths outside.

Perhaps, Claire thought, as she applied a generous helping of hand sanitiser by the hospital entrance, their baby would go on to achieve something spectacular. That was normal, wasn't it? She remembered reading about child prodigies made prodigious by overbearing parents. Olympians dropped off at school swimming pools before dawn broke. Runners carted up and down mountains for one more sprint, while stones rained away from their soles. She breathed in the alcohol fumes of the hand gel and tried not to think about the underlying scent of sickness and despair. It was impossible to ignore. It clung to her nostrils, took her back all those years. The clamps, her breathing, her dad.

Hospitals are strange places. They mark the beginning and the end. The hope and the fear. James had been blessed with uniquely good health. He had never been to A & E before. Hospitals are great levellers. They walked past the quiet of the oncology ward and entered the lift in silence. A hand jammed the door before it closed and made Claire jump. A stretcher wheeled in.

'Level three?' the porter asked. James shook his head and held one finger up.

The elderly woman smiled up at them. Her wrinkled mouth moved but no words came out.

'I think she's trying to say good luck,' the porter said.

Claire nodded thank you. She was rendered mute too. Her grandparents had died before she was old enough to retain memories. She never knew how to behave with old people. She panicked as they left the lift. Would the woman think she was mocking her? Claire didn't dare ask James. She was going to keep more of her worries inside now. Show him she was different. That she was ready for the inevitability of their new lives.

'I love you,' James said into Claire's ear, when they sat in the waiting room.

Claire took James's arm in hers and ran a finger over its dark hairs. She knew every part of that arm. She knew the constellation of moles, at what point James would flinch if she traced a finger up its tender pale side, and the way her head fit into the crook of his elbow. The arm had held Claire when she had almost lost the way. It had scooped her out of the whirlpool of disaster. That arm, that body, that person had been through everything with Claire for fourteen years. She had spent so long trying to know her husband.

When James proposed, Claire spent months agonising over whether she should change her name. James didn't care, he said; she could do what she wanted. Sally and Lily agreed Hansen was better than Brooks, her maiden name. It was more mysterious. Claire didn't want to betray the sisterhood, she said, but everyone knew she would change it anyway. She had always been like that: predictable. Her goals, her life, had always been small. The Goddesses offered something bigger, something she'd always wanted. Claire wished James hadn't been right all along; wished he'd never had to sweep in and save her. It was against everything she used to stand for. Independence and control.

But she loved him too – she loved him so much. She loved how he kept to his promise to look after her in sickness and in health. She loved his patience and excitement. His tendency to care and provide. He would make a wonderful, attentive father. Of that, she was certain.

After nearly half a lifetime together, Claire understood when her husband's silence was born out of comfort. As they waited to hear about the life they had created, equal in genes but unequal in physical burden, they didn't say a word. They were united by their desire to experience this milestone together. One Claire had wondered if they would ever reach. Around them, doors slammed shut and open, monitors beeped with life and without, and the world kept spinning without a care for Claire and James Hansen's feelings. Their relationship was still teetering on the edge but they had made it to nearly twenty-two weeks somehow. They rose when their names were called.

Claire lay down and shuffled around until the tiny body was visible on the screen, writhing white against a sea of black.

'Well, look here, we've got ourselves a wriggly one!' the sonographer said.

Claire couldn't stop staring. She saw their baby's thigh bone, and it was so real, so small, that her heart ached. She pictured the future of that thigh and the body it would support, the places it would go, while the sonographer continued to run through each part to check all was OK. The baby's heartbeat pulsed on screen and James placed a hand on her shoulder. She didn't need to turn round to know her husband was equally awestruck.

'Would you like to know the sex?'

'Yes,' they said, in unison, and James held her shoulder so tight.

It was all there. She was a daughter and she was healthy. They were parents to a baby girl. *Emily.*

Epilogue

Natural_NE_Mams
GatesheadGirl:
Hi everyone, thanks for letting me in. Reading through all these
posts has got me so excited. I can't wait to learn from you all!
I've always been drawn to the more holistic way of life and pregnancy definitely enhanced my interest. Sadly, I couldn't have the
water birth of my dreams as Emily was breech. I still don't feel able
to talk about what happened just yet, but I hope I'm up to it soon. It
was a really difficult time but the main thing is that Emily is healthy
and I'm finally home.

   We moved back here when I was eight months pregnant – there's
nothing like relocating 300 miles to kickstart maternity leave! I don't
know many other mams (just one, really, and we've drifted a little) so
Emily and I are so keen to meet up for some coffee and park dates
once I've fully healed. I hope that's soon. I'm trying to take things
day by day.

   What did everyone else do about jabs? The thought of causing
Emily any more pain is just devastating.

   Claire xxx

Acknowledgements

Thank you to Hannah Schofield, my incredible agent, for being the greatest advocate of my work. I'm forever grateful you found *Baby Teeth* a perfect home with Orion.

Thank you to my editors, Sam Eades and Sanah Ahmed, who transformed this book with their invaluable insight and wisdom. Thank you to the whole team at Orion who were involved in bringing this book to life.

I can't overstate how much I appreciate the friends and family who have cheered or consoled me since I started *Baby Teeth*.

A few special mentions, starting with the Tiffin Girls. Lucy Moy, thank you for consulting on some of the challenging medical scenes in this book. Sophia Butt, Tessa Pinto and Lilli McGeehan, thank you for two decades of soul-expanding silliness and the group chat that's my lifeline. Atousa Atkins, for being the best partner in reality TV-loving crime. And Ali Bartlam, for a friendship that holds me all the way from New Zealand.

To the whole Nottingham 'Herd' (you know who you are), thank you for making me laugh every day, and for the many early readers. Particular shout outs to Stewart Heard, Adam

Taylor, Sam Howard, Sinead Buckley, Liam McCullaugh, Steph Rew, Katie Browne, Amy Lodder and Lydia Drake.

Kam Scott, Miranda Drew and Felipe Sturgis, you've been fierce champions of *Baby Teeth* since day one and excellent ex-colleagues. Your enthusiasm and energy kept me going during crises of confidence.

Lucy Tomlinson and Ellie Simms, I can't tell you how much our friendship means to me, especially as editing this book collided with my own difficult journey to motherhood. Thank you for always, always listening.

To Pippa Tardi, family friend and wonderful midwife, thank you for all your input. And to Lacey, my midwife, who was always so intrigued by the concept of this book.

A humongous thank-you to my mum, dad and sister aka AJ, MJ and PJ. I genuinely don't know where I'd be without all your love and patience. Thank you for helping me believe I have something to offer the world. And to my grandad, thank you for your unwavering pride.

Thank you to the Silvani family too: Hannah, who delivered real-time feedback (next to me while I typed). Heather, who took the time to read the many versions of *Baby Teeth*. And Mike and Tom, for their calm support during my many meltdowns, book or otherwise.

Baby Teeth wouldn't be possible without my husband, Jack, who pored over every line approximately one hundred times. I'm sorry for everything I said whenever you dared to offer constructive criticism. And, to be serious for a second, thank you for always supporting my dreams and being such a loving and considerate partner. I love you to the moon and back.

Lastly, to my son, Robin, thank you for expanding my world and filling it with so much joy.

Credits

Celia Silvani and Orion Fiction would like to thank everyone at Orion who worked on the publication of *Baby Teeth* in the UK.

Editorial
Sam Eades
Sanah Ahmed

Audio
Paul Stark
Louise Richardson

Contracts
Dan Herron
Ellie Bowker
Oliver Chacón

Design
Charlotte Abrams-Simpson
Loveday May
Nick Shah

Editorial Management
Charlie Panayiotou
Jane Hughes
Bartley Shaw

Finance
Jasdip Nandra
Nick Gibson
Sue Baker

Marketing
Hennah Sandhu

Publicity
Sarah Lundy

Production
Ruth Sharvell

Sales
Dave Murphy
Esther Waters
Victoria Laws
Rachael Hum
Ellie Kyrke-Smith
Frances Doyle
Georgina Cutler

Operations
Jo Jacobs